NUBIA

THE AWAKENING

OMAR EPPS
CLARENCE A. HAYNES

NUBIA
THE AWAKENING

DELACORTE PRESS

Text copyright © 2022 by 72073 Inc.
Jacket art copyright © 2022 by Adeyemi Adegbesan
Map copyright © 2022 by Maxime Plasse

All rights reserved. Published in the United States by Delacorte Press, an imprint of Random House Children's Books, a division of Penguin Random House LLC, New York.

Delacorte Press is a registered trademark and the colophon is a trademark of Penguin Random House LLC.

Visit us on the Web! GetUnderlined.com
Educators and librarians, for a variety of teaching tools, visit us at RHTeachersLibrarians.com

Library of Congress Cataloging-in-Publication Data
Names: Epps, Omar, author. | Haynes, Clarence A., author.
Title: The awakening / Omar Epps and Clarence Haynes.
Description: First edition. | New York : Delacorte Press, 2022. |
Series: Nubia ; book 1 | Audience: Ages 14+ | Summary: In a climate-ravaged New York deeply divided by class, Zuberi, Uzochi, and Lencho, three teens of refugees from a fallen African utopia, begin to develop supernatural powers.
Identifiers: LCCN 2022012876 (print) | LCCN 2022012877 (ebook) |
ISBN 978-0-593-42864-1 (hardcover) | ISBN 978-0-593-42867-2 (paperback) |
ISBN 978-0-593-42865-8 (library binding) | ISBN 978-0-593-42866-5 (ebook) |
ISBN 978-0-593-64493-5 (international edition)
Subjects: CYAC: Ability—Fiction. | Social classes—Fiction. |
Refugees—Fiction. | Fantasy. | Fantasy fiction. lcgft | LCGFT: Novels.
Classification: LCC PZ7.1.E23 Aw 2022 (print) |
LCC PZ7.1.E23 (ebook) | DDC [Fic]—dc23

The text of this book is set in Adobe Caslon Pro.
Interior design by Jen Valero

Printed in the United States of America
10 9 8 7 6 5 4 3 2 1
First Edition

This is for my three children. Thank you for the eternal gift of fatherhood. I love you all beyond this world. —O.E.

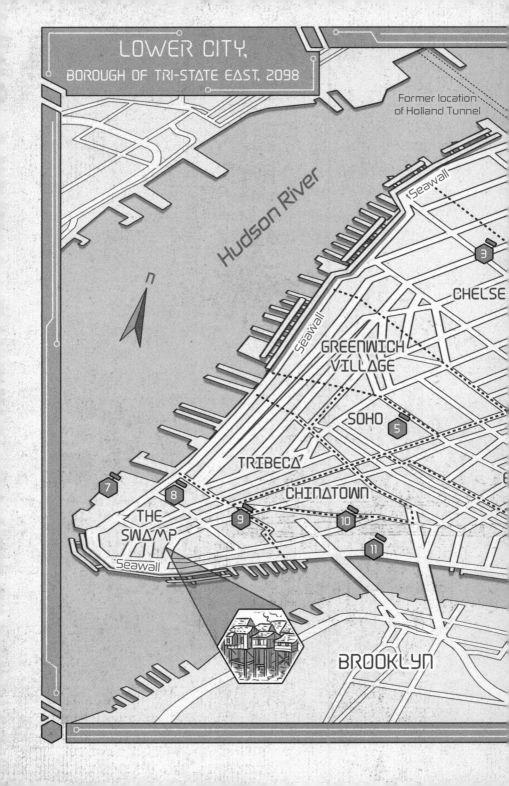

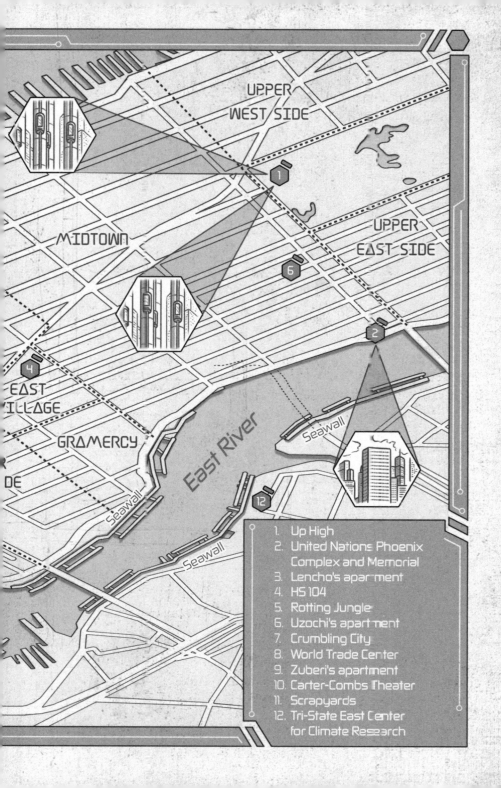

UPPER WEST SIDE

UPPER EAST SIDE

MIDTOWN

EAST VILLAGE

GRAMERCY

DE

East River

Seawall

Seawall

Seawall

KEY MOMENTS IN NEW YORK HISTORY

Preparatory Document for "Climate Refugees
of New York" Special Elective Section, HS 104

2059— first New York City seawall built in Inwood area
of upper Manhattan

2067— construction begins on the Up High, the world's
first sky city created with antigravity tech;
seen as residential option for the wealthy
concerned about rising sea levels

2071— first New Yorkers move to the Up High, soon
joined by host of other residents from around
the world

2072— the term "ascension" used for the first time by
Helios News commentator to describe process
of moving from lower city to the Up High;
becomes part of popular speech

2076— New York, New Jersey, and Connecticut break
away from the United States to form a new
independent government, Tri-State East (TSE);
its coastal counterpart, Tri-State West (TSW)—
consisting of California, Oregon, and Nevada—
is founded at the same time

2077— nu-raves first appear in city, a highly intelligent avian species cloned from traditional ravens; pigeon population radically decreases

2078— the United Nations Massacre occurs; scores of hostages are murdered, with terrorists apprehended by private militia later dubbed St. John Soldiers

2079— St. John Soldiers become primary peacekeeping force for TSE, which becomes only nation-state in Western Hemisphere to have fully privatized military/police force

2080— a group of female migrants from Mumbai working in education incorporate the principles of sexual consent into high school curricula across the city

2081— under second amendment to TSE's constitution, firearm possession made illegal nationwide with only specialized militia forces having access; mass transition made to stun gun and Taser tech

2082— series of storms descend on region, destroying parts of New York City's infrastructure, including subway system; additional seawalls

immediately built by St. John Enterprises; host
of Nubian refugees arrives

2083—large influx of refugees arrives from Caribbean,
including Jamaica, Haiti, Dominican Republic,
and Virgin Islands

2086—the Nubian Quarter is created in lower
Manhattan next to city's largest seawal ;
notable for being the only fully governmentally
subsidized neighborhood in New York

2089—clusters of Dutch climate migrants arrive:
responsible for design of vehicular hover
system that replaces subways

2093—the UN awards TSE biannual Lighthouse Prize
for its high rate of acceptance of climate
refugees; damaged lower-city economy
stabilizes due to real estate investments from
St. John Enterprises

Prologue

The streets of lower Manhattan were slick with rain, puddles glowing with light from the hologram news flashing across the buildings. The words FLOOD WARNING shone in red, continuously scrolling beneath the news reports. Those below in the Swamp kept their doors shut tight in response, or as tight as they could given the crumbling brick and mortar that made up their apartments. They, of course, were the lucky ones. Most of the inhabitants lived in archaic wooden shanties with aluminum roofs, sequestered in what had once been the financial district of New York City before the gleaming skyscrapers were demolished.

But whether the people were in apartments or shanties, each storm battered their homes even further, threatening to sweep them all away the next time the clouds darkened and the thunder roared. Each drop of rain spelled potential doom.

Still, those living below were strong. They built and rebuilt, using whatever materials they could to fortify their homes. They leaned on one another, holding tight to the community they'd carried across the sea. It wouldn't be the first time Nubians experienced a flood.

On this rainy night, a figure in a long coat slogged through the wet. They pulled their hood tighter against the chill in the air.

The figure's eyes moved to a holo-ad, watching the words blossom across the night sky amid the downpour.

Don't you want to ascend Up High?

Up High. The glorious promise of the sky city. The figure pivoted, taking in the terrain as far as they could. To the north stood the faint outlines of the sleek Central Park towers that ferried citizens to the heavens. In contrast, the south offered up a jagged brown seawall, one of several that loomed over the lower portions of New York.

The figure tilted their head back, gazing up at the promise itself. Above them, the city in the sky loomed large, glittering and bright, buoyed by its antigravity technology. Up there, the rain pattered gently on windows and roofs, never finding an open crack, never slipping through to aggravate the residents nestled inside.

Up High, a person wanted for nothing. Up High, rain was a steady melody to fall asleep to and not the stuff of nightmares.

Footsteps made the figure turn. They ducked closer to the nearest building, letting shadows swallow them whole. They watched for someone to appear, looking left and right as only one who knows they're being followed does. They waited, their breath white in the cold air.

The night was quiet, save for the rain. It beat steadily. Soon, it might stop completely, only to be replaced by an intense heat that would burn skin and take one's breath away. There was no telling with the weather. Not anymore.

But for now, the rain hid the sound of the footsteps as they started again. The figure, still pressed against the wall, found themself pulled back to the words of the holo-ad.

Find yourself in the sky.

Find yourself Up High.

The figure hugged themself against the chill.

They took a step forward, letting the light of the holo warm their face with its radiance, their arms falling to their sides. For a brief moment, they forgot about the rain.

They didn't see the person behind them until it was too late.

Chapter 1

Zuberi

Each punch brought Zuberi a bit closer to peace.

The bag she was working was ancient, peeling in places, with lopsided stuffing that left her knuckles smarting after the beating. She was going to need to do some rehab on it soon, otherwise she'd just be punching leather. Zuberi stepped back from the bag, taking a breath in the cool morning air. She rubbed absently at the silver scar on her chin, tossing her loc'ed hair away from her face as she forced herself to slow her breathing.

Zuberi knew that part of mastering the fighting forms was mastering the breath. It couldn't be all punching and kicking. Ever since her father had started to train her in Nubian fighting forms, he'd stressed the importance of mindfulness, of honing one's thoughts before landing each blow. Her father had drilled this philosophy into her brain ever since she was small, when it was her tiny fist connecting with his palm in their living room.

Now Zuberi had more than outgrown training in that

living room, mostly because it doubled as her bedroom. So she'd gotten creative, something she'd never had a problem with. Sometimes she'd train in an empty warehouse; other times she'd train in the scraggly Hudson scrapyards with their open access to the river. At school, there was the gym, which she used on occasion. But she preferred places in nature, one of the reasons she made the trek so early to Minerva Park. Nature, with its serenity and stillness, made it easier for her to find an organic connection between the human body and the outer world, an intention deeply embedded in the Nubian forms. Given that the city was mostly devoid of nature, though, she had to rely on the small offerings of trees and shrubs found in Minerva. There, Zuberi had her special hidden places where she could practice, like her little patch off to the side of the abandoned playground where there was a sturdy-enough tree to hang the trusty punching bag she'd bought cheap from one of her neighbors.

She had to admit it felt good to get out of the Swamp, as much as she loved her hood. The Nubian Quarter wasn't an actual swamp, of course, but that was what everyone had called it for as long as Zuberi could remember. She'd asked her father once why the quarter had been blessed with such a nickname, and he'd just shaken his head. He knew that when Zuberi asked a question—no matter how innocent it seemed—she usually had about five others in reserve.

The Swamp was where most Nubian refugees lived, a last resort after they'd fled their homeland and arrived in New York back in the early-2080s. Nubians couldn't find even the most menial jobs and were shut out of the renters' market by landlords, so they had no choice but to lease cheap plots of land held by the government in the city's abandoned financial district, which had since moved Up High. They'd been expected to fail, or so Zuberi's father told her. It had been through sheer Nubian will and a sense of community that they'd managed to build and maintain their homes there, humble as they might be.

Nubian will was behind most of the things Nubians had. Zuberi had seen it all her life. Her own father's determination to pass down the fighting forms was a testament to that, too, how he made sure she not only learned them all but could enact each of them in her sleep.

She turned back to the bag, shifting her weight as she landed more blows before switching to high kicks. She crouched low, her legs shaking from the exertion. She must've already been out in the park for at least an hour, and she was feeling it everywhere. Didn't matter. Pain was part of the process, and she welcomed it with open arms. Punching and kicking and maneuvering around the bag every day helped Zuberi deal with whatever she needed to deal with before she could be a "regular person," as Vriana liked to put it.

On the next punch, she connected with a sharp corner of the bag. Bright pain zinged up her arm and she stepped back. It was then that she heard a voice, a whisper.

Zuberi's head whipped around as she sought the source. She didn't expect to be in the park alone—many people used it for recreation and, in some cases, a home. But this early, it was usually quiet. Zuberi swiped at her brow before catching sight of something stirring in the brush across from her.

"Someone there?" she called out, flexing her fingers.

More stirring. Zuberi swore she heard a sort of gasping sound, followed by a cough.

She bit her lip. It was impossible not to hear her dad's voice in her head, telling her that this could be a trap and to run away—now. As the head of his own security company, he knew every trick and scam in the book. The city was rife with desperate people, and desperation made people dangerous.

But Zuberi also knew that if some mugger was hiding in the brush, they'd picked the wrong girl.

She took a few tentative steps toward the brush. As she got closer, a cool April breeze kicked up, making her shiver. She blinked at the dust stirred up around her, then opened her eyes again.

There.

At first, Zuberi didn't know what she was seeing. It was like a wisp of air, something both completely there and not, like a spark of electricity zipping over an exposed wire. Here and gone again, more than shadow but not by much. A wisp of a figure, barely discernible in the haze of morning. She blinked again, thinking the morning's exertion was getting to her.

And that was when the wisp sharpened.

A woman appeared, with long braids over her shoulders and eyes that glowed in the beams of sunlight that fell through the branches of the trees. Her gaze settled on Zuberi, piercing, unforgiving. She wore long robes, her arms crossed. Zuberi felt as if she was being judged, but for what?

The woman's eyes drifted down, and Zuberi started. There, on the ground, two feet poked out from behind a tree. A woman—the same woman who Zuberi saw clearly floating just above—was passed out, tucked into a hollow in the tree trunk beneath an array of branches that held a school of nu-raves. Her eyes were closed, her head slumped forward. Her skin was tinged purple, drool dribbling down her chin.

Zuberi recoiled.

Goddess . . .

She knew what she was seeing, even if she'd never seen it so up close before. She knew by the way the woman's veins swelled on her hands and how her cheeks hung slack that these were the signs of Elevation.

Elevation. Even the drugs that swarmed the city were laced with promises of Up High living. It made Zuberi's stomach churn, especially now, as the woman in front of her twitched.

But while Elevation explained the woman's condition, it didn't explain the figure floating above her. The woman continued to stare down at her in judgment through and through. That gaze, it reminded Zuberi of her father and her aunties. It reminded her—

Suddenly, the figure was gone. Zuberi squinted, then closed her eyes, then opened them again. The air was clear, empty. She stepped back, crossing her arms and squeezing them tight to her body. She felt dizzy.

She'd pushed herself too hard, clearly. Hallucinations were a problem with dehydration and overexertion. Her father told her so all the time. And when Zuberi looked back up at her empty water bottle, she knew she'd done way too much this morning.

Below her, the woman groaned, and Zuberi stepped back. Part of her wanted to wake the woman up, make sure she was okay. It was what Vriana would do, after all. But then she remembered her father's warning about strangers yet again.

So she left, deeply uneasy as she made her way home to shower and get ready for another day at High School 104. It would've been easier to do if all she had to worry about was class, but the woman's eyes followed her every step of the way, vicious and narrow no matter how Zuberi tried to shake them off.

By the time she reached the worn façade of 104, the morning had brightened. She entered the building and passed through the Taser and e-dagger detectors, finding the campus mostly empty since it was still fairly early. She could hear the occasional sounds of lectures droning through classrooms, signs of life thanks to those who took on the extra zero period. Beyond that, there were small knots of students leaning against concrete walls or huddled around benches. She saw one kid drawing long black lines down the side of a slab of concrete with a heavy marker, his moves lazy and unhurried. She watched to see what he was writing, though she had her guesses. Judging by the sun emblem on his jacket, he ran with the Divine, one of the gangs her father was always chasing away from the stores he ran security for.

"Beri!"

Zuberi jumped at the sound of her name, though as soon as Vriana appeared beside her, she relaxed. It was as instant as a hot bath, the way her best friend could always make her feel better. No matter what was going on, Vriana was the salve.

"Girl, I've been looking for you *everywhere*," Vriana said, pulling her into a quick embrace. "I'm exhausted and it's only morning."

Zuberi laughed. "Sorry. Just got here. What's up?"

Vriana flashed a toothy grin as she took hold of Zuberi's arm, guiding her to a nearby bench to sit. "I want to go check out those boys from the Divine Suns who're running track this morning," she said. "Did you see their muscles? Mm, mm, mm, oh-so-fine Divine."

Zuberi grinned and shook her head. Another day, another Vriana crush. They came in waves, almost as dependable as the dawn of a new day. It wasn't as if the love wasn't reciprocated, either. Zuberi would bet currency that her best friend was one of the most crushed-on kids in their grade. Even non-Nubian kids flirted with Vriana, a feat that Zuberi would've declared next to impossible given the rampant prejudice Nubians faced.

Of course, it wasn't hard to see why people fell for Vriana, considering she was beauty incarnate. Where Zuberi was athletic leanness with a streamlined, subtle personal style, Vriana was effortless curves wrapped in trendsetting fashion. Today, she was wearing dark blue jeans with lightning-bolt rips on the thighs, paired with a neon-pink kente tee knotted just above her hip to show off a sliver of skin. Vriana had a warmth that shone through all over, from the way she spoke with her hands to the gleam in her brown eyes, often accentuated with a rainbow of colors that Zuberi knew she never could've pulled off. Today, Vriana had lined her eyes in silver and gold, a perfect counterpart to her navy-and-magenta braids, which were swept up in a side bun. With her braids up, Zuberi could see the thin plate earring that Vriana always wore.

"Beri? You listening to me?"

Zuberi blinked. No, she hadn't been listening. Like so many of her peers, Zuberi had been briefly wrapped up in taking Vriana in. You'd think multiple years of friendship would've dulled the effect, but Vriana still struck anyone she met into a brief—and embarrassing—stupor. Zuberi felt a bit better when she saw a boy across the way literally trip over his feet to look at Vriana before running into a wall.

"Sorry," Zuberi said, shaking her head with a laugh as Vriana looked over her shoulder at the boy. "I was just checking out your eyeliner."

"Oh, it's perfect today, right?" Vriana said, tapping the side of her right eye. "You wouldn't believe how long I spent on it. Anyway—the hot Divine—"

"Hang on," Zuberi said, raising her hand. "Didn't you just start dating that girl from chem?"

Vriana scowled. "Right. Samantha. She got crazy possessive, so I broke it off last night. I was going to text you but it was late."

"You broke it off? Vri, you'd been talking about that chick nonstop for days. I mean, *Sammie* this, *Sammie* that . . ."

"And it was going well and fine until she started interrogating me about where I'd been and who I'd been hanging out with after the second date. *And* asking me why I wasn't answering her messages right away?" Vriana made a dismissive gesture with her fingers. "Um, no, unacceptable. That's just a controlling relationship waiting to happen. And you know my freedom is too important to me to be dealing with possessiveness."

Zuberi rolled her eyes. "Goddess give me strength. All right, okay. Continue."

"Thank you," Vriana said. "Anyway, I've got my eye on this one Divine guy, Zaire. Really big and hunky . . . and *juicy*. I need you to do some recon for me. He seems like the strong, silent type, but just in case he's actually an asshole—"

"Girl, you're saying you'll break up with someone for being too possessive, but a full-blown *Divine* kid is okay?" Zuberi scoffed, shaking her head again. "He's literally in a gang. As in, hurts people on a regular basis."

Vriana dug through her scholar-pack, waving her free hand absently at Zuberi.

"He's just misunderstood," Vriana said. "Trust me. We have some classes together and he seems so sweet and sensitive. And besides, not all of the Divine are savage. Like I said, if you do the recon—"

"Which involves what, exactly?"

"Well, you know, since you're also the strong, silent type, you'll be able to tell if he's a good guy."

Zuberi snorted. "That literally makes no sense."

Vriana extracted a notebook, one she'd decorated with a variety of sparkling stickers, and began flipping through the pages. "It makes perfect sense. Maybe you can invite him for one of your morning workouts."

The mention of the workout sent a shiver up Zuberi's

spine, and she worried her lip. Vriana looked up at her and raised an eyebrow.

"What?" Vriana asked, pausing her notebook flipping. "Something happen this morning?"

Zuberi shrugged. She didn't like to hide things from Vriana, mostly because Vriana could be counted on to dig and dig until she unearthed whatever it was that Zuberi was trying to keep a secret. Like when Zuberi had stumbled over to her house on that horrible night . . .

She turned away from the memory, trying to force her mind to stay on the current problem. Unfortunately, that meant focusing on what she'd just experienced in the park.

Had she really seen a spirit?

Zuberi caught her best friend's worried gaze. She knew Vriana would want to know every detail of what she saw and help her work through it. After all, Vriana fancied herself an amateur therapist—and she wasn't half bad. Still, even if Zuberi wanted to be honest with her friend, what could she say?

"Nothing," Zuberi said. "Just got kind of spooked while I was working out, I guess. Felt a little woozy. Probably didn't drink enough water."

Vriana's face relaxed. "I'm always telling you that you don't hydrate enough."

Zuberi smiled and tapped her friend on the shoulder. "Sage advice."

Vriana hooked her free arm through Zuberi's and dragged them both to their feet.

"Come on," Vriana said, leading the two of them toward the

opposite side of the school where more students were starting to filter in. "If we hurry, I bet we can catch the end of the
practice. Oh, and you can quiz me for history."

She passed the notebook to Zuberi, open and flipped to
where she'd written her notes.

"Ugh," Zuberi said, looking at the pages. "I forgot. It's an
essay test, too right?"

"Yep," Vriana said with a sigh. "And completely unnecessary. I don't care what a bunch of dead guys did a billion
years ago. They could be teaching us something interesting,
like how we should take care of our bodies and relate to each
other, but noooooooo. It's always gotta be about why this old
dead guy hated this other dead guy and . . . oh, guess what?
They helped jack up the world and then they died."

Zuberi bit her lip. It was one of the things she and Vriana
would never agree on, no matter what. Vriana was smart, one
of the smartest kids in their grade, but there were subjects
she cared about—psychology, chem, and lit, for example—
and subjects she loathed. History fell into the latter category.
She claimed it was because she liked to focus on the present,
but for Zuberi, you couldn't appreciate the present without
also knowing the past.

It wasn't like Zuberi was in love with their history class,
especially since their preceptors always gave them the same
rehashed versions of Tri-State East events: the climate catastrophes, the building of the first seawall in New York, the
creation of the sky city, and so on. Lessons were always taught
with the air that the creation of Up High had saved so many

and created a new age where everyone had the chance to succeed. Nubians, the people who had come to this city after their own land was destroyed, were completely forgotten.

Still, learning history was important to Zuberi, even if she got a watered-down version. At least she could fill in the holes, uncovering what people were hiding about the system. And she could uncover the lies told by folks like Krazen St. John.

It was the kind of thing that could get Zuberi ranting for hours. How Krazen St. John's promise of a better life Up High was a big piece of the problem. Something for the lower-city residents—particularly Nubian refugees—to chase after so that they never stopped to realize that it was *because* of the Up High that they suffered. How many funds went Up High rather than to the lower city where they were needed? Why did Up High residents always get the best tech, the best medical attention, the best everything, while those in the lower city dealt with crumbling roads and decrepit buildings and streets crawling with St. John Soldiers?

"Beri, you're doing it again."

She blinked. Vriana had nearly marched them all the way to the field, though they were currently walking through the trailers that held foreign-language classes on the outskirts of the school. The area was mostly deserted, save for a few groups of kids huddled together along the edges of campus. Behind them, covered in thick grime, was a once-yellow HS 104 CREATES STARS sign that had been defaced numerous times. It was a fairly depressing part of 104, and that was saying something.

"Sorry," Zuberi said. "What'd you say?"

"Going into your own world again," Vriana replied with a huff. "Ignoring my pressing test needs. Don't worry, though. We're almost there."

"Right," Zuberi said, trying to stay present. "You wanted—"

A rock zipped past Zuberi's face, so close that she felt a rush of wind on her cheek. She whipped toward the source to find a tall, lanky boy leaning against one of the concrete pillars, his lips curled into a cruel smile. His friends behind him smirked and sneered.

Zuberi's eyes swept over them, from the snaking tattoo on one of their necks to the web insignias scrawled on the sides of their jackets. All part of a gang, dubbing themselves the Spiders.

In Zuberi's last two years at 104, she'd watched as gangs slowly became more ubiquitous. It had started with small interactions in the hallway, the way different crews glared at each other, and had moved on to an uptick in tagging chairs, walls, toilets . . . anywhere that could be reached, really. Then, of course, there were the fights. With each mix-up, the gangs got a little bolder. It was one of the reasons why Zuberi fully intended to tell Vriana—no matter how "nice" Zaire seemed— that gang members were off-limits.

Case in point, the Spider asshole now staring Zuberi down. He was thin with yellowing teeth, no doubt the result of whatever form of Elevation he was taking. She glared at him, wishing he would evaporate on the spot.

"Hello, ladies," the skinny boy said, picking up another rock. "Don't y'all look good."

Zuberi fought to keep her fists unclenched.

17

She moved to keep walking, but before she could, two boys she hadn't seen stepped in front of her and Vriana. Immediately, her breathing spiked.

It won't be like last time, she told herself. *Calm down.*

Next to her, Vriana laughed, a high, tinkling sound.

"Throwing rocks to get our attention?" Vriana teased. "Are we in second grade?"

The skinny boy kicked off from where he was leaning, striding toward them, nearly closing them in.

"Oh, believe me," he growled. "We're far from that."

Vriana still smiled, both hands tightly gripping the straps of her scholar-pack. "Good. Then you'll let us get to class."

"You weren't going to class," said the boy. "You were going to watch those Divine losers. But don't worry. We'll forgive you."

Zuberi glanced at Vriana, seeing her friend's smile falter ever so slightly.

"How 'bout you back the fuck up, you skanky zombie," Zuberi said, eyes cutting to the boy again as she stepped forward, forcing him to take a step back.

His head lurched toward her, a look of disbelief on his face. "What'd you say to me?"

"You heard me," Zuberi said, realizing that she knew this fool's name from hearing other Spiders shout him out on campus. "Back the fuck up, Kal. We don't want to talk to you."

He sidestepped her, moving in on Vriana. "No problem. We'll talk to your friend."

Kal's eyes traveled down the girl's body, lingering on her chest and thighs before he raised his eyebrows gleefully at his friends. They snorted with laughter as panic gathered in Vriana's eyes.

"We're leaving," Zuberi said, grabbing her friend's hand. It was shaking.

You're running again, Zuberi scolded herself. *You could take every one of those guys. So why are you running?*

But now wasn't the time, not with Vriana by her side. Even if she could take them, it wasn't worth getting her best friend hurt.

It didn't help either that, when she looked at the boy's eyes, she saw the woman from earlier. Strung out. Alone. And still, the look of judgment.

"Come on," Zuberi said, her voice barely a whisper. "Let's go."

Vriana nodded. She didn't question why Zuberi steered them away from both the Spiders and the Divine on the track field, moving them straight to class.

But Zuberi still felt the look of the Spiders on her back. She knew that she'd just become a target.

She didn't mind.

Let them try.

Next time, she'd show them exactly who they were messing with.

Chapter 2

Uzochi

Uzochi's favorite class was his zero-period special elective, with its roster of rotating topics. Here, in the early-dawn course that was only taken by students who wanted to excel, he found peace. In this class, no one judged him for arriving five minutes early or for his color-coded notes (yellow, orange, and royal blue being his favorite hues). No one laughed behind their hands when he soared to the top of the digital scoreboard during review games. No one whispered among their friends while he tried to concentrate on his tests. No, in zero-period special elective, Uzochi sat among peers who, like him, were dedicated to something greater, who *really* wanted something and were willing to sacrifice an extra two hours of sleep per day to achieve it.

A few students had parents who forced them to take zero period, but honestly, Uzochi didn't mind that. He understood parental pressure all too well.

"This will all be worth it," his mother would sometimes

tell him as he packed for school before the rest of the neighborhood woke up. "When we ascend, you'll look back on your choices with pride."

Uzochi's eyes swept the room, taking in the other students. Each of them sat at their desk, organized in rows with their digital notebooks open. He heard the usual light *tap-tap-tap* as his peers chose their answers for this morning's quiz. Sitting a few rows behind him, his classmate Sekou absently twirled a tablet pen in his hand. Sekou was one of the students who Uzochi would've guessed was here because of his parents, but he also had an effortless cool that meant he belonged anywhere. He could join the students clowning around in regular history and then the next day put his head down and ace the tests in special elective. Sekou moved through 104 like water, fluid and malleable, able to fit into a variety of spaces.

Uzochi was envious. He couldn't be water. He'd tried, but he believed himself to be more like stone. Immovable, rigid.

Instantly, a modulated voice chirped, "Eyes on your own paper, students."

Uzochi's gaze flicked over to the droid positioned at the center of the classroom, its digital eyes scanning from corner to corner. The whir of the robot was white noise to Uzochi at this point, as were the quiet *ping*s that swept the room after its scan. On a couple of his peers' desk screens, he saw the warning signs flashing: *ACADEMIC DISHONESTY DETECTED; THIS IS A WARNING.*

No such warning popped up on Uzochi's desk, though he

had read a different message in green: *If you're done with the test, please move on to the essay assignment posted on your class stream.*

Uzochi had turned in his quiz approximately five minutes ago, not that he was counting. His gaze moved to where his teacher, Preceptor Ryan, sat at her desk, casually swiping at her own desk screen. Uzochi knew she was grading tests from her other classes. She didn't always do it, but he could tell when she did. She crossed out sentences and circled things with her tablet pen, using a free hand to rub her temple. Sometimes, Uzochi swore he even heard her thoughts drift through the classroom, but he knew that was just the lack of sleep creeping in.

He glanced at the digital clock on his desk. Twenty more minutes. He'd hoped his peers would finish their tests fast enough so that he could get a jump on his next class's lecture notes, but clearly that wouldn't be happening.

He sighed, pulling up the essay assignment on his digital notebook along with a separate tab for notes. Then he read the prompt, highlighting key phrases with his tablet pen as he went.

Essay Prompt: Using primary source documents, consider the impact of immigration on New York's economy and population following the Great Storms of 2082. Identify pros and cons to ultimately determine whether immigration was a boon or disadvantage for the city. Be sure to consider multiple perspectives in your argument.

Uzochi bit his lip. When they'd first entered this section

of the elective—the part titled "Climate Refugees of New York, 2082 and Beyond" in his textbook—he'd hoped that this was the point when his people's history would finally be acknowledged by his school. After all, how could Nubians be left out of the material when they were so many of the refugees in question?

His hopes had been buoyed when Preceptor Ryan had rolled in one of 104's only two holo-projectors, something that usually signaled that a lecture would be special or interesting. Uzochi had sat up as Ryan paced in the loose navy jumpsuit all preceptors wore, waiting for her to tell the story of his people.

She gave a short overview of how global climate catastrophes drove migration to the city, asking the class to refer to the timeline document she'd transmitted, and then moved on to focus on Nubians. Uzochi had leaned forward, ready for her words.

"Soooo, smack-dab in the middle of the Great Storms of 2082, thousands of Nubians reached the shores of New York by boat. They'd supposedly arrived from a remote island that had remained unmapped for centuries. It's important to note that these claims have *not* been substantiated." Preceptor Ryan pursed her lips, the skepticism on her face palpable. "They settled mostly in the lower regions of Manhattan, eventually clustering in the Nubian Quarter, though some were lucky enough to find better homes farther north and in the outer boroughs."

Next to Preceptor Ryan, a crisp three-dimensional image

had appeared above the projector—a brown seawall looming over rows and rows of shanties all resting on thick, criss-crossing stilts. Uzochi knew the area all too well . . . the Nubian Quarter, more often referred to as the Swamp.

"Immediately, their arrival put a strain on the economy," Preceptor Ryan had continued. "Adult Nubians rarely joined the workforce, which isn't too surprising given that the vast majority of the population remains uneducated, holding blue-collar jobs like security guards, domestics, street vendors . . . Of course, some Nubians *rise above* this. A few excel as athletes and artists. But, unfortunately, the general pattern has been one of poverty, and it's a vicious cycle. You all know of the young people in the community who've turned to gang life."

She'd looked meaningfully around the room, and plenty of students had shifted uncomfortably. In her gaze was the unspoken question, "Are you next?"

"Now, of course, there are new programs to help Nubian refugees excel," Preceptor Ryan said, clicking to her last slide, an image of Krazen St. John awarding one of his annual Rise Above scholarships to a tall Nubian girl with a gigantic smile holding a huge check—the scholarship Uzochi planned to apply for senior year.

Beside the beaming girl, Krazen St. John stood slightly off, his bald head shining under auditorium lights and the gray circuitry of his implants glistening on his neck and hands and the left side of his face. His olive skin was otherwise covered up by one of his trademark caftans, which swept the ground.

"Thanks to these programs," Preceptor Ryan finished, "we've been able to help build up the community. But it's not easy to break cycles of stagnation. It's why I'm so proud of those of you who are here."

Her eyes had glittered meaningfully, and Uzochi knew he wasn't the only one who avoided her gaze. He understood that her comments were directed toward the few Nubians in the class.

"Now," she'd continued. "Moving on to other refugees impacted by rising sea levels . . ."

The image of Krazen St. John then morphed into a video of the flooded canals of Amsterdam, marking the end of what Preceptor Ryan had to say about Nubians.

Uzochi hadn't known what to think after the lecture, only that it all felt wrong. The problem was, Nubians were always associated with the horrors of 2082, as if they'd somehow brought over the storms that had left parts of New York permanently flooded. Uzochi knew the message well—that Nubians were untrustworthy, bad luck, omens of doom, purveyors of weather-based witchcraft. But he'd hoped his teacher would have more to say about the time. Part of him had even dared wish that she might correct the prejudiced stories instead of repeating what most people said about Nubians barely contributing anything to New York.

One look at his test, though, told him that not only did her lecture cover all that she had to say about his people, but Uzochi was expected to repeat it for his essay.

A message from Sekou popped up on Uzochi's screen. It wasn't the school's official channel but his personal one, one he—and every other student who knew better—had created through a hack. Uzochi glanced up at Preceptor Ryan to check that she was still grading and looked back at the message.

Sekou: *This essay's some bullshit.*

Uzochi caught his breath. He agreed with Sekou. Of course he did. But typing that? Even if teachers couldn't see his screen's content through standard monitoring systems, Preceptor Ryan might get up and walk around the classroom and spot his message. But she *was* grading, obviously . . . Still, he'd just need to keep his response neutral, to be on the safe side.

Uzochi: *Yeah, I was just looking at it. It's kinda hard.*

He looked over and saw Sekou shaking his head. A flurry of messages appeared on Uzochi's screen.

Sekou: *Hard? It's not hard. They want the party line even with the ton of Nubians that attend 104. Fuck that. She wants pros and cons? How about how my dad was forced to work as a street vendor for years before getting a sucky construction job? How about how we live in the Swamp because that's the only place they let us live? Nah. I'm telling the truth.*

Uzochi felt his chest tighten. He knew Sekou was right, but writing an essay like that would definitely get his friend into trouble. Sure, Sekou was half Nubian, half Italian, but he was open and proud about his Nubian heritage. Uzochi didn't exactly have a choice in sharing what he was. With his particular set of features, he was Nubian through and through, and he was fine with his ancestry. But if he wanted to get anywhere in life, he had to earn that St. John scholarship and ascend.

Uzochi's fingers hovered over the keyboard. He didn't know what to type. He caught Sekou's eyes, bright, waiting, and he knew before he answered that whatever he said would be a disappointment.

Up front, the droid began to whir louder. Uzochi looked up to see that several students around him had their mobiles out, whispering frantically about something.

"Students," Preceptor Ryan said, standing up from her desk. "Devices away. You know better."

The students exchanged looks but then stowed their devices, returning to their work. Uzochi didn't miss that many of them had been messaging, just as he and Sekou had. Sure enough, a new message from Sekou popped up on Uzochi's screen.

Spiders and Divine getting into it again. Security's already broken it up. Don't know why they do this shit at school.

Uzochi breathed a sigh of relief. This, at least, he and Sekou agreed on. Uzochi started to type back, but a new message appeared first.

Is it true your cousin's running with the Divine now?

Uzochi's fingers froze on the keypad. He knew the answer to the question but didn't want to tell Sekou. The shame already burned through Uzochi constantly.

He occasionally saw his older cousin in the hallways of 104, happy to pass him by as quickly as he could. Lencho Will was the kind of guy who rapidly filled up space with his arrogance and posturing, something Uzochi had no time for.

And now, based on everything he knew, his cousin was running with the Divine.

Uzochi glanced at Sekou, who was clearly waiting for his reply. He worried his lip and then began to type.

I dunno. Hope not. He'd be stupid to do that.

There. Now it was obvious—at least to Sekou—where Uzochi stood.

Another message popped up.

Have you talked to him? Bad shit happens to people in the Divine.

Uzochi tried not to look annoyed, wanting to send a snide message in response. Sekou clearly didn't know Lencho. You didn't just "talk" to his cousin. Speaking to a concrete wall yielded better results. But something told Uzochi that Sekou wanted a real answer.

The bell for next period rang through the room, harsh and piercing, saving Uzochi from having to reply. Everyone emptied out, including Sekou, while Uzochi took time to pack up. He didn't need to be part of the crowd, especially if a fight had just been broken up. He zipped his pack and turned to leave just as one of next period's students walked into the room. Uzochi's heart nearly fell out of his chest.

Zuberi.

He knew the girl from the halls of 104, the statuesque Nubian with the slight silver scar along her chin and cloud of midnight locs. In the English class they shared together last semester, she sat quietly in the back and slipped out as soon as the bell rang. Occasionally, she wore those bursts of color associated with descendants of Nubia—a sash of cerulean here, a scarf of topaz there.

The most incredible girl Uzochi had ever seen.

She threw her stuff down next to her seat and immediately

started typing on her desk screen, not wasting a single minute. Just like he would've, getting straight to work.

"Uzochi? Did you need something?"

Preceptor Ryan's voice cut through the room, and Uzochi immediately wished the ground would swallow him up. Because now Zuberi was staring at him, right when he was looking like a complete fool.

"Uh, no," he said quickly, shouldering his scholar-pack. "Just leaving. Um . . . yeah. Bye."

He avoided looking at Zuberi, but he could've sworn she was smirking. He walked quickly past her desk, mentally kicking himself the entire way.

Maybe there should be a special elective on talking to girls, Uzochi thought. He would take it in a heartbeat.

Chapter 3

Lencho

"Dude, I'm telling you, it would be a gold mine."

The air around Lencho was heavy with the scent of spices and smoke pouring from the line of food trucks parked along the streets near 104. Kids from school were crowded all around, eager to fill up on the daily offerings. Some chose the cheapest options, while others . . . well, they weren't loaded exactly, but they had currency to exchange.

Currency Lencho was desperate to get his hands on.

"I'm telling you, these kids'll buy anything if we sell it to them the right way," he muttered. "We'd have a constant stream of income. Enough to—"

"Lencho, it's school. We gotta draw the line."

Aren's voice was deep, heavy, the sound of a boy who'd truly grown into a man. And even though he was only slightly older than Lencho, that year of being out of 104 had aged him beyond just his voice. He sported a mane of black-and-brown curls and a long beard that he hadn't worn when he was at school, along with new tattoos and a few scars encircling his arms. And though Lencho was the taller of the two, Aren's presence was weightier. More powerful

It was why, Lencho knew, Aren was a natural leader for the Divine, why he'd been chosen as general and able to rise up the ranks so quickly. But—and Lencho would've never said so out loud—Aren's tough visage wasn't always mirrored on the inside. He drew too many lines. As far as Lencho was concerned, it was costing the Divine.

And it was costing Lencho.

"The Spiders don't care," Lencho said. "They sell to kids in my grade and lower. I know they do."

Together, Lencho and Aren made their way through the makeshift market that lined the path of almost every kid heading home from 104. Beyond the market were sooty brick buildings and streets where rusted hover cars glided past, their engines a steady hum. Merchants without trucks found space on the sidewalk, hanging over makeshift pits of fire, roasting pans heavy with fried eggs or insects or arachnids. It was a bustling place, full of voices and the sound of clanking utensils.

Lencho had brought Aren here so that he could see the possibility. In fact, he'd begged Aren to meet him here after Lencho had gotten off school. He'd spent his classes brainstorming how it would all work. How they could get Elevation cheaply from their usual sources, but instead of pouring it into the streets—where their regular clientele was primarily made up of those already addicted—they could find new customers, kids their age eager to experiment. The plan was foolproof.

"The Spiders are the reason *not* to do it," said another voice from behind Lencho. He turned his head slightly, finding Lara trailing after them, a whipped yogurt in hand. She looked intimidating as always, with her chiseled face and shaved head. As she tilted her head at Lencho, judgment leaked from every pore.

Lencho hadn't wanted Lara to be there today. As Aren's right-hand lieutenant, it was technically Lara's job to overthink every new move the Divine Suns made. But it didn't mean Lencho loved having her around, poking holes in his plan before he even had a chance to defend himself.

"Right, moving in on their turf and transactions. I get it. But we can handle them," Lencho said. "Besides, they're too high and mighty as it is. They're getting arrogant, and someone needs to shut 'em up."

Someone, Lencho thought wildly, *like me.*

Lencho had been in the Divine for only a month or so, and he wasn't taken seriously. He was just another kid trying to prove himself, but other kids didn't have the stakes that Lencho had, didn't have his promise.

Aren steadied his gaze.

"Look, man, I know you want to do this and resolve our supplier issue," he said. "But I've got a line, okay? No schools, no Nubians. There're too many of us who go to 104. We don't hurt kids, and we don't hurt our own."

Lencho clenched his fists together in the pocket of his hoodie, forcing himself to breathe. It took every part of him not to tell Aren that he was fucking this up majorly, that life was shit and sometimes you needed to do what you needed to do, scruples be damned. But in the end, he fixed a smile on his face and nodded.

"Sure," he said. "Respect."

He caught Lara's eye, the smirk clear as day on her face. He hated when she looked at him like that.

"Keep it up, sweetie," she said, giving him a pat on the shoulder like he was a dog. "You'll make something happen someday."

"It's true," said Aren. "Just keep your eyes out for opportunity. You want some stuff to sell for later, maybe when you're back in your hood or uptown?"

"No" was what Lencho wanted to say. Selling kept him firmly in groundling territory, and he wanted to be a leader. But what choice did he have? So he nodded, and Aren passed him a small bag of Elevation, which Lencho quickly stowed in his pocket, hiding the iridescent purple pills that easily attracted attention.

"It's good to see you, man," Aren said, giving Lencho a light pound on his fist. "I like how your minds always moving. Lara and I got some shit to do, all right? But we'll talk soon. Light be with you, bruh."

Lara said nothing, barely waving goodbye as she and Aren walked away.

Lencho tried not to look as hurt as he felt as the two of them left the market. He'd have to make do with what he had, or, at least, he'd have to come up with more reasons why his plan was the right one. His eyes swept the crowd in frustration as he was forced to ignore the plethora of potential consumers for the Divine. He felt antsy, like he needed to make some sort of move.

"So it's true then."

Lencho turned at the sound of the voice. There, in the crowd, stalking toward him, was one of the last people he wanted to see right now.

Uzochi already looked unreasonably preppy with his spiffy brown jacket and gray slacks and shiny scholar-pack, but it was the smug, holier-than-thou look on his face that really pushed Lencho over the edge.

"What's true?" Lencho said as Uzochi stepped in front of him.

"That you've joined the Divine," Uzochi said, eyes narrowed.

Lencho looked past his cousin to make sure Aren and Lara had disappeared into the crowd, and then he shrugged.

"Yeah, it's true," he said. "What about it?"

Lencho took in the scene. He let his gaze travel to the beefy construction workers who sat nearby on the crumbling curb, eating scorched mealworms and peppers off wooden kebab sticks, and the women in flowing skirts and trousers and tunics with little kids in tow. He didn't see any adults he recognized. He needed to make sure there weren't any nosy aunties nearby who'd say something to Uzochi's mom. He'd never hear the end of it, the suggestion that he was pulling Uzochi away from his schoolwork and over to the dark side. The side where you ran with gangs.

As if Lencho would want a mouse like Uzochi running with him. He tried to imagine what the other Divine would say if Lencho even so much as suggested bringing his cousin into the crew. Uzochi, sanctimonious preceptor's pet who thought he was better than everyone. It was bullshit.

"Why would you do this?" Uzochi asked, shaking his head, oblivious to Lencho's thought. "Those guys fight over nothing."

"*We,*" Lencho corrected, folding his arms over his chest, "defend our turf. There's a difference."

Uzochi scoffed. "Turf, you say, like you own territory. But guess what? You don't. It's just . . . pointless."

"Right," Lencho said. "I should be reading more, right? Buy into that goody-goody ascension nonsense like you? Kiss the ass of the same people who call you a shack fucker?"

He swept his hand to where the words GO BACK TO THE SWAMP were scrawled in paint across a nearby poster advertising one of Krazen St. John's newest "social welfare" programs. More crap that people like Uzochi were desperate enough to buy into.

"*If I just read enough books and follow all their rules, maybe they'll let me in,*" Lencho said, his voice high and cruel and mocking. "Wake up, dude. At least we're getting what we're owed in the Divine. Some of us have actually had to grow up."

Uzochi's look of shame and pity never wavered as he kept shaking his head. He looked like he wanted to say something but held back.

Lencho felt like he was suddenly seeing his cousin for the first time. *Uzochi . . . is an uppity ass.*

"You know what, just leave me alone, all right?" he said. "I can't look like—"

35

"Like what?" Uzochi interrupted. "Like I'm your family? Because I am."

Again, sparks rippled through Lencho. He closed his eyes to try to quiet the sensation, and then his gaze returned to his cousin.

"Blood's just blood," Lencho said. "I don't need it."

"Look—"

Uzochi started speaking, but almost instantly, he stopped. His eyes went wide, like he'd just heard or experienced something . . . horrible. Even for Uzochi, it was weird as hell.

"Dude, what?"

"Did you hear that?" Uzochi said, eyes still wide as he turned around. "Something . . . someone screamed."

Now he knew it. The constant studying had finally gotten to the kid.

"Over there," Uzochi said, suddenly moving. "Come on!"

Lencho wanted nothing to do with his cousin, but the terror in his eyes was real. And so, with a hesitant look over his shoulder, he followed Uzochi from a distance, matching his pace.

They ran out of the market, turning down a nearby alley. At first, Lencho was about to curse Uzochi out for losing his shit—until Lencho saw the girl.

He knew her from school, barely. Zuberi. The badass fighter chick with that little silver scar.

And she was currently pinned against the wall by a damn Spider, his elbow lodged against her throat.

Chapter 4

Zuberi

"See what happens when you disrespect us? Told you you'd pay."

Zuberi had known they'd try something. All day, Spiders had mad-dogged her when they saw her in the halls. She'd disrespected and humiliated one of their own, after all. But other things had called for her attention and Spider bullshit had been pushed out of her mind.

She'd been leaving school when it had happened again, same as that morning. A group of guys gathered near 104's exit, taunting each other while they played some game on their cracked tablets. Zuberi had barely noticed them, had given them a passing glance, and then, when she tilted her head up, she'd seen something else. Floating figures, shifting slightly in the air.

She'd stared at them, blinking rapidly, like they were images that wouldn't fully load on one of her screens. She'd stood completely still and continued to look at the phantoms, squinting hard, desperate to parse out what she was seeing.

And then, of course, one of the guys had snorted with laughter, and the figures had evaporated on the spot.

Was it still dehydration? Exhaustion? Zuberi didn't know. She'd told Vriana she needed to go straight home, though, sensing that maybe she needed to take a nap. What she *really* wanted to do was train more with the forms, but somehow that didn't seem like the best idea.

She'd decided to walk through the market, thinking maybe she needed to eat, and wound her way through the crowds and the food trucks, taking in each menu to decide what she'd grab for the road. But then she realized she'd lost whatever appetite she'd had because of the odd visions. Deep in thought, she slowly walked past the lines of trucks to a more deserted corner of the market marked by rolling trash and abandoned vehicles.

"I'm telling you, no. My answer won't change. I'm not selling that shit to Nubians."

Zuberi had stopped short when she heard the voice, one she faintly recognized. She turned her head, realizing it was coming from behind a gutted hover van.

"Aren, I hate to admit this, but Lencho's right, we need to branch out," said another voice—a girl's.

Moving silently on the tips of her toes, Zuberi crept closer to the voices, inching up to the side of the van and daring to peek around its huge rear fender. She immediately recognized the boy. Aren was a Nubian who used to go to 104, with rumors circulating that he'd dropped out to run the Divine full-time.

Zuberi didn't like eavesdropping, wasn't her style. But

here was possibly concrete info she could give to Vriana about exactly why she needed to avoid the gang. After all, there was no doubt in Zuberi's mind what these two were talking about. The Divine sold Elevation, which led to damaged folks like the woman Zuberi had seen earlier slumped against the tree. And maybe they didn't sell to Nubians, but *someone* was selling to her people. In the past few years since the substance had hit the market, Zuberi had watched several Swamp families deal with constantly drugged-out relatives battling Elevation addiction. It wasn't pretty.

"We focus on the customers we have," Aren said. "They're loyal."

"They're hooked, sure," the girl said. "But they're too far gone, too poor. And we need to up our numbers. You know we're at risk of not being able to pay back our suppliers unless we make more sales. *Significantly* more sales. You're always the one going on about taking the Divine to the next level, how we need to act like pros."

Zuberi waited for the answer from Aren. She remembered him, a funny, cool kid with a laugh like a bolt of lightning. Always seemed older than he was, but this? This sounded above even him.

"We'll figure it out," he said. "I don't want to talk about this anymore."

"Aren—"

Zuberi realized just in time that the conversation was over and they were about to head her way. She shuffled off to the side just as quietly as before, ducking into an alley to hide. She watched them from the shadows, Aren and his mystery

Divine girl, as they strolled back into the market crowd and disappeared.

It was then that she'd heard the nearly hysterical laugh of Kal and several other Spiders behind her, waiting in the dark.

Zuberi barely had time to register what was happening, realizing that this was becoming a very unfortunate day. They'd caught her unaware, she'd give them that. It was how the asshole in front of her had gotten his hand around her throat, a move he was about to regret.

Rage crystallized in Zuberi's body, running hot, then cold, then hot again, Kal grinning in the background, letting one of his cronies do the work. She shut her eyes to let fury settle into her legs, her arms, her core, her hands . . .

Today, she would *not* be running away.

She clenched her fists, angling her leg to knee the closest Spider in the groin. She'd strike him hard, and then she could take out the others. It would be simple, her mastery of the fighting forms ready to be unleashed. She would—

"Let her go!"

Both Zuberi and the Spider holding her whipped their heads toward the voice. There, standing in the alleyway, was someone Zuberi would've never expected to see. Uzochi Will.

Uzochi.

She knew him from a couple of classes. Studious, well-mannered, and hardworking, with his hair often in fastidious cornrows and his clothes crisp, neat. The kind of guy who kept his head down and didn't ask for trouble. Someone her father would've said "had his head on straight." She knew Uzochi was waking up early for zero-period electives, having seen him that morning leaving class as she settled into first period.

But beyond that, Zuberi hadn't learned much about the boy. He was quiet and kept to himself, which Zuberi could relate to. Otherwise, she knew him in the way so many young Nubians knew each other, through rumors and stories and passing comments. Her father knew his mother, just like everyone else who had roots in the Swamp.

So why was it that when Uzochi showed up, Zuberi felt a weird ripple through her entire being?

It was like the moment in the park when she'd known there was something—someone—there before she'd found the Elevated woman. Because now, when Uzochi's eyes met Zuberi's gaze, something dark and heavy and bright and loud hit her all at once. Something otherworldly.

Something much more dangerous than the hand on her neck.

Chapter 5

Uzochi

Uzochi's hands trembled as he clutched the straps of his scholar-pack, fear adding lead to his legs, lights starting to flicker in his eyes. There was no way he could handle the gang by himself. The Spiders surrounding the girl turned to him and grinned, knowing he was fresh meat that they could easily devour.

Zuberi's eyes suddenly flashed in his direction, landing squarely on Uzochi, her gaze so direct that he stumbled. He'd never looked at her, not like this. He watched her watching him, holding his breath as she did.

But then, as quickly as they'd locked eyes, she was pulled back into the fight. Zuberi gripped the fingers of the Spider holding her throat, a sharp cracking sound filling the alleyway, and swept her left leg under his feet, sending him to the ground as he shrieked in pain. Another Spider ran up to her and slammed his fist into her side. She landed on the ground as well, breathing hard.

Uzochi knew he should go forward and help her, but he

was frozen. As Zuberi struggled for breath, her eyes flashed open, landing firmly on Uzochi once again.

"What the hell, dude?" she yelled at him. "Get out of here!"

As she spoke, something slammed into Uzochi, something impossible to explain. Rage . . . ferocity . . . terror . . .

. . . all coiled into one.

The emotions were Zuberi's—somehow, he knew it, deep in his gut—and they hit him like a brick to the stomach, so hard that he doubled back.

"I . . . I'm trying to help," Uzochi said, trying not to sound as wounded as he felt.

"Yeah, well, I've got this, and I don't need any more distractions," she said, spitting blood onto the ground as she swiftly stood up and glared at the gang. "You assholes done?"

"This your boyfriend?" snarled the skinny kid. "You think this fight's over now 'cause he's here?"

"Are you kidding?" A Spider girl cackled from behind the kid. "I've seen this one around. Her boyfriend's nothin' but a nerd. A nasty Nubi nerd. I've got him, Kal."

She picked up a metal pipe lying on the concrete and dragged it beside her, approaching Uzochi. "Could've just minded your business," she snarled.

Uzochi didn't move as she circled. He couldn't have even if he'd tried, the fear in his bones freezing him to the spot. This close, he could see the purple veins pulsing in the girl's eyes, her teeth chattering, her hands jittery. A metallic odor oozed from her skin. She was high on Elevation, no doubt about it.

The skinny kid smirked, pushing up his jacket so that his

Spider tattoo was visible. Uzochi knew the boy's name, Kal, after hearing his stupid crew shout him out all the time on campus.

"Right," Kal said. "And I'll finish the girl."

Uzochi swallowed hard. He'd been roughed up by gangs before. He would've preferred to reason with them, but he didn't think that was happening.

"Hey, dumbass, what's your fuckin' problem?"

Uzochi breathed a sigh of relief. His cousin *had* followed him. As Lencho took his place next to Uzochi, the tight fear in his chest began to unravel. Lencho was sinewy muscle, a head and a half shorter than Uzochi but with a presence that made him seem bigger.

"Man, get outta here unless you wanna get your ass beat, too!" Kal yelled.

Lencho made no move to leave. "You're a joke!" he shouted. "Lording around here with your crew and acting big, but you're small. Inferior. You . . . ain't . . . shit."

Kal's eyes widened.

"As a member of the Divine Suns, I invoke gang law. I challenge you to duel one-on-one," Lencho said, baritone voice booming through the alley. "Keep your li'l crew out of this. Just you and me. Or are you scared of being taken out by a skanky Nubi?"

Kal's nostrils flared, the boy's fury emanating from his skin. "You ugly-ass, monkey-faced roach-eater. I don't need help to take care of you!" he shouted back, his fists opening and closing at his sides. "I accept your challenge."

The other gang members hooted. An afroed boy with a patch yelled, 'C'mon, Kal, mess him up!"

Uzochi slowly moved backward, planting himself against a wall as the Spider ambled toward his cousin.

Then suddenly Kal charged, shoving Lencho's shoulder. Right as Kal made contact, Lencho grabbed the boy's hand.

"Hey, let me go, man," Kal said, his voice shaky as he struggled to yank himself free.

Lencho's frown slowly morphed into a toothy smile.

"No problem," he said as he released Kal's hand.

Glowering, the Spider let loose a roar and swung a left hook. Lencho dipped low, evading the blow.

Uzochi watched with his heart in his throat.

Kal swung again, his punch swift, tight. Again, Lencho ducked, avoiding contact.

Then, in a rush of motion, Lencho jumped high and smashed his foot into Kal's jaw.

The boy staggered back. Lencho moved in, leaping to hit Kal again, a knock in the forehead here, a blow to the mouth there. Lencho's speed increased as he jabbed at the Spider's torso. And then he tackled Kal's midsection, wrapping both arms around his waist and wrestling him to the ground.

Uzochi blinked. A light had appeared around Lencho and Kal. A light that seemed fluid, stringy . . . almost alive. He shook his head to try to clear his sight and looked away.

Zuberi was watching him. Her eyes were wide with . . . fear? Or something else? Her gaze darted back to Lencho and Kal, and then to Uzochi, her mouth hanging open.

"You . . . you . . ."

But the words didn't come forth. Instead, she scrambled back on her hands and bolted out of the alley. Uzochi wanted to follow her, but the sound of crunching bones made him turn.

Kal had been thrown to the ground, groaning as he struggled to get up. Blood streamed down his face. He ran forward, swinging again. And again, Lencho dodged. He punched Kal once more, and then reconnected with his fists, twice, three times . . .

The gang quieted. Kal was moving more slowly, his arms limp, feet shuffling. Lencho danced back and forth in front of him with ease, his gait fluid as the larger boy started to slouch, lower lip sagging, knees bending. He looked way too heavy, his massiveness burdensome.

And Uzochi felt heavy as well, as if he'd been drained of energy, a pain penetrating his core.

The gang leader wobbled. Lencho connected with one more jab and Kal tilted over, hitting the ground.

The eye-patched Spider broke from the group and ran into the busy market.

Lencho stood over Kal, who was motionless, his head tucked into his chest. "Get up!" he yelled, giving the boy on the ground a kick. Then he bent over and rocked Kal's limp body, pounding his back, his head, his arms, grabbing his shirt. "Get . . . up!"

"Lencho, stop. Stop. You won already!" Uzochi shouted, rushing forward. As he grabbed Lencho's arm to pull him away, he noticed the blood dripping from Lencho's hands. Kal's blood.

"You won," Uzochi said again, his voice gentle as he gestured to the Spider crumpled on the ground. "Let it go."

Lencho looked over at his cousin and blinked, as though coming out of a daze. He stared at the hands restraining his arm.

"What the hell, man?" Lencho said, yanking himself from Uzochi's grip

Suddenly, movement caught Uzochi's eye. He turned to see someone from the market running toward them, a security guard, no doubt. And when he got to the alley, he saw the boy on the ground. Barely breathing, blood everywhere.

Lencho's hand was on his shoulder, pushing Uzochi. Zuberi was already long gone. Uzochi instinctively knew he only had one choice, and he didn't hesitate.

Uzochi ran, not looking back.

Chapter 6

Lencho

Lencho moved fast, keeping his eyes focused ahead, his chest out, his pace brisk. Thankfully, Uzochi matched his stride.

Finally, they were far enough away that Lencho felt safe stopping, confident that they were out of reach of prying eyes and the risk of being overheard. Lencho stopped, and Uzochi nearly ran right into him.

"What the fuck were you doing?" Lencho demanded, turning on the other boy. "You wake up today and decide to lose your damn mind?"

Uzochi bristled. "You're seriously asking me that? After you pummeled that guy into the ground? He was passed out, Lencho. What if you—"

"Whatever I did, he got what he deserved," Lencho snapped. He didn't want to think too long about Kal lying there on the asphalt. There would be consequences. Attacking the gang leader was one thing, but what Lencho had done . . . he might as well be asking for open warfare between crews. If Aren was against him selling Elevation at school, then he definitely wouldn't want him doing this.

Still, he didn't feel too bad. The Spiders were known to pick on Nubians for no damn reason, and Kal was notorious for his racist slurs. Lencho still remembered the first time he'd met the gang leader, how Kal had laughed in his face and called him "bushy Nubi trash."

So yeah, Kal had it coming. He wasn't going to let his cousin get all high and mighty about an ass-whupping. He glared at him for good measure, daring him to say another word.

Uzochi opened his mouth to speak and then shut it, shaking his head. He looked at Lencho with something between shame and pity, that same look from earlier in the afternoon, a look that burned. Lencho swore something inside him snarled.

"Should I have let the asshole take a swing at you?" he said. "You and I both know one punch would've finished you off."

Uzochi crossed his arms. "Whatever. This is exactly what I was talking about."

"Yeah," Lencho said. "Same. I said you couldn't handle yourself, and guess what? I was right."

Uzochi's face took on a pained expression, as if he'd just been walloped, but Lencho didn't care. He turned and walked away, leaving a slack-jawed Uzochi to do whatever it was a preceptor's pet did. Lencho didn't need him and didn't need to be worrying about his ungrateful ass.

What he did need was somewhere to direct the energy

that was coursing through him. Rage flared in his chest, the red in his vision pulsing. Agitated. It was as if he'd kick-started something that he couldn't temper, and the longer he walked, the headier he felt.

Lencho stomped on. The terrain changed as he reached the section of lower Manhattan where old tenements dominated the landscape, some housing rent-paying city residents, while the abandoned properties sheltered the homeless and gangs. Lencho dodged large pools of water in the streets, the aftereffects of last night's rainstorm. The pools were an inconvenience, but they were nothing compared to what others dealt with farther south in the Swamp. There, the drain networks were always undermaintained, pipes only cleared when Mayor Culliver needed a photo op. And even then, the work seemed incomplete and never-ending. A good downpour easily clogged the drains with garbage, causing sewage to float in mini-ponds and rivers; most of the shacks used as homes were built on stilts for that very reason. Every now and then, especially after a storm, a shack tumbled down into the filth, taking with it those unlucky enough to be home. And that didn't take into account the seawall itself, new cracks always appearing with pockets that needed to be filled in, tempting fate every day they were left unaddressed.

And here was Uzochi, ready to ignore it all as long as he earned a scholarship and ascended. Ready to stomach how Nubians were treated as long as he was one of the special ones. Uzochi was wrong. You could only take power by seizing it, and Lencho had learned that a long time ago.

Today, the lesson had just been more literal.

The fight had been . . . different. Lencho knew that. When he'd connected with Kal, when he'd touched him, that was when he'd felt truly alive. It was more than invigoration. It was almost as though Lencho had taken something from Kal. Lencho realized he couldn't fully describe the sensation but knew how he felt, like someone had plugged him in and turned the power way up.

Picking up his pace, Lencho took his hands out of his pockets, the dried blood sticky as he opened his palms and flexed his fingers. He made his way down Lafayette Street, past a host of wrecked buildings two or three stories tall. At the corner of Broome, he paused. He was more jittery by the second, and he couldn't go home like this. Couldn't—

The sound of footsteps made him whirl around. For a moment, he expected Uzochi, lost with his tail between his legs. But the streets were empty. Still, Lencho's jaw clenched. He wouldn't put it past the Spiders to jump him after learning what he did to Kal. He'd been lost in his own mind. Sloppy. He needed to focus.

He forced himself to move. The streets remained mostly empty, though Lencho swore he could still hear the *thwap-thwap-thwap* of someone following him. Paranoia. He was still way too amped up from the fight.

He turned down a different alley, clenching his fists, trying to swallow up the energy. He shut his eyes, taking deep breaths. His head was going to explode. He was—

This time, there was no denying the steps. Someone was

there. Lencho whipped around, ready to attack whoever was following him, ready to end them there and get his peace.

When Lencho opened his eyes, he found that he wasn't alone. But the person in the alley with him was no one of consequence. It was a man with a long white beard, scraggly and dirty, wearing clothes that hadn't been washed in weeks. He was digging through the bodega's trash can, and when he looked up at Lencho, the white that had settled on his eyes was reflected in the light of a nearby holo-ad.

Was he blind? The man returned to the trash, not paying Lencho another second's attention. His couldn't have been the source of the footsteps that Lencho had heard. In fact, the steps had stopped.

Lencho continued to observe the sightless man, finding himself drawn to the stranger. He crept over slowly, quietly, instinctively, noticing once again the sensation of sparks against his skin. The same sensation he'd experienced when Uzochi was near. The same sensation he'd felt when fighting Kal.

He needed to experience what he felt when he touched the Spider leader. When he hit him. That elation and energy.

It had been wonderful.

He wasn't thinking when he rushed forward, driven by a bottomless hunger. It took Lencho less than five steps to cross to where the man was standing by the dumpster, Lencho's hand suddenly on the man's shoulder.

A force of energy flowed into Lencho's fingertips, blossoming in his neck and chest and spreading through his limbs. He closed his eyes again just as he grabbed the stranger's arm.

Somewhere distant, Lencho thought he heard the man cry out. Maybe he even tried to pull away, but Lencho's grip was viselike. All he knew was the spark of energy rushing into his veins, making him whole again. A transaction of the strangest sort. All of his anxiety vanished and he was transformed into nothing but pure possibility.

This touching strangeness was his salvation, and right now, at this moment, it was all he needed to be free.

A dog barked down the street, breaking Lencho's concentration. His eyes flew open and he jerked away from the man. He caught his breath as the stranger crumpled before him, a soft moan escaping his lips. Lencho knew he should care. As cold as others thought he was, he *did* have a heart. Yet his conscience didn't come into play as he turned and fled, something wild and untamed and exquisite thrumming in his veins.

Lencho stopped to pull energy from three more people he found slumped in shadowy corners of the city, each one adding to the euphoric feeling that buoyed him as he moved farther south. He was unstoppable, his mind and body an electric current that moved faster and reacted more quickly than ever before.

After the third person, though, Lencho noticed that something was different. The euphoric high he'd experienced was absent, replaced by a wall of fatigue that fell over him, an aching all over. He wondered if another draining could somehow boost him again, but even as he considered it, more aches sprang up all over his body.

. *Better not push it,* he thought. Evening was setting in. Time to go home, whether he wanted to or not.

Having walked almost two miles, he made his way to a hover bus stop right at the border of the Swamp, the shanties on the periphery of his sight. He soon boarded the M20, ignoring the glares from passengers taking in the state of his clothes as he rode north toward his neighborhood in Old Chelsea. He swore he could taste the tingling energy of their bodies, sweet on his tongue. It was a fading sweetness, though, like candy eaten hours before, an aftertaste that Lencho didn't love.

He got off at his stop, distracted, starting in earnest to wonder what was happening to him, and walked one block west to the apartment building where he lived, one of the few glass high-rises that remained in the area. He passed by a food cart, the scent of roasted crickets and barbecued chicken enveloping him. Children sitting on a rusty iron bench smacked their lips as they ate off blocks of wood with their parents. He let himself into his building and entered the waiting elevator. The doors shut and he was enclosed in shadow, the only light coming from a dim bulb and an illuminated "8."

A minute later, he turned the key and walked into his apartment.

"Where the hell have you been?"

Father's loud voice, right at the door. Father's massive hand. Palm and fingers immediately connecting with Lencho's cheek and chin.

"Where were you?" Kefle roared.

"Wait. Dad, I . . ."

Kefle slapped him again before he could finish.

"Stop . . ." Lencho held up his arms to protect his face. He quickly glanced up at the antique white-and-black clock hanging over the doorway that led to the kitchen.

5:57.

Shit.

Weeks ago, Lencho's father had instructed him that on the first and third Mondays of the month, when he had afternoons off before working night shifts at the droid center, they would enjoy a proper meal as a family. Lencho should be home no later than 5:45 so dinner could be served at 6:00.

With all that had just gone down, Lencho had forgotten that it was indeed the first Monday of the month. Dinner was never served late.

"I will ask again, where were you?" Kefle demanded. "And . . . Lencho, what happened to you? Your clothes and hands?"

Lencho focused straight ahead, staring at a wall, heart pounding, not wanting to look at his dad looming over him. From the corner of his vision he spied his mother, Leeyah, in the living room, arms wrapped around her torso.

"Boy, you walked through the streets like this?" Kefle continued. "What were you thinking? You know how we're regarded by the people here. My son should not be seen . . ."

Lencho's cheek was throbbing, his father's hands hard, callused.

I'm not gonna cry, he told himself.

". . . think of your mother. The time she takes to prepare your garments . . ."

Steel, he thought. *Please.*

Lencho focused on one of his father's mounted staffs, the wood chipped and dry. He blinked. The vigor Lencho had felt earlier was completely gone.

"Boy, look at me," Kefle demanded. "LOOK AT ME!"

Lencho swiveled to his father, who grabbed the lower half of his son's face between thumb and forefinger.

"What . . . did . . . you . . . do?" Kefle asked.

"I'm sorry for being late," Lencho said, voice cracking. "I lost track of time hanging with friends, and in the market, I fought a guy who's been hurting our people." He made sure to leave out that his "friends" were members of the Divine. Lencho's father had no idea he'd joined a gang.

"What?" Kefle pressed.

"I fought . . . I fought this kid who bullies Nubians," Lencho answered. "I won."

"What?" Kefle asked again, his face twisting in anger.

"I beat him, Dad," Lencho said, his father's grip still strong around his jaw. "For us. For Nubians."

And the tears came.

Kefle absorbed the words, his grip on his son loosening. He took a step back, Leeyah's eyes remaining averted.

"You're not to be late to this house again," he said, voice low. "Be ready for dinner in ten minutes. Clean yourself."

Dinner was served at 6:10.

Showered, scrubbed, in fresh pants and a magenta tunic,

Lencho kept his head down through the meal of rice, crickets, spinach, and spiced goat. His mother did the same. Kefle sat erect in his chair at the head of the table, shoulders back, chest out. Lencho ate slowly, fear morphing into anger. The red returned to his sight, this time with a noise building in his ears.

A roar.

Why am I putting up with this? he asked himself, remembering the power he'd felt coursing through his body not even an hour ago.

As Kefle sliced his portion of goat, Lencho was struck with memories of the last few years at home. Kefle's enraged face as he cursed Lencho out for leaving his jacket on the couch. Kefle cuffing Lencho because Lencho forgot to turn off the light after he'd left the kitchen. Backhand slaps, one after the other, for getting home late or responding to a question with a smidgen of attitude. Kefle had once forgotten that he was wearing his quartz ring—a Nubian treasure he'd saved from the cataclysm, a prized mark of princedom—and opened a gash right above Lencho's right brow, leaving a mark.

His father's words from the past ate up all other sounds in the room. Lencho, barely able to do anything right, merely mediocre at scholastic endeavors. Unfocused. Outside of some proficiency in the fighting forms, a regrettable waste of royal blood.

Kefle placed his utensils down next to his plate.

"Do not waste your time on other Nubians," he said to

Lencho. "Our family is most important, and being careless with family time, with *my* time . . ."

Lencho clutched his fork and knife over his plate, his nails biting into his palms.

"Son, do you understand me?" Kefle pressed.

The phantom memories floating in Lencho's head stopped as he looked at his father sitting at the head of the table. For the first time, he saw this man for who he was.

"You know what, Dad," he answered, "I do understand. Who cares. Fuck you."

Leeyah gasped and dropped her fork, the ensuing clang filling the room. Kefle stared back at his son, mouth dropping. "What did you just—"

"Fuck you, Dad!" Lencho yelled. "You're a fuckin' fat swollen rotten jackass and I've had enough of this shit!"

Lencho shot up from the table and made a beeline for his room, slamming the door and turning the lock. There was a loud, tinny crash and the stomping of feet and the pounding of fists on the door and Kefle yelling, "Open up, you insolent bastard. Open this door!" Lencho could hear his mother wailing in the background as he paced his room, hands on his head, tears streaming down as he peered at the ruined outfit he'd thrown in the corner.

The pounding continued. Lencho's tears dried up. He stopped pacing and stood still, his fear leading him down a new path. What if his father kicked down the door? He quickly scanned his room, searching for anything he could use as a weapon.

And then the pounding ceased, followed by the soft shuffling of feet and the slamming of what Lencho recognized as the front door to their apartment. Kefle had left. Lencho tried to breathe, wiping snot from his face.

He unlocked his door and stuck his head out to make sure the coast was clear. The door to his parents' bedroom was closed. He imagined his mother inside doing that sulking thing she always did after Kefle hassled Lencho, though he'd never stood up to his dad before. Not like this.

He didn't want to stay in the apartment, didn't want to look at the beige walls or the stupid staff from Nubia or the plates of uneaten food on the dinner table. He grabbed his jacket from a hook by the door and quietly left.

On the ground floor, barging through the building's main glass door, he was hit by the huge holo-billboards floating across the street and shielded his eyes from the lights. News alerts scrolled continuously under advertisements hawking everything from gourmet lepidoptera sauce to the latest sheer bodysuits from J'Amore. A neighbor had once mentioned to him that the unceasing light, especially at night, was what made the rent on their block lower than the surrounding properties.

He dashed down the block, needing to get away from the holos as well and find someplace quiet. Maybe he'd head to the Divine HQ. Maybe—

Then he heard footsteps once again. These were heavy, the sound of boots on pavement, unlike the lighter steps he'd heard before. Lencho turned, finding himself face to face with a St. John Soldier.

The stun gun hit him in the side before he could breathe. Pain rocketed through his body, and then he felt something hard and tight close on his wrists.

"This is an arrest," the soldier said. "Don't struggle."

But Lencho couldn't have even if he'd tried. Something was injected into his arm and his vision blurred. He was drifting into blackness.

In an instant, he was gone.

Chapter 7

Zuberi

Zuberi didn't breathe for at least an hour after the clash with the Spiders. At least, she didn't breathe easily. The memories of the fight, of the day, really, were like shifting sand, and she simply couldn't find her bearings.

It wasn't a new feeling, not exactly. Ever since the day Zuberi got her scar, she'd had those moments when she gasped for air and crumpled to the ground, lost. But eventually she'd find herself again by closing her eyes and counting her breaths. She could bring herself back from the brink the same way she trained her body: one number at a time.

Today, though, Zuberi couldn't count. She couldn't do anything but struggle against the nightmare of the fight. What she'd seen and felt.

Because of him.

He'd distracted her, giving the Spiders time to close in. To *hurt* her. That was one of the cardinal rules of fighting, wasn't it? Focus on the threat at hand. Think ahead if you can, but don't get so distracted that you lose sight of the danger of now.

Uzochi had taken her advantage as a superior fighter and ripped it to pieces, all because he wanted to play hero. And when it came down to it, he didn't even step up.

But Lencho did.

Zuberi knew him and his arrogance and the hardened way he stomped through the halls. At one point, Vriana had even whispered about having a potential crush, but Zuberi was adamant that was just a bad idea. There was no softness with Lencho, no room for giggles or bright stickers or a whimsical spirit like Vriana's.

And yet, again, the moment Zuberi saw him . . . the ripple. As with Uzochi, clear as day in her mind.

Power.

When Lencho's hands had touched Kal, she'd noticed . . . something. Almost like lines of energy thrumming between them. She'd looked between the boys and wondered what it meant, and why, once again, was she seeing things?

And then Kal's figure had appeared above him, just like the woman earlier floating in the air.

It was Kal, right down to the bloodied face Lencho had given him moments before, but he was translucent, staring down at his limp body. He pulsed with something more than anger as he screamed, and then he turned his wide, bloody eyes at Zuberi.

And that was when she'd had to get out of there.

Zuberi had managed to grab her scholar-pack and dash away from the market, thinking that maybe Kal was dead after Lencho's attack, that she was seeing his soul leave his body. But then, of course, she'd remembered the other figures she'd seen . . . the ones of those who were clearly alive, written off as hallucinations.

She ran and ran, sprinting down Third Avenue until the street turned into Bowery, slowing down only when the pain became too much, her breath ragged and a dull ache starting to arch up her side. Zuberi eased into a light jog, trying to convince herself that she wasn't crazy, trying not to feel guilt over leaving the fight.

What's happening to me?

Why was she seeing phantoms? She'd never experienced anything like this in all of her seventeen years. As her jog turned into a measured gait, Zuberi ignored the surrounding hubbub of lower Manhattan, with its tenements and street vendors and steady stream of hover vehicles, and went deeper inside.

Spirits . . . why am I seeing spirits?

Zuberi suddenly remembered a story her father used to tell her when she was little about a Nubian woman who spoke to ghosts. Her father had said spirits followed this woman wherever she went, asking her why they'd died. Her answer to the ghosts was always different. Sometimes she replied that something tremendous and much larger needed them more. Other times, she declared that life was cruel. Eventually, her father said, she stopped talking to them at all. She chose to focus on life instead of death, even though ignoring the spirits was difficult.

"That's not a happy ending," Zuberi had argued when she was a child.

Her father had squeezed her hand, his voice gentle. "No, it's not, Beri. But sometimes we get the endings that we need to hear."

Zuberi had thought about his words for some time. She still thought about the story all these years later, especially as her father only occasionally spoke about Nubia. Was she becoming like that haunted woman, destined to be followed by random ghosts? But no, this was different. She was seeing the spirits of people who weren't dead, or at least she hoped not, thinking of Kal. Goddess, it was too confusing. She needed to talk to someone. . . .

She continued to try to work through her nerves by walking, her feet carrying her farther south. Once she reached the Swamp, she saw no reason to stop, finding a smidgen of comfort in being among her people. She walked through their own market area, a spiderweb of stalls strategically situated between the shanties, the ground wet from the recent downpour.

Zuberi eventually drew closer to the area's seawall, its crumbling brick façade usurping her vision. Just ahead, she spotted a small crowd. Several St. John Soldiers were standing nearby as well.

She stopped at the group. "Is something going on?" she asked one of the militiamen.

The soldier's eyes found hers, already set in a glare under his headgear.

"Mr. St. John's giving a press conference."

Of course. One of the many St. John press conferences where he talked about how much he helped Nubians and other people in the lower city. She kept walking, getting as close to the seawall as she could, stopping at the low concrete partition that had been placed about a dozen feet away. The wall snaked along the far edge of the quarter, running parallel to Water Street, an irony Zuberi wished she could ignore. With patches of scaffolding sprouting from its surface, construction workers were continuously working on the atrocious-looking thing, their labor droids constantly buzzing around with flocks of nu-raves flying overhead. Like most of the lower city, the seawall was falling apart, with Zuberi finding it insane that the Up High was sustained in all its shiny splendor while the city could barely maintain a measly brick barrier.

As Zuberi's gaze roamed upon one particular chunk of brick where a tiny sun had been tagged, she heard the booming sound of music. That could mean only one thing.

Krazen St. John was about to speak.

Chapter 8

Sandra

"It is an honor to be here with you all today, addressing important issues . . . together."

Sandra St. John knew her father's speeches by heart. Or, at the very least, she knew their intentions by heart, their mechanisms and the ways they were sewn together. He always used words like "together" and "we" and "uniting," making it clear that he and the people were working as one. Sandra had once counted the use of "we" in one of his addresses fifty-seven times.

Overkill? Maybe, but he was fine with that. Nothing that Krazen St. John ever did was unintentional. No, every word, every move, was calculated. An orchestra of action. From the moment he stepped out of his office and put his face in front of the seemingly endless array of cameras keeping track of his every move, Krazen was ten steps ahead of everyone.

It was Sandra's goal to be able to know and anticipate every such step, to be her father's daughter.

"As citizens, we look to our leaders for hope in these

troubling times," Krazen continued, standing on the small stage that had been hastily erected for him here, right by the seawall's partition. He looked taller from where Sandra sat, slightly off to the side, watching him rapturously as she'd been ordered to. That was good, for if he looked impressive to Sandra, he must look like a giant to the crowd.

It would've been easier, of course, to use an augmented holo and project his image here. But the people who lived below criticized Mayor Culliver for overusing holos to present live speeches, saying it showed a lack of trust in his constituencies. They said so in one of numerous polls conducted by her father's employees, polls that were then analyzed and dissected by different branches of the St. John machine. People here preferred to see their leaders in the flesh and speak to them face to face whenever possible. They wanted to be truly seen, truly heard. No matter how advanced the holo tech was, it couldn't replace the feeling of a handshake. And so Krazen had made the trek to the seawall near the repugnant place they called the Swamp, bringing Sandra along.

She had calculated her look for the occasion, researching pictures of the neighborhood seawall, crumbling and dilapidated as it was, finding it gray and brown and covered in mold. As a result, she'd worn her own muted colors, a loose navy jumpsuit that wouldn't look too over-the-top. Her crimson hair was pulled back in her signature ponytail, and her makeup was neutral. She looked solemn, respectful. Even her silver jewelry was understated. The shoes had been the hard part, as the ground near the seawall was uneven, but a pair of dark leather boots fit the bill perfectly.

"I have heard your complaints," Krazen said, and Sandra tracked his gaze as it swept over the small crowd. Locals, mostly Nubian, each of them carefully selected from the larger mass of people just down the street. A mix of young and old. A few babies held in their mothers' arms. A look of hardship tinged the crowd, which was, of course, exactly what Sandra's father wanted to show. How in need these people were, with their archaic devices and unsophisticated ways.

"The mayor has abandoned the seawall," Krazen continued, shaking his head as murmurs of assent swept through his audience. "He has deemed it 'a minor inconvenience.'"

Anger swiftly boiled up in the crowd. Every person in the Swamp knew that the seawall was the primary thing that stood between the surrounding community and sheer destruction. Each day that ticked on without necessary repairs was a potential death sentence, and Krazen knew that.

"But I know how important this wall is to all of us, how *essential* it is for our safety and survival," Krazen said, holding his chin up. He outstretched his hands for effect, slivers of circuitry glistening along his forearms as the sleeves of his caftan fell to his elbows. "Which is why I have offered to invest the funds necessary for a complete overhaul."

Cheers erupted, and Sandra allowed herself to smile. Underneath the cheers, the sound of the waters beyond the wall churned. For a moment, Sandra dared to wonder what would happen if the wall crumbled right now, falling apart. She would drown in the river, or possibly, one of the many St. John Soldiers would pluck her out to safety. But others would die. . . .

"However," Krazen said, a slight frown transforming his face, "I can only make such an investment if the mayor allows it. I've outlined my plans for this generous donation, but I must admit to you all, this initiative depends on his willingness to work with me. It is my dear hope that we can reach an agreement soon."

"We, we, we." The word was doing a lot. Sandra knew from her eavesdropping that her father had asked the mayor for quite a lot in return for his repair of the seawall, more than the mayor was probably willing to give.

And so Krazen had done what was necessary. If the bargain couldn't be won honestly, then he would rely on manipulation.

The crowd continued their enthusiastic applause as drone cameras clicked around them. Krazen gave a final wave, and Sandra stood to join him, maintaining her sympathetic smile. Early evening was falling around them, kept at bay by the lights that hovered overhead. Soon, darkness would cover this place, hiding the cracks in the seawall that Sandra saw so clearly now. She tried to imagine a toe or a heel hitting the wrong place, how everything would splinter . . .

Such odd thoughts.

Sandra followed her father off the stage to where his ever-present assistant, Tilly, waited. She sported short, bobbed hair and a crisp cream coat with matching trousers, her pristine clothes a stark contrast to the grime of the alley. Everything about her screamed glamour in a way that Sandra felt was just a touch too obvious, from the two slim silver rings adorning her manicured hands to her brown skin, which was free of a single blemish or freckle save for the slivers of circuitry lining her neck. Her hazel eyes blinked at Sandra, and Sandra found that something odd twinged inside her.

She examined the feeling, digging deeper to find the root of the problem. It was what her meditation coach was always telling her, how she needed to isolate the parts of her mind that she wanted to build and work through her emotions. A strong mind, she was told, could do wonders, and Sandra absolutely refused to be weak.

The feeling, she decided, wasn't jealousy, as one might expect. No, it was suspicion. Tilly had been her father's favorite scanner, recently promoted to personal assistant, and Sandra simply wasn't sure about her.

"Excellent as always, sir," Tilly said to Krazen. "Lots of great sound bites."

"Yes, well, let's make sure to get the highlights out to the right people," he said, tapping the side of his head to activate his implants and check his comm. "And I want as many people as possible interviewed about the seawall before they leave."

"Of course," Tilly said, her eyes once again finding Sandra. She had the distinct feeling that Tilly wanted her to leave, which was exactly why she stayed put and smiled instead.

"Is there something else?" Krazen asked, his voice devoid of the charm he'd just held so effortlessly onstage. He didn't like to be kept waiting.

"Well, actually," Tilly said, "there *is* a development that we should discuss. Something . . . interesting's been found."

Now she didn't just glance at Sandra. She looked. Pointedly. So, unfortunately, did Krazen.

"Well, let's talk in private, then," he said. "Sandra, you'll take a separate car."

She hated to be dismissed, but her father didn't need to know that. He also didn't need to know that she had her own ways of finding out his private business. Such acts felt disrespectful, but subterfuge was sometimes necessary. Sandra was looking out for his—their—best interests.

"Of course," she said. "I'll see you when we're back Up High."

"I'll be busy tonight," Krazen said, his voice curt, cutting. Sandra kept her face neutral, ignoring the sting as he turned and left with Tilly.

It was actually better, she decided, that he was busy. If he was busy, then she could do some investigating with little fear of discovery.

She'd get the answers she needed, whatever way was necessary.

Chapter 9

Uzochi

Uzochi sat on an azure couch, exhaling, continuing to zone in on the energy at his center, feeling it fill his heart, head, and limbs. For more than an hour, he'd been planted there, refusing to rise until his body was settled, staring at the sofa's fabric, its color reminding him of the strange blue light that had continued to reappear in his vision since he'd left the fight near school. By the time he'd made it home to Kips Bay, he was shaking. He'd gone straight up to his apartment, unable to do anything but sit . . .

. . . and breathe.

The trembling had slowly lessened until he was somewhat himself again.

When he'd first gotten home, all Uzochi had done was pace, moving from the kitchen to the living room. The apartment he shared with his mom was small, so he'd circled the entire front area more than two dozen times, still shaking as his thoughts swirled.

His head was a mess. The fight, the light he'd seen, Zuberi, his cousin . . .

Lencho.

He'd replayed what happened in his mind over and over. He'd never seen his cousin like that, practically vibrating with rage. And the way he'd leveled Kal . . .

But it was what Lencho had said to Uzochi outside school that played on a continuous, barbed loop.

At least we're getting what we're owed in the Divine.

Uzochi wasn't a fool. He knew that Nubians had never gotten a fair chance in the Swamp. But he also knew that joining the Divine Suns wasn't going to give Lencho anything other than a criminal record or an early death. If Preceptor Ryan had seen the fight, she would've just glared in revulsion at those assembled and declared, "Told you so."

And, Uzochi thought with his own disgust, she would've been right. At least about his cousin.

It was different, though, with Zuberi. She couldn't have been fighting because she wanted to. He didn't know who had instigated what, but he was certain she hadn't walked up to several gang members and asked for a brawl.

Her eyes. They were burned into him, along with her rage. Even now, back in his house, he could feel the emotion pulsing through his veins.

The pacing hadn't quieted his mind, so Uzochi had settled on the couch. He generally wasn't into meditation, always feeling like he had other things to do with school, but at that moment, he needed quiet. His mom, in contrast, was

73

always meditating, pressing Uzochi to join her, so he tried to remember what she'd told him. He sat, attempting to clear away the distracting thoughts, seeking peace through stillness, twisting his cornrows around his fingers. Eventually, he did feel calmer, the edge of the day subsiding.

Uzochi had been trying to figure out why he'd jumped into the fight, or at least tried to jump in. So unlike him. But the answer soon came to him. Zuberi needed his help.

Fat lotta good that did, he thought. He wondered where she was, if she was all right. Uzochi couldn't stop thinking about how striking and regal she was. How *fierce* she was in the fight. But then, those intense emotions he'd experienced in her presence. Bizarre . . .

He shook his head. *Okay, mister, back to the real world . . .*

For Uzochi, his path forward was to mind his business, focus on his goals, and avoid the messiness of life. Because of his diligence, he was way ahead of the game academically, having already earned enough credits to graduate from 104 as a junior. Nonetheless, he was all about taking as many advanced classes as he could while engaging in extracurricular activities. His goal was to become a preceptor's assistant senior year and take a full slate of college-level electives. His academic counselor had advised him that this would seal the deal, that he would most certainly earn a Rise Above scholarship to one of New York's Up High universities. A dream. He would finally ascend, maybe even do an exchange program with other Up Highs in London or Paris or Mumbai one day, after making sure his mom was settled in the sky as well.

Uzochi stared at the bevy of awards on his desk, including

the pair of gold Mind Czar trophies he'd received for earning the highest GPA at 104 during his freshman and sophomore years. He was a shoo-in to receive the award again in less than two months when junior year was done. His heart swelled with pride.

Lencho's words threatened to echo in his mind again, but he pushed them away. It was jealousy, plain and simple, the same jealousy his peers had, why they made their snide comments. Even those like Sekou, who Uzochi admired and appreciated, simply didn't have his commitment to the future.

He couldn't let words and attitudes make him feel bad. Uzochi decided he'd focus on his schoolwork, as it always helped him recenter.

Okay . . . what first? He decided on Spanish, and then maybe he'd start on that essay for Black lit class and draft the agenda for the Intercultural Alliance meeting next week. Uzochi thought about turning on the holo-projector to play the Helios News special on the anniversary of the UN Massacre, feeling a connection to the iconic building slightly north of where he lived. But no, he didn't need holos in the background while handling schoolwork. He was still too unsettled.

Focus, he reminded himself. And so he did, sitting at his desk, which was nestled in a corner of the living room next to the two massive shelves that held his library of books, losing himself in reading and graphs.

By early evening, Uzochi realized his mother would be home soon and it was up to him to make dinner. He headed to the kitchen, commenced meal prep, and, after placing the food in the oven, went back to the living room, a big bag of seaweed chips in hand to tide him over until dinner as he studied some more.

He was grateful when, a little after 6:15 p.m., his mother arrived at the apartment, pulling him from his work.

Com'pa entered, as she always did, laden with her job's chunky, outdated laptop hanging from her left shoulder. For the past few years she'd toiled as a nurse for the elderly on the Upper West Side of Manhattan and the southern Bronx, only recently getting promoted to assistant supervisor for her agency. The promotion was deemed a miracle by other staffers, considering she was Nubian. But Uzochi knew the truth, that Com'pa constantly pushed herself to be essential and exceptional. One glance at the laptop told Uzochi that she'd brought work home and was planning to go over administrative files well into the night.

"Dear heart, it smells delicious," Com'pa said, bending down to take off her work sneakers. "Is that roast chicken?"

Uzochi nodded, breathing in the aroma of chicken with couscous and parsley, a dish Com'pa had showed him how to make years ago. "I added some fresh peppers today."

She nodded, next shrugging off her long jacket. "I've taught you well, dear heart. A genius and a chef. What a gift to the world."

Uzochi smiled at the compliment, just happy he could do a little something for his mom after a long day. They ate together at their tiny kitchen table, their meal served on cracked blue plates. Com'pa and Uzochi didn't speak, not right away.

Uzochi knew that his mother often needed time to decompress, to slowly peel away the mask she wore at work. Here, with her son, she would let her hair down and speak freely in her true accent. Uzochi had watched the switch happen for years, how she'd flattened her speech when speaking to most New Yorkers while saving her authentic voice for other Nubians.

Even with his mother's sometimes chipper demeanor, Uzochi had also come to realize that a heaviness slowed her steps, filling the walls of their apartment and resting on the shelves overrun with his history books and novels and the wooden replicas of shea trees she'd carved. The trees were flanked by Com'pa's hand-drawn illustrations of Uzochi's father, Siran, and aunt Mira, the only people mentioned the few times she talked about her past. An extremely rare occurrence.

Uzochi knew this was why he had to push himself so that they could both ascend. To rise above the weight. His mother had carried too much for too long.

"Dear heart," Com'pa said, startling Uzochi out of his thoughts, "you seem distracted."

Uzochi bit his lip. Of course she noticed. She saw everything.

"Just something after school," Uzochi said. "Lencho . . . got into it with a gang, the Spiders."

Com'pa took his words in and put down her fork. "Your cousin started a fight?"

Uzochi shook his head, looking down at his plate. "No. They were attacking a girl. Um, a really nice girl." Heat rushed to his cheeks as he spoke. "So he stepped in and challenged the leader of the Spiders to a . . . well, um, a duel. It's like, some sort of gang thing. And Lencho won."

The words felt wrong, ridiculous, even. Uzochi thought of the blood splattered on the ground, smeared on his cousin's sleeve. To say he "won" made the fight sound like a game.

"What about you?" Com'pa asked.

Uzochi looked up. "What do you mean?"

"You saw all of this," she said, "because you were watching?"

She didn't say it with disdain, not openly. But the words stung Uzochi just the same.

"I tried to help her," he said, words tumbling out. "The girl. I wanted to reason with them. But . . ."

He hesitated. He was getting to the parts of the day that were still messy and tangled in his mind. The odd sensations he'd felt and the strange blue light and how Zuberi had affected him . . .

The jitters had returned. He picked at his chicken, feeling like something was needling the back of his skull. A headache, maybe, but sharper. Deeper.

"But Lencho got there first," he finished.

"I see," Com'pa said, shaking her head and leaning back. She continued to focus her gaze on Uzochi, and he squirmed under her stare.

She sighed. "I thought he might have joined some sort of gang, as you call it. My friend Efua thought she saw him with a group of hooligans not far from the Swamp. I should say something to Leeyah."

Uzochi couldn't help but laugh. What would Leeyah say

or do that would make her son listen? Uzochi hadn't seen his aunt in years, but he could remember her, quieter than anyone he'd ever met, with no control over Lencho. Even when they were kids, Uzochi remembered how his cousin would visit with his mom, the loud boy running through the house, screaming and making shooting sounds at the top of his lungs as he acted out scenes from his favorite sci-fi show, *Our Cosmic Majesty*. Leeyah never tried once to corral him.

That, she left to Kefle.

Uzochi knew why his mother would rather speak to Aunt Leeyah. Uncle Kefle had always been brutish, quick to misunderstand. Before, Com'pa had tried to keep their families connected, especially after they had all first come over from Nubia. But too many dinners had ended in bitter remarks, with his uncle enraged. And thus Uzochi had stopped spending time with his father's side of the family until he began attending 104, seeing Lencho occasionally.

He and his mom were alone in some ways, but Com'pa still remained connected to the Nubian community, even though she and Uzochi had managed to get out of the Swamp, and she'd made friends throughout their current neighborhood. People genuinely adored her, and it was rare that their house was empty on a Saturday. Someone always stopped by for a chat, which was when Uzochi would put on his headphones and turn to his books.

"She was worried this would happen," Com'pa said, again breaking through Uzochi's thoughts. She must've missed his laugh, or was choosing to ignore it. "I wonder . . . perhaps I should speak to Lencho."

Uzochi balked, almost choking on couscous. "Why, Mom? He won't listen to you. You should have heard what he told me. He basically said he hates his family."

Blood's just blood. I don't need it.

Com'pa took a sip of water. "Lencho is young. He doesn't know better."

Something shadowy and spiteful kicked inside Uzochi, pressing on the ache in his skull.

"I'm young," he said. "And I'm not joining a gang."

"Dear heart, of course you aren't," Com'pa said. "But Lencho . . . you shouldn't be so hard on him. We all handle things differently."

It was always this excuse, wasn't it, for Lencho? His cousin could've made better choices, could've spent more time with Com'pa and Uzochi, could've studied harder. Yes, his father was horrible, but at least he *had* a father.

Uzochi had no one except his mother, but he didn't use that as an excuse to slack off or do things like join a—

A scream ripped through his mind.

How am I going to pay for this? . . . What are they going to do to me? Where will I live?

A voice that Uzochi had never heard before. Words drowned out by sobbing.

"Uzochi?"

He clutched his head, feeling as though he needed to hold his skull together or it would shatter. More words entered his mind, this time in a different voice.

They're not going to accept me. They're going to throw me away like trash.

More crying, but the screaming was gone. Now it was just words, and more voices falling on top of each other in a cacophony of anxiety and fear.

Uzochi felt hard floor as his chair clattered behind him. His mother flew to his side, her hand on his shoulder, her voice lost to the tidal wave of sound in his mind.

. . . tell them I'm sick? We can't afford the treatment . . . never get better. They don't need to know . . .

Uzochi started to cry as a flash of blue light blurred his vision. He shut his eyes, gradually forcing them open when he realized the light persisted.

Com'pa was next to him, a splotchy shadow among the blue. He looked into her eyes and saw her fear. And then the fear was in his body as well, seeping into his bones, the pounding in his chest unyielding. He turned away from his mother, fighting for breath as the voices pounded in his head.

I can see the dead, but they're not dead. So who are they? And what am I?

This voice stopped him because he knew it. Hours earlier, the same voice had demanded to know "what the hell" after he'd stepped into an alley.

Zuberi.

He shut his eyes and focused on her voice, wading through the storm of pleas and demands and questions that plagued him. He paddled through them until all he heard was Zuberi, the blue almost blinding.

What's wrong with me?
What's wrong with me?
What's wrong with me?

It was her voice, and then, suddenly, it was Uzochi's, too. Her question became his question. He let go of her voice and held on to his own, somehow finding the strength to will everyone else in his mind to be quiet.

When he opened his eyes, Com'pa was still staring at him. The fear was still there, threatening to drown him, but he couldn't hold it back any longer. He couldn't bear the blue light or the voices if they returned, and so he shut his eyes.

This time, he saw black and knew nothing more.

Chapter 10

Lencho

Lencho awoke, feeling like he was being strangled. He gasped for air, his arms heavy at his sides. He instinctively punched out with his hands, but quickly realized he had limited mobility. He was being held down by something tight, restrictive.

Sheets. He was in his clothes lying under crisp white sheets.

He blinked, forcing his eyes to register the room he was in. The space was clean, cleaner than any room he'd been in, and across from him was a floor-to-ceiling painting of the sky.

No . . .

Not a painting. It was a window. Lencho was looking straight into fluffy white clouds and an early dawn breaking across the city.

Shit. How long had he been out?

"Careful. You don't want to sit up too quickly."

Lencho whipped around, the sheets tugging against him as he moved, fists already raised. The woman standing in front of him was the last person he would've expected to see, presuming he was in some sort of cell. She was sky city bourgie through and through.

"Mr. Will, hello and good evening. My name is Tilly Montaigne," she said. "I represent someone who's interested in meeting you."

He stared at her, trying not to let himself be distracted by her poise and beauty. Where the fuck was he? Lencho had never been arrested, but he had a feeling that most arrests didn't end like this.

"'Scuse me?"

"I apologize for the way we brought you in," Tilly continued, the hint of a smile on her lips. "The officers who were directed to seize you weren't aware of quite how special you are. They have, of course, been dismissed."

Lencho stared at her. "What?"

"You are, as I'm sure you've deduced, Up High," Tilly explained. "We noticed you were in need of medical attention, and we attended to that on your behalf. Now that you're up, it would be best for you to learn why you're here from the source himself."

"Whoa, whoa," Lencho said, holding up his hands. "What do you mean, medical attention? What'd you do to me?"

She laughed, a melodious sound that tickled the air. "Just cleaned up the cuts on your face and arms, Mr. Will. I assure you, nothing nefarious is going on."

He glared at her. He didn't like being spoken to like this, like he was a fool who didn't understand how things worked. This was weird.

And was he really Up High?

"Now, why don't we begin the meeting?" Tilly said, tapping something behind her ear. Lencho realized with a start that she clearly had cybernetic implants. He knew about implants—potent tech with an extravagant price tag, something only available to Up High residents, according to the holos—but he'd never seen them used in person.

Suddenly, a door that Lencho hadn't realized was there clicked open and someone walked through.

No.

Not someone.

Krazen St. John himself, dressed in a cream caftan, stepped into the room, a pair of soldiers standing just outside the newly revealed door. As he entered, the portal melted back into the wall, leaving Lencho staring at the most powerful man in Tri-State East.

"Lencho Will," said Krazen, the silver circuitry of his implants glistening in the light of the window. "It's a pleasure to meet you."

All Lencho could do was stare. He was beyond confused, beyond perplexed. First, he'd thought he was arrested, and now . . . ?

Krazen chuckled. "I take it you don't know why you're here?"

"Uh, no," Lencho said, feeling the tug of a nervous smile. "Not a clue."

Krazen walked over, sitting in a nearby chair, Tilly continuing to stand. Lencho felt beyond awkward, being in this weird bed, having Krazen St. John only feet away from him.

"My assistant, Tilly," Krazen said, nodding at the woman, "reported back to me about you."

"*He's* your boss?" Lencho said, unable to process all that was happening.

Tilly's smile stretched ever so slightly. "I'm his personal assistant, yes. And his scanner. It's my duty to keep an eye on the lower city and report anything . . . unique. And given how gifted you are, I had to let Mr. St. John know immediately."

Lencho's brain stuttered over what she'd just said. *A scanner.* He didn't know what that was. And there were other words he was struggling to understand . . . like "gifted." "Gifted" was a term normally ascribed to guys like Uzochi who got perfect scores on their exams. Lencho had never earned a perfect score on anything.

"Tilly tells me she witnessed something . . . well, something very rare," Krazen said.

"I've been watching you," Tilly added, her voice light and airy. "We keep tabs on all dealers of Elevation."

"Hold on," Lencho said. "I don't know if I should be talking about this without, um . . ."

What was he trying to say? Representation? A parent? Whatever. He wouldn't be admitting anything to these people until he knew what was going on.

"Relax," Krazen said, holding up a hand. "We're not concerned about your petty dealings. Well, not in the way you think we are. But the point is, Tilly observed more than your Elevation machinations."

Tilly nodded. "It began with what happened on the street."

She placed two fingers on the inside of her wrist, tapping circuitry, and behind her, a holo appeared. There was Lencho, approaching a stranger. With another button, the image became a video. Lencho staggered up to the man, putting his hands on his body, Lencho swearing he saw the wisps of red that limned the edges of his vision when he drained someone. Then the video showed the man collapsing, with Lencho standing over him. He turned this way and that, and then, like a rocket, took off down the street.

Shame flooded Lencho at the sight of what he'd done, particularly as the camera stayed on the man hunched over in the street.

"It's impressive, Lencho," Krazen said, his voice soft. "Nothing to be embarrassed by."

Lencho couldn't respond. His eyes stayed on the holo, finding it difficult to look anywhere else. Understanding settled in. It was *her* footsteps he'd heard earlier. Tilly. She'd watched him drain all those people, taking their essence. How had she kept herself hidden? Could implants make people invisible?

He looked up at her, ready for an expression of disgust. Even if she didn't know what he'd been doing—*he* didn't even really know what he was doing—she'd seen the way those people collapsed after he was through with them. How he'd left them there to rot.

But Lencho discerned no disgust. In fact, Tilly's expression never shifted from its polite, engaged interest.

"Then, of course, there was the fight," she said, tapping her wrist again.

This time, Lencho couldn't watch. He knew as soon as the holo appeared with him and Kal what it would show. His eyes found the floor, unable to look up.

"Tilly," Krazen said, drawing Lencho's attention. "Perhaps Mr. Will and I could speak alone."

The holo disappeared. Tilly nodded and turned, retreating quickly from the room, leaving Lencho and Krazen St. John alone.

He hated that he felt like he could cry, but it was too much. The fight earlier with Kal, the draining rampage . . . and then, the argument with his dad. How was he supposed to deal with any of this?

"Mr. Will," Krazen said. "Am I correct in assuming that you're a member of the Divine?"

Lencho nodded. He couldn't do anything else.

"And is your gang comprised of all Nubian teens?" Krazen asked. "Most of whom are around your age?"

Again, Lencho nodded, not really understanding why the guy was asking him these questions.

"And am I also correct that you're selling Elevation, but you aren't quite hitting your numbers to pay back your suppliers and are in danger as a result?"

Lencho's neck almost snapped, he looked up at Krazen so fast.

"I'm a powerful man," Krazen said. "You don't deserve to struggle, Lencho. A gift like yours is special, and I can help you learn more about it."

Lencho spoke carefully, still confused. "What do you mean, 'a gift'?"

Krazen stood up. "I'm afraid I'll need a bit more confidence in our relationship before we take this discussion any further. But let's make a deal. Bring your fellow Divine members to meet with me, and we'll discuss how to handle your Elevation problems . . . and your gift."

Krazen tapped his inner wrist, just like Tilly had. The door slid open again, and she appeared. Had she been waiting outside, ready to be summoned?

"Tilly will give you my information," he said, walking to the door. "When you're ready, we can discuss further."

She walked over to Lencho, his dirty, cracked phone in her hand. He was too overwhelmed to be annoyed that she'd taken it in the first place. All he could do was watch Krazen St. John as he padded to the door. Only then did Lencho realize that the man was barefoot.

"You should know that I'm quite generous to those in my company," Krazen said, swiveling slightly. "If it's your goal to ascend *permanently*, that could very well be a possibility. It's all up to you, Lencho. And I believe you'll make the right choice."

Then he was gone, and Tilly stepped in front of Lencho, holding out his mobile. She held the device delicately between her fingers, as if it was something foul that she loathed to touch.

"Whenever you're ready, just say or type his name and his contact information will appear," Tilly said, her soft fingertips brushing Lencho's as he took the phone back.

"Right," he said, feeling more embarrassed by the second in her presence.

"It's been a pleasure to meet you, Mr. Will," she said with a nod as she stepped back. "I look forward to seeing you again."

He stared at her, too mesmerized to speak. This close, she seemed to glow. He looked back at his mobile, his fingers hovering over the keypad, the phone looking like a piece of junk compared to these people's implants. He actually had Krazen St. John's information right here in his hand.

Suddenly, there were guards on either side of him and he was whisked out of the bed and instructed to put on his shoes. In less than a minute, he was walked to another portal that appeared in the wall, a portal that Lencho realized was an elevator.

His time Up High had just come to an unceremonious end.

Chapter 11

Uzochi

"We're live with Professor Cassandra Johnson, lower-city histories scholar, here to talk to us more about the increased militia presence currently seen in certain neighborhoods in Tri-State East. Professor Johnson, welcome to *World Village Report*."

The sounds of the holo-news floated into Uzochi's consciousness, the words blurring together with the fragments of his last dream. He'd been walking the streets of his neighborhood, a younger version of himself struggling to move faster as the sidewalk disintegrated beneath his feet.

"Happy to be here, James. But let's be real about what we're talking about. We're not speaking of 'certain' neighborhoods. We're speaking of poor neighborhoods, refugee neighborhoods, plain and simple. And we need to call it like it is. Because even if it's become the norm to have a giant tank parked down by the local bodega, it wasn't always like this. New Yorkers did *not* walk the streets surrounded by military vehicles. They just didn't. Yet most of the viewers of your show who live in the lower city constantly see roaming militia squads."

Uzochi didn't open his eyes. In the dream, he was pinned between the sidewalk crumbling before and behind him. He was going to fall into the abyss. But then he looked up and Zuberi was there, shouting something he couldn't make out.

"And remember, New York has the largest concentration of climate refugees compared to any other city in North America. These people have suffered enough, and they hear the message that's being sent loud and clear: They aren't trusted here in our city. In what's become *their* city."

Jump! Uzochi thought Zuberi was yelling. But where would he jump to?

"Cassandra—I mean, Professor Johnson—these militia groups are keeping all of us safe, including the refugees. If the people living in the lower city are seeing it that way, they're projecting."

Uzochi held out his hand. Zuberi could help him. She could float down to him and grab his hand. She could save him.

"I adamantly disagree, James. If St. John Soldiers are meant to be a privatized replacement for traditional military units, fine, but they should be utilized sparingly. At this point, these squads are just a way for Mr. St. John to showcase his control over the lower city as he sits fat and happy above us."

Zuberi didn't reach back. She looked at Uzochi and her eyes narrowed.

Who the hell are you? she said.

The sidewalk disappeared beneath Uzochi, and with a scream, he rocketed to the depths beneath him. He waited for his feet to strike the ground, for the bones in his ankles to break—

"Uzochi, are you awake?"

His eyes flew open and he sat straight up, gasping for air.

He was home, on the couch, under a suffocating blanket. He didn't know what time it was, but fragments of light were slipping in through the tiny holes in the frayed curtain that hung in front of the apartment's sole window.

"Son, talk to me. Are you okay?"

Uzochi closed his eyes, forcing air in through his nose. He slowly centered himself in the room, in the present. When he could, he opened his eyes again, taking in everything. Com'pa was near him and had muted the holo-news that had seeped into his dream. The *Village Report* host, James S.E. Bradley, was gesturing wildly with his hands as his guest rolled her eyes and gesticulated right back.

"Mom, what happened?" Uzochi said, finding his voice tremulous. She handed him a cup of water, and he downed it in a single gulp.

"You passed out, that's what happened," she said, taking the cup from him and refilling it from a pitcher on a nearby tray. She was already dressed in her nurse's uniform. "You scared me half to death. I took your vitals over and over again to make sure everything was okay."

Uzochi took the refilled cup and drained it thirstily. Com'pa smiled a bit, but then concern spread across the soft lines in her face.

"Dear heart, are you all right?"

Uzochi set the cup down and pressed a hand to his

temple, trying to remember what had happened before he blacked out. He remembered the flash of blue light, same as at the fight. And something . . . something with voices. One in particular, but the longer he was awake, the fainter it all became.

It wasn't something he could tell his mom. The sensations and visions were all too muddy, and if he told his mom he was hearing voices and seeing lights, she'd cart him off to a counselor. Or maybe even a med center. Uzochi couldn't properly sort through anything right now. His head still ached and he was completely famished. How long had it been since dinner?

"What time is it?" he asked, looking around.

"A little before six in the morning," Com'pa said, checking the time projected at the bottom of the holo-news. "I nearly called for a medic. You woke up a few times in the night . . . son, I was worried."

Six in the morning? That meant he'd been out for the entire night. Of course his mom was worried. He knew she'd be ready to cart him away to a doctor.

Uzochi sat up, kicking off the repressive blanket. He was in his pajamas, which meant his mom had changed him out of the clothes he'd worn to school. A deep embarrassment stirred inside him. He was nearly grown and his mother was treating him like a child.

Lencho's words returned. *Some of us have actually had to grow up.*

"Uzochi . . . ," Com'pa said, putting her hand on his.

He yanked it away, immediately regretting the hurt that

flashed on his mother's face. He knew this wasn't her fault. She was just trying to be a mom.

What was the matter with him?

"Sorry," he said quickly. "I just . . . um, I feel a little out of it."

"But why?" Com'pa pressed. "What's going on? Please, tell me."

He shifted on the couch. What could he possibly tell her?

"I ate something bad at school, I guess," he lied, and he saw in her eyes that it was his first mistake.

She clucked. "Uzochi, just stop. You never hide things from me. Come now."

"I'm fine, Mom," he insisted. He needed a moment to figure out the significance of the dream and the nonstop voices he'd heard in his head last night. Maybe the stress of the day had gotten to him? With confronting Lencho and the fight? "Really. Maybe I was just, I dunno, dehydrated. Can you let it go?"

She stared at him, then stood up, shaking her head.

"Just like your father," she said, looking away from him. "Stubborn."

At those words, Uzochi perked up. Com'pa never talked about Uzochi's father, her grief constant but silent. Siran had died when Uzochi was a baby, before his family even made it to Tri-State East. When Uzochi got a bit older and asked about his dad, all Com'pa would say was that the storm had been horrible, that Siran had tried to save everyone from the cataclysm that destroyed Nubia, that he would be so proud of

Uzochi. Then her eyes would mist, and Uzochi never wanted his mother to cry. So he stopped asking questions but never stopped wondering.

A fresh opportunity had now arisen. He glanced at the illustration of his father that rested on the shelf nearby. If Com'pa's portrait was accurate, he and Uzochi shared the same eyes and nose, though Siran had a thick, curly beard.

"Mom, can you—"

His question was interrupted by a soft pulsing sound that filled the room, followed by a charming woman's voice. "You have a visitor," said the digital announcer perched under the top of the apartment doorframe. It was one of the few modern innovations Com'pa had bought in the lower city years ago, purchased from a Swamp street merchant specializing in sky tech. She felt safer using the device, as their building had no real security.

"Ah." Com'pa glanced toward the announcer. "Announcer, image of visitor, please," she said.

A live feed of a man standing in front of the apartment door was projected to the main room of the apartment. The desaturated holo flickered, the announcer being an older, outdated model. Though the image was shaky, Uzochi saw that the visitor had a big wad of gray-white hair and wore a modest tunic.

Com'pa went to the door and opened it, the feed blinking out. "Hello, hello!" she said to the man standing outside, pushing aside the sadness that had just filled the living room. "Adisa Elenkwa, please come in, wise spirit brother. And please pardon the untidiness. It can't be helped. My son and I are in a . . . situation, as you've heard."

"Com'pa Will, sister, thank you so much for your hospital-
ity," Adisa said with a slight bow as he entered the apartment.
"I came as soon as I could after we spoke."

Uzochi sat up. He knew Adisa, of course. Every Nubian
did. He was one of the most popular community elders,
someone to be deeply revered. But Uzochi didn't know what
to make of Adisa being here. The few times he'd come over
before, Com'pa had not-so-subtly told her son he should go
study at Bellevue Park.

"Adisa, do you remember Uzochi?" Com'pa said.

"But of course," the elder replied. He walked over to where
Uzochi sat, his lined face severe. He stooped down slightly.
"Uzochi Will, hello. Are you well?"

"Baba, hi. Um . . . I . . . ," Uzochi said, searching his memory for any of the standard greetings Nubian kids used with
elders. "Yeah, um, I'm fine."

Adisa and Com'pa exchanged a knowing glance. Uzochi
hated when adults did that, having their own unspoken communication as if he wasn't there.

"Actually, I'm way better," he said, standing up suddenly.
"In fact, I think I'll take a shower. I can still make it to school."

"Dear heart," Com'pa said, hands fluttering. "Don't you
think—"

"Excuse me, please," he said, trying to sound as polite as
he could while fighting the increasing ache in his skull. The
last thing he needed was to have another spell in front of his
mom *and* an elder.

Com'pa looked again at Adisa, who just watched Uzochi.
Judgment, clear, sharp, and Uzochi didn't know what it was

about. Usually he loved to be judged because he was always prepared for the test at hand. But right now he was in the dark, and he loathed the feeling.

Uzochi bowed, hoping his mom would forgive his rudeness, and turned on his heels to the bathroom.

It was the only door in the house he could lock, given that he slept on the pullout bed in the living room. When he shut the door, he kept the lights off, fearing that any extra stimulation might set off a headache.

Get it together, Uzochi, he told himself.

He turned on the water and stood under the spray until he no longer heard Adisa's voice through the thin walls. His mom would soon have to leave, too. As long as Uzochi was up and moving and seemingly okay, he knew she would go to work. If memory served him correctly, she'd be working in the Bronx today and so would take their used hover car to head uptown.

He was proven right when he dressed in the bathroom and went to the kitchen, finding a short note from her and a packed lunch. Part of him wanted to leave it out of a spite he didn't understand, but he pushed the feeling aside and placed the bag in his scholar-pack. The reality of the morning set in, including how he'd basically ignored Adisa—a horrifying example of disrespect—and given his mother a hard time. He blamed his irritability on stress from the previous day, promising himself he'd make it up to her later.

Chapter 12

Zuberi

At school, Zuberi kept her eyes open for signs of the Spiders, surmising they'd find a way to retaliate against her eventually. Vriana, who Zuberi had filled in about the incident, must've had the same thought, though she wouldn't say so explicitly. Instead, she never left Zuberi's side unless they had different classes, and even then, she walked Zuberi to her class before leaving to go to her own. Zuberi finally had to tell her she was fine, to cut it out. After all, she knew she could take them . . . as long as she stopped seeing weird floating figures above everybody's heads.

It turned out that Kal had been hospitalized but was expected to make a full recovery. And even though the fight happened off campus without any witnesses besides Zuberi, Uzochi, Lencho, and the gang, that didn't stop the entire school from speculating. Gossip about the incident dominated everyone's IMA* social media feeds. At least no one seemed to know that Zuberi was involved—a lucky break. Her dad didn't need to know she was fighting gang members, even if it had been justified. He was adamant when he trained Zuberi that fighting was a last resort, something to be used only in self-defense or extraordinary circumstances. Easy enough for him to say. He didn't go to 104.

In addition to watching out for Spiders, Zuberi also kept a close eye on Uzochi, who seemed to be walking around with a strange sort of energy. She caught him glancing at her more than once between periods, only to look away and scuttle off. She had so many questions for the boy, none of which she could actually ask. The light she'd seen during the fight. The way he'd stared at her, like he could see all the way through to her soul. And the spirits . . . she wanted to ask someone about them. Anyone. But then she would've seemed insane.

Luckily, the ghosts had abated . . . at least, for now. Zuberi kept herself as busy as possible during her classes, and thankfully, she only saw her peers in front of her, nothing floating above their heads. She was beginning to think yesterday's happenings had all been a fluke, one she was grateful to put behind her.

For her last block, Zuberi had a free period, while Vriana had science. To kill time, Zuberi headed straight for the school's massive gym. As she walked there, she passed one of the security guards. Her dad had his own thoughts about 104's security, how they only protected certain students (sometimes) and were more concerned with appearances than actual safety. Zuberi thought it was a microcosm of what Krazen St. John wanted to turn the entire city into, a place where there was an immediate response for those Up High and a delayed, even nonexistent one for Nubians and others in the lower city.

Still, she didn't need to be on the wrong side of security. When the guard looked up at her, she flashed him the pass embedded in her mobile that told him it was her free period. He nodded, and she walked on, letting out a breath.

The yellow-walled gym was empty, as it always was during this period. Zuberi knew the gym's schedule like the back of her hand. Here, she could train in peace. She didn't have the collapsible metal staff she often trained with, as it would have been considered a weapon on school grounds, so today she would inhabit the forms without additional tools. She didn't need to enact all seventy-two defensive and offensive positions. No, she would practice moving from her core, relying on only her body to ground her.

She practiced the forms for forty-five minutes, exulting in her serenity and strength as outstretched limbs and arched hands glided through the air, a roll or flip added here and there. Her father had been so proud when she'd started to improvise during their practices, proclaiming that back in Nubia only the best warriors knew how to play with the forms while honoring core positions.

By the time the school bell signaled that final period was done, Zuberi was sweaty and breathless but clearheaded. The forms were exactly what she'd needed. Always were.

"Knew I'd find you here," Vriana said several minutes later, poking her head into the gym. "You ready?"

Zuberi nodded, wiping sweat from her brow with a towel and then following her friend out. Most of the school had already cleared—kids at 104 rushed off campus in a mass exodus at final bell—but there were some stragglers. A few looked at Zuberi as she and Vriana passed, making eyes at Vriana. She was as beautiful as always in an off-the-shoulder floral blouse, so Zuberi wasn't surprised.

Together, the girls slowly made their way to the Swamp to do homework at Vriana's. Zuberi picked up a beetle-yogurt wrap at the sole cafe across the street from school, her eyes still on the lookout for Spiders. The farther downtown they walked, the more activity around them seemed to pick up, and by the time they passed Reade Street, the aroma of food carts was heavy in the air. They walked past the usual rows of tenements and empty storefronts. Zuberi occasionally glimpsed the abandoned, skeletal buildings of Battery Park City in the distance, the only high-rise buildings in southern Manhattan that remained undemolished. Upon hitting Warren Street, they reached the rows and rows of shacks on stilts that had come to define the Nubian Quarter, thirty-five square blocks in all, interspersed among the ruins of the old financial district. Even though there were still pools of water after the big downpour two days ago, the street was relatively dry.

Vendors were out hawking their wares in enamel tents, selling kente dresses and tunics and tees with knockoff designer logos and random home knickknacks and fufu with tomato soup and plantains made kelewele style. A couple of vendors even had outdated tech from the Up High that they were selling for a discount. Countless piles of cedarwood supplied by St. John Enterprises lay between the tents, a Swamp necessity, as someone's home always needed repair. When heading to Vriana's section of the quarter, Zuberi loved to let her gaze linger on Romantico's, the only Nubian fusion restaurant in the city, with its mix of West African and Mediterranean dishes. The sight of the venue's neon-red awning jutting over the sidewalk made her smile.

What she would have loved to avoid was the sight that seemed to suck up all the space in the neighborhood. The Swamp's red-brown brick seawall loomed above.

"You know, with all the money they have Up High, they could fix this in a day," Zuberi said, shaking her head in disgust, remembering Krazen's press conference. "It's like they *want* us to live like this."

Vriana scrunched up her nose. "Yeah. Maybe."

"Doesn't it make you mad?" Zuberi pressed.

"I mean, I guess," Vriana said, hesitating. "I mean, yeah, honestly, sometimes I do get mad. But what am I going to do? And so many people have it worse."

Zuberi bit her lip. "Yeah, but that's all part of the same problem. And unless we do something about it—"

"Before you start rage-spouting, can we talk about the more immediate problem? You know, how you were about to fight an entire *gang*?"

"Vri, I had to," Zuberi said. "I was jumped."

"I'm not saying it wasn't badass," Vriana said. "But maybe . . . I dunno, play it cool for a bit? We don't need you fighting everybody."

Zuberi bristled. "I *don't* fight everybody. They came for me, and I fought back."

Vriana looked up to the sky. "Okay, Beri, you're right.

You're a perfectly content person. It's not like you wake up at the crack of dawn to go punch and kick imaginary people in the park."

"I do not 'punch and kick imaginary people in the park,'" Zuberi said. "I train."

"Because that's a normal hobby for a teenager."

"Well, yeah, it is," Zuberi said. "My dad said Nubians used to train all the time from when they were kids."

"Then let's be grateful we aren't in Nubia," Vriana said.

Zuberi had to bite her lip to keep from snapping at her friend. There was no reason for them to get into it once again. They simply held different worldviews. Vriana didn't have that burning desire to connect with her heritage the way Zuberi did. And Vriana thought Zuberi was way too political, too angry and *militant*. (Zuberi so hated that word.)

But maybe she could talk about the visions she'd been having? The spirits? Knowing Vriana, she'd find a way to explain the visions with science of the mind. Actually, maybe that wasn't such a bad idea to discuss. Maybe that was the problem. Zuberi just needed more information.

"V," she said quietly. "Is there some kind of, um . . . mind condition you've read about where you see, uh, figures? Like spirits . . . of people?"

Vriana paused, blinking eyes that today were lined in pink.

"You mean like a medium or a psychic?" she asked.

"No," Zuberi said. "Not dead people. More like . . . I dunno. Just figures. Floating. And they look back at you."

Vriana tilted her head. "Gonna have to be more specific, Beri."

Zuberi sighed, finally giving in and telling her friend all that she'd experienced, the woman in the park, the kids after school, Kal and Uzochi and Lencho. The ghosts and the glowing. She let the words sit there between them, waiting for her friend's answer.

Vriana considered this, pursing her lips intently, her demeanor serious. "Sounds like some kind of psychic ability, but I don't know."

Zuberi bit her lip. Great. Now she just felt like more of a freak.

She turned to Vriana. "Well, have you ever felt like you had some kind of . . . I dunno, ability?"

"Oh, absolutely," Vriana said.

Zuberi stopped walking. "What?"

Vriana smiled, mischief returning to her features. "I can make anyone feel better just by talking to them. And I do mean *anyone*."

Zuberi forced a smile, squeezing her friend in a side hug.

"You sure can," she said, even as she felt hollow and disappointed by the response.

Zuberi stayed quiet for the rest of the walk to Vriana's as her friend picked a new topic of conversation, namely, her psychology class. Zuberi half listened as they walked until, suddenly, Vriana stopped.

"Hey," she said, "who is that?"

There on the ground was a man slouched against the corner of a building. He was groaning, just like the woman had in the park, but his pain was beyond hers. He was clutching his stomach, body shaking as he sobbed.

Vriana and Zuberi exchanged looks. Beyond the man, Zuberi saw the usual dotting of St. John Soldiers patrolling the Swamp. Two were relatively close, clearly having a casual conversation while the man nearby moaned in pain.

"Excuse me," Vriana said, waving at them. "I think this guy needs some help."

They paused their conversation to look at the girls. For a moment, Zuberi thought they might ignore the request, but then the soldiers approached, each of them glancing at the man.

"Elevation junkie by the looks of it," said a soldier. "No doubt an overdose."

"We'll make a call," said the other. "You ladies be on your way."

Vriana clearly wanted to argue, but Zuberi pressed a hand to her arm. She didn't trust St. John Soldiers as far as she could throw them, and she didn't need them coming up with reasons to pay attention to a pair of Nubian girls.

"Just let 'em handle it," Zuberi whispered. "We'll keep walking."

They'd barely gone a few more steps, though, when they heard another voice.

"He'll come out of it. Eventually."

Zuberi whirled around, fists already up and ready to fly. But the boy who appeared, seemingly out of the shadows, wasn't a Spider.

It was Lencho.

Goddess, why am I constantly running into this frickin' boy?

"Fancy seeing you here," Vriana said, her smile instantly radiant. "We missed you at school."

Lencho's face twitched, as he was probably trying to figure out whether Vriana was serious or mocking him.

"Um, my friend wanted to thank you, by the way," Vriana said, her words becoming more hesitant. "For saving her ass."

Zuberi glared at Vriana. "I didn't need saving," she said to the boy. "By you *or* your cousin."

Lencho kept his distance, staying in the shadows of one of the few trees planted in the Swamp, its wood hollow and white with death. He looked over at the soldiers, but when Zuberi followed his gaze, she saw that they'd already returned to their conversation and were strolling away.

"Sure," Lencho said. "But anyway, don't worry about the guy. He'll be fine."

"How do you know?" Zuberi asked. "You sell him the drugs he's on?"

Lencho's eyes narrowed. Had she hit a sore spot?

"Just saying you don't need to worry," he said. "And maybe don't start shit with any Spiders right now, all right?"

"It's good advice," said Aren, striding up behind Lencho. He'd brought along another boy who Zuberi didn't recognize. He was massive, completely solid with arms like boulders, making both of the other boys look tiny in comparison. Next to her, Vriana let out a breath.

"That's Zaire," she whispered.

Zaire seemed to have caught wind of the whisper, and he glanced over at Vriana. He looked like the kind of guy who possibly smiled once every ten thousand years, but for the beauteous Vriana, his lips quirked ever so slightly.

"We were looking for you, Lencho," Aren said. "Gonna

head back to HQ. We were worried you might've gotten . . . distracted."

He wagged his eyebrows at Zuberi and Vriana, which made Zuberi roll her eyes and Vriana giggle.

"I was just heading back, too," Lencho said, stone-faced as ever. "You didn't need to look for me, though."

"Eh, we look out for each other," said Aren, grinning at the girls. "What about you, Zuberi? Looking to enlist? We can always use a real fighter."

"So this is you living the life, huh? Selling people Elevation and leaving them wrecked," she said, unable to help herself. "Stand-up guy."

Aren just laughed. Next to him, Zaire leaned over and whispered something, then nodded toward the St. John Soldiers in the distance.

"We should probably get moving," Zaire said, his voice louder now. In fact, as he spoke, it was as though his voice was a steady rumble that reverberated through the Swamp, echoing all around them.

Zuberi blinked. She was losing her mind. No, the boy was just speaking. Nothing was rumbling. Nothing was—

In a flash, Zaire glowed green. His eyes swung to hers and he stared, saying something she couldn't hear. Then suddenly there were two Zaires, one floating above, scowling at her, another on the ground.

Her chest tightened.

"No," she whispered. "Not again."

"Beri?" Vriana asked, tugging on Zuberi's sleeve. "You okay?"

She was not. Aren's spirit suddenly appeared as well, hanging from his body. And then Lencho . . .

Lencho glowed red, everything around him drowning in the glow.

No.

No.

What was happening to her?

"Beri," Vriana said, her voice more insistent. "Talk to me. What's happening?"

Zuberi turned to look at her friend. She stared at her, blinking, as Vriana's spirit detached from her body, sashaying into the air.

"No," Zuberi whispered. "It's not possible."

"Hey," Aren said, his voice nearing a shout. "What the hell's wrong with her? She havin' a fit or something?"

Was she? Zuberi's head whipped back and forth, taking in the translucent figures floating above. She backed away.

"I dunno," Lencho said. "But we should go—"

"Nah, man," Aren said. "We gotta get her out of here. Hurry before those St. John assholes notice."

Zuberi wanted to go. She needed to. But the figures were watching her, and she needed to know what they were. Why they were following her.

"What—"

Lencho's hand was on her wrist, dragging her forward, a grip unlike anything she'd felt before. He was heat, a raging fire singeing her skin, the kind of burn that zipped all the way through her body. At once, the floating figures vanished and steady breath returned to her lungs. She blinked, looking down, as Lencho dropped his hold on her.

"What do you see?" he asked, his voice a harsh whisper. "What do you see in me?"

Zuberi met his eyes, and when she did, she swore she could see a hint of red behind them. But it wasn't anger that she found. It was wonder.

Who was this boy? And what could he do?

Then someone else had her hand. Vriana. Zuberi let herself be led away by her friend. She couldn't speak, and Vriana didn't press her. They walked until they reached the juncture between their two homes.

"Was it the spirits you told me about?" Vriana asked quietly.

Zuberi nodded. She needed to get home, to sort out her thoughts.

Vriana squeezed Zuberi's hand.

"I don't know what's going on," Vriana said, "but you know I'm here for you, right?"

Zuberi nodded, even though she didn't know anything at the moment.

"You're going to be okay," Vriana said. "I promise."

She pulled Zuberi into a hug, and Zuberi let herself sink into the embrace. Because at least for a moment, Vriana made her feel safe.

Chapter 13

Lencho

Lencho stomped through the Swamp, his mind whirring after what had just happened with Zuberi. After slipping away from his gang, he'd managed to drain that guy in the crook of a derelict building, the experience so sweet, so beyond electric, his body feeling dynamic and strong as he took what belonged to another. But then those girls had chosen to walk up. Why, why did they have to linger? Every second they'd stood there, talking to those soldiers, Lencho had thought he'd surely be found out. Of course, he didn't know exactly what he'd be found out for. . . . He still didn't fully understand his so-called gift.

But Krazen St. John knew, which already felt like one too many people.

"Lencho, man, hold up," Aren called from behind him, pulling Lencho from his thoughts. He was headed for the Rotting Jungle, the Divine's headquarters and his home away from home. Possibly his only home now that he'd evicted himself from his parents' place. Unless . . . well, unless he took Krazen up on his offer.

"Man, what happened?" Aren asked, Zaire stepping up behind him as the three came to a stop.

Lencho looked around. He was paranoid about being followed now, expecting Tilly to pop up around any corner. He didn't feel safe here, out in the open, revealing secrets to Aren.

"Can we talk at the Jungle?" Lencho asked.

Aren looked at Zaire, then back at Lencho. After what felt like a lifetime, he nodded.

They walked quickly then, Lencho feeling like his body was on fire. He'd hoped draining would leave him calm and energized, helping him cope with the aftermath of everything that had happened yesterday and this morning. But instead, he'd spent the day hopping from one high to another, unsettled, jittery.

And what had just happened with Zuberi? He hadn't wanted to touch her, not with all the draining he'd been doing, but he'd reacted by instinct, trying to snap her out of her trance. Touching her was different, a sensation unlike anything he'd experienced before. Almost as if there was something greater surging in her blood.

The experience had left him even more confused—the last thing he needed. Now it was late afternoon, and he still didn't have a clue what to do when it came to Krazen's offer or figuring out his gift (which was a bit disturbing if he thought too much about it) or continuing to push for Elevation sales at 104.

There was one thing he knew for sure, though: he

wouldn't be going back home. This had been confirmed when he'd been dropped back off down in the lower city. When he checked his messages, his mobile had been filled with threatening texts from his father, all of them about how he'd shamed his parents and how he'd pay for his flagrant disrespect. The most recent text had told him not to bother coming home if he was unable to offer a proper apology for his behavior, and Lencho decided to take his father up on the offer. Kefle was the one who should've apologized to his son and wife for the years of abuse and terror. But whatever, all good. Like he'd told Uzochi, blood was just blood. He had another family, a chosen family, and it was time he moved into that new life completely.

The trio of boys quickly walked north, soon approaching the eight-story tenement the Divine Suns referred to as the Rotting Jungle. The building reeked. Even though most of the crew squatted there every night, Lencho was sure no one ever bothered to wipe down its floors or walls or properly take out the garbage. Still, the smell did act as a sort of security feature, since almost no one entered the property by accident.

"Let's go to my place," Aren said, stepping up behind him. "And, Zaire, let's debrief later, all right?"

The massive boy nodded, heading off to his own room at the other end of the Jungle. That left Lencho and Aren to take the first set of stairs to their right, walking up to the next floor, a shadowy space of corroded partitions and familiar, random objects. The ancient wicker bookshelf missing its right half. The overturned baby carriage covered in dust, its hover platform broken.

Lencho spotted a couple of Divine hanging in a corner under a big window and gave them a wave and head nod. The girls waved back, smiling. Keera sometimes worked uptown while Nneka was an off-and-on student at 104; both lived in the Jungle full-time. Other than their chatter, the space was quiet.

On the second floor, Aren led the way to where his door was open, revealing a turquoise-and-ivory Nubian flag tucked in a windowsill. Lara was there, lounging on a battered couch with a small holo-projector in her hand, the light from the 3-D images of a reality show reflecting off her face. Lencho figured she must've swiped the projector from a street merchant, a new, shiny little treasure.

"Hey," she called over her shoulder, grinning at Aren and then Lencho. "So you found the runaway?"

"Not a runaway," Lencho said quickly. "I was, um . . . detained."

Lara sat up on the couch. "You were arrested?"

It was technically true, so he nodded.

"What?" Aren demanded, grabbing Lencho by the shoulder. "They charge you? Why didn't you say anything?"

Lencho shook his head. "It's all good. I didn't say anything because it wasn't a big deal. And no charges were filed. I threw my stash into a trash can once I saw the St. John Stoneheads coming. They, uh, questioned me and kept me in one of their stupid vans for the night, just being assholes. But they let me go this morning."

Which wasn't technically a lie. Lencho looked from Aren

to Lara, hoping against hope that she would leave. He didn't want to tell Aren about Krazen's deal with her here.

"I, um . . ."

"Fuck, man," Aren said. "Rough night, huh? At least they let you go."

Lencho just nodded. He was trying to figure out how to pitch Krazen's deal, but the words were dry in his mouth.

"And those girls," Aren said. "What were they doing?"

"They found some guy high on Elevation," Lencho said, thankful for a question he could answer. "One of my customers. I got rid of them. And they're just kids, anyway."

Lara sucked her teeth. "So are you. Speaking of, what's this about the Spiders wanting to retaliate? One of their leaders, Kal, ended up in the hospital."

Lencho's blood ran cold. How much more shit could he take? Sending a boy to the hospital? Could he even return to school?

Aren turned to look at him, and Lencho shifted uneasily on his feet.

"They were attacking some Nubian girl," he said. "Actually, Aren, they were attacking that girl we just ran into—Zuberi. And my cousin tried to get involved, and I had to fight 'em off by myself 'cause my family ain't good for shit. But it was a clean duel. If Kal says anything, it's on him."

Aren and Lara glanced at each other. Lencho shifted anxiously. What'd they expect him to do? Stand there and do nothing?

Lencho knew many of the Divine didn't trust him. There

were whispers that he'd eventually run back to his cushy life in Old Chelsea when things got tough, that he only wanted to join a gang for kicks without understanding the stakes. Why else would someone with Lencho's options get involved with a crew full of ratty orphans with dead Nubian parents, who'd run away from foster care? Besides dealing Elevation, the Divine relied on theft, muggings, underground security jobs, and body work to survive. Not an easy life.

Taking down a Spider leader, though, showed that Lencho wasn't afraid of the risks. It sent a message that the Divine were formidable, something to be reckoned with, and Aren and Lara needed to acknowledge that.

"Look, it was necessary," Lencho said. "And it proves my point from before. We need to send a message to the Spiders, and now we've sent one. And . . . I still think we need to reconsider selling at 104. If it's not Elevation, then we sell protection, or maybe even tech hacking. I dunno. What I do know is it's untapped turf."

Aren considered this, rubbing his chin. Lencho held his breath, feeling in his bones that this was his chance. This was his moment.

But then Aren shook his head, and everything inside Lencho deflated.

"Not yet," Aren said. "At least, not on the Elevation. I'll consider the other two, do the potential numbers with Lara. I just think laying low is the better option here. Sorry, bruh. We gotta deal with this Spider fallout before we do anything else."

Fallout. That was what Aren saw him as right now. A consequence that had to be dealt with.

"You need anything else, man?" Aren asked, stepping closer. "I know it's been a hard couple of days. Remember, we're family. So if there's something you need, just ask."

"Actually," Lencho said, hating that he had to ask this, considering the circumstances, "I need a room. I . . . um, left my parents' place."

Lara studied him, then her gaze darted to Aren. "Fifth floor's open," she finally said. "Choose a spot."

Aren nodded. "Take it. We're happy to have you. And let me know what you need . . . toiletries, extra clothes. I got you."

Lencho nodded, hoping he looked grateful and not sulky. Shame engulfed his body. He probably seemed beyond pitiful, going from a nasty fight to being arrested to having no place to live. And more than anything, he wanted to run outside and find someone to drain.

"Thanks, and light be with you," he managed to say to them both, even though the Divine slogan felt hollow. He left the room after they returned the sentiment, buzzing a little as he went to his new spot on the fifth floor, choosing the studio that looked the least run-down. At least they'd said yes to this. It wasn't much, just an empty space for him to roll out one of the spare straw pallets left for squatters, plus a slanting sink and a rusted toilet and shower in the bathroom. But at least it was home.

There would be things to deal with, obviously. He barely had any currency to his name, and Aren still wasn't seeing his point of view.

No, Lencho had to grab ahold of himself, leave behind tired ways of thinking. He had new connections now, *magnificent* connections, and something was happening to his body that was extraordinary.

He just had to figure it out. He couldn't waste this opportunity, not when this was the kind of connection many would kill for, even goody-two-shoes Uzochi. He imagined his cousin's face if he showed him the holo now embedded in his phone.

The holo. Lencho couldn't help himself. He had to make sure it was real, that it hadn't been a dream. He closed the door to the studio, pulled out his mobile, and whispered the name.

"Krazen St. John."

Immediately a holo sprang from his mobile. Lencho's phone had never had holo-projection capabilities until he'd reached the sky.

And there Krazen was, turning in Lencho's new room. The icon of Tri-State East. And that wasn't all. There, on the screen of Lencho's mobile, a phone number and an address. Below it, the words *I look forward to meeting you and your friends.*

Lencho's mind buzzed. He swiped the holo away, eliminating the light before anyone saw it through the crack at the bottom of his door. His mind was fuzzy, his limbs heavy and aching from the long day. He'd figure out what to do tomorrow, he decided. He needed to chill for now and make sure to get a good night's sleep, was all. Then he would be able to think clearly.

Unfortunately, when he tried to sleep hours later, his straw cot wasn't forgiving, leaving him to toss and turn as the night wore on. He thought of home, of his bed with the blankets his mother had knitted him. The shower that he could've taken, one that ran clear rather than dirty brown. He replayed the angry words he'd said and heard over the past couple of days, felt the tingle in his hands and arms and thighs and feet that told him his body was begging to drain someone.

Where did this power come from and why did he have it? Krazen St. John had the answers, and it was time for Lencho to make moves, to really prove to the Divine who he was.

Chapter 14

Sandra

Sandra rested her hand on one of the countless consoles that filled the huge atrium, the coldness of the steel providing a pleasant bite to her fingers. She needed to stay focused, to feel alert despite the late hour.

Dozens of holo-screens occupied the atrium's central space. Fifteen scanners sat at their consoles, eyes attuned to live video feeds of different parts of the lower city as they typed notes on anything that seemed out of the ordinary. Though Krazen's street cameras had first been used to surveil what went down at his construction sites across the lower city, he'd eventually hired a rotating staff of scanners to monitor the screens 24/7, paying special attention to what happened under the cover of night. *Don't sleep on what goes down in the dark,* he'd once said to Sandra. *The leverage you can gain on people who think no one's watching.* This meant that the atrium was always buzzing with activity, even when the rest of Tri-State East slept soundly.

Sandra never spoke to the scanners while they worked.

This was partly because Krazen loathed distractions, particularly those affecting his employees. A distraction, he said, led to sloppiness, and sloppiness led to lost profits. So even though Sandra walked through a room full of people, her heels click-clacking on a spotless marble floor, no one spoke to her. No one made eye contact. Once or twice, she thought she saw a pair of eyes slide in her direction, but they always snapped back to their screens before she could catch them outright.

The scanners didn't trust her. She didn't mind. Sandra preferred that they saw her as dangerous. It made things simpler for everyone when she wasn't underestimated.

She walked the length of the atrium, her off-white duster skimming her ankles. Beneath it, she wore a simple pair of fuchsia leggings and a plain pink tee, no makeup. But even if she was dressed casually for her personal standards, she'd made sure she put on her simple but elegant gold hoops. Without the hoops, she might as well have been naked.

Tilly's station was empty, yet to be filled by a replacement, as Sandra knew the other woman still sometimes returned to her console. She paused at the chair and examined the desk. Sandra wasn't surprised to find that Tilly's station was clean, minimal, like the others. Her father didn't allow for any personal effects. She recalled that one scanner from Queens had tried to prop up a tiny picture of his wife only to be summarily suspended for a week. He was the same fool who once called her father "Krazen" to his face instead of "sir" or "Mr. St. John," not realizing that the only people the Sky King allowed to use his first name were his adoring public and his daughter. The silly scanner's ascension status was almost revoked.

Ever since the press conference, Sandra had been trying to figure out what her father was up to. She knew Tilly was somehow at the root of it, and as a scanner, she had access to intel that others did not. Which was why Sandra was here.

Tilly's screen was on and her cameras were still open, which meant that she might actually still be nearby, as it wasn't like her to leave information like this unsecure. Not that it was really private information. Any of the scanners could review the atrium's data streams. But Tilly had pinned specific feeds to her desktop. Why?

Sandra peered closer, watching a clip in the corner that she realized consisted of video captures, not live feeds, replaying again and again.

It was a feed close to Union Square, one of the easier places to scan, as the area's infrastructure was well maintained, if a bit ancient—as was everything down below. Still, there, on Twenty-Second Street, something in the video caught Sandra's attention.

A boy, or perhaps better to say a young man, maybe mid-teens. Sandra's age. She tapped the screen, zooming in on the video. He was slim and athletic with what some would call Nubian features, and he was bending over someone. His hands were on their face and shoulder, almost as if he was holding them still. Suddenly, the boy stood up, shoving the person abruptly aside. Then, with an ungodly speed, he burst from the alley.

Who was he? And why was Tilly so interested in him?

She clicked on another recorded feed. There was the boy again, hovering over someone else, a man it seemed. Then he was stepping away, breathing hard, watching the stranger on the ground. Then . . . two girls, walking up to the same man, who appeared to be severely distressed. Desperate. Sandra leaned closer to take them in, her gaze flicking between each of the people on-screen.

"Sandra?"

She froze at the sound of his voice, immediately pulling away from the screen. She took in the tiniest breath, schooling her features into the placid mask she always wore for the lord of the sky.

Sandra turned, smiling at the corpulent man standing at the other end of the atrium.

"Krazen," she said, bowing her head slightly. "I was looking for you."

He chuckled, his circuitry-laced hands crossed behind him as he strode toward Sandra, his steps not making a sound despite his massive weight. He walked barefoot, as he preferred to do in his private offices, the beige caftan he wore sweeping the floor, its hem embroidered in a curlicued gold trim. She met him in the middle of the vast room.

"You were looking for me on a screen?"

Sandra tossed her long ponytail back over her shoulder, glancing at the scanners.

"I know you like to keep an eye on staff," she said. "You want to see productivity. I thought you'd be making your rounds here soon."

Krazen considered her. "You were right."

Sandra let her smile widen. "I used the evidence and facts before me to make a decision. Exactly what you taught me."

The edge of Krazen's lip twitched, as close to a full smile as he generally gave his daughter.

"Well, I think it's time for you to return to bed," he said. "You're not having trouble sleeping again, are you?"

Sandra's smile faltered. When her father wandered the atrium at all hours, it was because he was a dedicated leader. When she did so, it was because of a deficit.

"No . . . Father," she said, purposely using a term of endearment. "I only wanted to check on their progress."

"I thought you were looking for me," he said, his voice roughening ever so slightly.

Sandra swallowed. She caught a scanner watching her, and she tensed. She must never show weakness. Krazen knew that, so why was he exposing her in front of his employees?

"Can we speak privately?" she asked.

Sandra instantly loathed the insecurity in her voice—a rare stumble. She straightened her back, trying to put the moment behind her.

Krazen's gaze was as cold and unrelenting as the marble floor. He regarded her for a moment. Sandra tensed for rejection.

"Swiftly," he said. "I have a meeting."

She sucked in a breath. Of course. Her father always had meetings. Was it with the mayor, more threats to get him to accept the seawall deal? Or one of the media execs, to make sure Krazen continued to receive favorable coverage on the holos? Or was it with Tilly about the "something" she'd discovered?

He waved her outside, leaving the scanners to their swiping.

"You shouldn't be bothering the scanners," he said, turning to Sandra in the passageway. "I can't allow distractions."

"I apologize," Sandra said, wincing at the reprimand. "I only noticed that Tilly wasn't at her console—"

"Tilly," Krazen said, "is on private business for me, and as my personal assistant she is no longer bound solely to the atrium. You'd do well to remember that before you go poking your head in scanner business."

Sandra swallowed. This was the fine line she was always dancing across. She needed to be assertive but demure. Confident but deferential. Promising but not an obstacle.

"Apologies, Father," she said. "I'm simply eager to learn the business." *And to figure out why Tilly is watching some Nubian boy in a grubby lower-city alley.*

Krazen chuckled, the condescension in his tone unmistakable. "I admire your diligence, Sandra. But now—"

He paused midsentence—someone must have started speaking into his main comm—and he turned from his daughter, considering whatever was being said to him.

"Yes," he said, the circuitry on the left side of his face distorting his profile. "I'll be in my office. Of course."

He glanced at Sandra. "Good night, child. Head to bed."

She nodded. Part of her wanted to follow him as he strode in the opposite direction, but there was no testing Krazen St. John. An order was an order.

Back in her room, Sandra took a shower before climbing under the covers, her sapphire silken sheets matching her pajamas. She pressed the buttons on a control panel that opened the domed window overhead, revealing the twinkling stars that dotted the night sky, the luminescence so bright that she could clearly make out the contours of her room. One of the perks of having a penthouse in the sky city's tallest tower.

As she stared at the stars, Sandra started to strategize. She needed to figure out what Tilly and her father were up to and why they were watching a random boy. Maybe it was time for her to do some scanning of her own, to more fully develop her own networks. Something was up. She could feel it.

The face of the handsome boy in the alley lingered in Sandra's memory as she slowly drifted off, the beginnings of a plan forming in her mind.

Chapter 15

Uzochi

"It's time now to analyze one of the most tragic moments in our city's history—the United Nations Massacre of 2078. It was on this day twenty years ago that a league of ecoterrorists took over the world-renowned complex, murdering eighteen on-site personnel and taking scores of hostages while demanding reparations for those displaced by rising sea levels."

Uzochi had never struggled to stay awake during class. It didn't matter that he had to get up early for special elective—he was always wide awake, enraptured by the material and determined to learn.

But today was different. Ever since he'd passed out earlier in the week, he was in a constant state of fatigue, one that he worried would tip him over into another incident of blue lights and heightened emotions. He spent his classes on edge, keeping his mind focused on the subject matter so that he didn't nod off or lose his grip on reality. For whenever he found himself slightly drifting, the voices threatened to slip in.

He'd sense them on the edge of his mind before jerking back to the present. Faint, phantom-like mumbles and whispers tapping at his skull. Persistent and annoying, popping up no matter how hard he tried to focus on the tasks at hand. He forced himself to revisit notes he'd already written or type up complex answers to his teachers' assignment questions . . . anything to keep himself plugged into class and away from the voices. It left him utterly exhausted by the end of the day so that all he wanted to do when he got home was crash.

But there was no peace at his place, either. He was thankful that Com'pa had been working the night shift for the week, that she didn't see him pacing around their living room, jumping from his desk every time he heard a voice in his head, looking around the apartment, bewildered. And then his body felt . . . strange. For days, he'd barely managed to finish his homework before tiredly crawling into bed, not waiting up for his mom. His eyes shut, and Uzochi knew only blackness until he awoke the next morning to do it all again.

This had been his life for days now, though the whispers had quieted down since the previous night. Still, Uzochi's ability to focus was failing, especially given how Preceptor Ryan was droning on. Paying attention would've been easier if the information was new, or even if she'd added a fresh spin to her lesson this year, possibly unearthing some previously unknown facts to keep it engaging.

But no. It was the same as last year when Uzochi took special elective. Ryan wouldn't deviate from her scripted lesson on the UN Massacre.

"It was a harrowing situation, to say the least," she said, pausing to point to a graphic on the projected holo hovering in the front of the class. The image showcased the exterior of the main United Nations complex, one of its sides hollowed out and crumbling from a blast. Uzochi felt like he had seen the photo thousands of times in his life. He knew, staring at the destruction, that he should feel something. After all, he usually did feel something every time the anniversary came around, especially as he lived less than a mile south of the site of the attack. He felt for the families who'd received those terrible calls and for the horror the hostages had faced. But today, Uzochi had nothing left to give.

"Officials from the newly created Tri-State East were blindsided by the siege, and the city's anemic police force was deemed inadequate for the task at hand," Preceptor Ryan declared. "Yet, after a standoff of almost thirty-seven hours, the threat was neutralized through the intervention of real estate mogul Krazen St. John and his militia squads."

Preceptor Ryan clicked the slide forward again, replacing the image with the classic shot of Krazen embracing one of the hostages. It was a Nubian woman with salt-and-pepper hair, tears running down her face as she clung to the big man who'd saved her life. Something about the image turned Uzochi's stomach, and he glanced back to where Sekou sat.

Sekou hadn't spoken to Uzochi much since the day of the essay. Like the rest of the school, Sekou had heard about the fight—or rather, he'd heard the popular version, that Lencho Will had beat up a Spider, the version that all but left out Uzochi and Zuberi. Uzochi was fine with this, but it meant he wasn't sure what Sekou knew, exactly. Either way, Sekou didn't seem thrilled to talk to him. The least of his problems, really.

Uzochi swiveled back to the front before Sekou could return his look. Focusing on his notes, Uzochi wrote down what the preceptor said even though he already knew the story by heart: ". . . threat neutralized by Krazen St. John/militia."

The savior, people called him. And it was true. He had saved so many lives that day. And yet . . .

Lencho's words from the week before floated back.

If I just read enough books and follow all their rules, maybe they'll let me in.

Uzochi sighed. He couldn't be letting his cousin get into his head. In fact, he would've liked to forget that afternoon with Lencho entirely.

Of course, that hadn't gotten easier, not with Lencho strutting around the school. Apparently his involvement in the fight, though the stuff of rumors among the students, hadn't reached the eyes and ears of preceptors and administrators. Or at least the ones who really mattered. His freakin' cousin, such a lucky guy.

Uzochi had thought that hitting someone hard enough that they had to be hospitalized and getting away with it might've humbled Lencho, but apparently not. He seemed totally fine, which, in itself, was a problem.

One of Uzochi's teachers had said something about it. Preceptor Jordan, who taught calculus. A few days after the fight, he'd shaken his head at Uzochi as he packed up at the end of class. Uzochi'd barely been able to focus on the preceptor's complex equations, so he didn't hear Jordan when he first spoke.

"Sorry?" Uzochi said, realizing the teacher was speaking to him.

"That cousin of yours," Jordan said. "I hope you won't be following that path. I heard about his extracurricular activities the other day."

The words had been a gut punch. All his hard work to earn his preceptors' respect, and Lencho was sowing doubt.

He assured Preceptor Jordan that he and Lencho weren't anything alike, but the comment haunted him just as much as Lencho's words.

"Of course," Preceptor Ryan continued, drawing Uzochi back to the present, "this event signaled the rise of the so-called St. John Soldiers in New York, with his private squads receiving special clearance from the government to act as agents of the law. While sometimes a source of controversy, the militias are generally regarded as the gold standard for urban security and policing."

It was this, Uzochi knew, that so enraged his cousin and Sekou and others. The "gold standard" of policing was what, according to them, put so many Nubians and other poor lower-city kids in jail. But wasn't that the fault of those who pursued crime in the first place? Uzochi believed that Lencho *should* have been arrested for what he'd done, especially since he knew that, if Lencho was running with the Divine, he wasn't just getting into fights. He was sure Lencho was running Elevation, a nasty thing that destroyed people's lives.

And yet Lencho—and the rest of the Divine—were out on the streets.

"Right, so let's get down to the meat of today's lesson," Preceptor Ryan said. "You're all familiar with the events of the UN Massacre, but we need to dive deeper. I want you all to answer the questions on your tablets that I've posted, but when you respond, you should be thinking specifically about how this moment was a course correction for our fledgling nation. In that moment, terrorism could've easily overtaken life as we know it, but thankfully, we had the resources and resolve to forge a new direction."

With a flourish, Preceptor Ryan gestured to the holo of Krazen St. John and the Nubian woman.

"Just imagine, for a minute, what life would be like if Mr. St. John hadn't been there that day."

A lot better than this bullshit. Get that asshole off the screen.

Uzochi sat straight up. Had someone really just said that out loud?

Maybe I can reuse the essay I wrote on this last year.

Uzochi whipped around, taking in the room. What was going on? Students couldn't be saying these things so brazenly without consequence. He turned to Ryan for her reaction, but she was yawning.

"Pardon me," she said. "Long hours grading your essays last night."

Which were horrible and made me question all of my life choices.

Uzochi blinked. Had Preceptor Ryan just insulted the

entire class? As he looked around, no one so much as shrugged. A few kids seemed bored, and a smaller fraction were visibly annoyed, like Sekou. But otherwise, the class looked like it always did.

Which meant . . .

No one was speaking these things out loud. He was hearing them in his head.

Does she even read what we write?

I swear, she wants me to fail.

I need to pick up another shift at work to pay for Dad's meds.

That quiz in trig later is gonna kill me.

They came rapid-fire, one thought collapsing over another. Uzochi shut his eyes tight, trying to tune them all out. He needed to get back on track with class. He'd let himself slip too much.

Except he no longer felt fatigued. In fact, he was buzzing with energy. It was . . . copious. Dangerous. He tried to breathe, forcing his eyes to open again.

"If you have any questions, watch the included videos with the assignment," Preceptor Ryan told them, taking a seat at her desk. "And stay focused, please. No distractions."

Hopefully, some of the Nubians here know better than to get involved with filthy gangs. But I doubt it. They're all the same.

Uzochi's insides went cold. He swung his gaze back to Preceptor Ryan, who was now scrolling on her own tablet. He'd known that was her voice as clearly as if she'd spoken aloud.

He was imagining it. He had to be. His teacher would

never harbor such thoughts. And why was she thinking about gangs in the first place?

"Preceptor?" A quiet student near Uzochi piped up. "Could you help me with this?"

Preceptor Ryan didn't look up from her tablet. "In a minute. Checking student work."

Maybe if she actually read the directions, she wouldn't need me . . .

The voices had quieted in Uzochi's mind, all save for Ryan's. Uzochi looked from her to the student, a quiet girl with coils cut short close to her shoulders. Uzochi recognized her from when he used to live in the Swamp; she'd always made sure to wave hi when they spotted each other in class.

At Preceptor Ryan's dismissal, though, the girl had shrunk in her seat. She bit her lip, turning back to her tablet. Uzochi thought he might see the threat of tears.

Uzochi got up from his seat and went to the girl, bending down next to her even as her eyes widened.

"Hey," he said. "I can help you."

"Student out of assigned seat!" the droid at the front barked. "Student out of assigned seat!"

"Uzochi?" Preceptor Ryan asked. "What're you doing?"

An angry thought floated across Uzochi's mind. He wanted to say something along the lines of "Your job!" But he forced himself to swallow the statement.

"Could I help her, please?" he asked instead.

Ryan's eyebrows rose. For a moment, he thought she would refuse. But then she waved her hand and smiled.

"Of course," she said. "Thank you, Uzochi."

Normally, Uzochi would've swelled at the words, but now the gratitude rang hollow. He pushed it aside, choosing to focus on the girl and her work.

"Right," he said. "So, what do you need help with?"

For the next fifteen minutes, Uzochi worked with the girl—her name was Tasha—and found that the voices quieted as he did so. Maybe it was that Preceptor Ryan had gotten so far under his skin that he refused to hear anything else, or maybe he was just imagining the voices. But whatever the reason, Uzochi relaxed for what felt like the first time in days.

Tasha's word-processing software was causing her tablet to crash every time she tried to link to the class lesson, so Uzochi helped her download the program he used, quietly giving her a few additional tips before heading back to his seat.

Soon, the bell rang. Tasha walked over to his desk.

"Thanks, Uzochi," she said, smiling.

"No problem," he said, smiling back. "Lemme know if you ever need help again."

She nodded, turning to head out of class as Uzochi gathered his stuff.

"That was quite generous of you, Uzochi," Preceptor Ryan said as he moved to the door with his scholar-pack.

He looked back at her. In all that time, she'd never gotten up from her desk.

"Yeah," Uzochi said. "Thanks. She just had some outdated software."

Preceptor Ryan sighed. "I figured as much. The configurations of basic tech are completely beyond that girl. For the life of me I don't know why they put her in this class. Students should be more prepared."

Uzochi stared at the teacher, remembering her voice in his head proclaiming that all Nubians were the same. And now she seemed to think it was beneath her to help one of her students with a small problem.

"Well, I don't agree—"

"Hey, Uzochi?"

He turned, surprised to see Sekou waiting for him in the doorway.

"Can you help me with something?" Sekou asked, glancing not-so-subtly at Preceptor Ryan. It was clear that, whatever Sekou needed help with, it wasn't something he wanted their teacher to hear.

Thankfully, she simply smiled. "Go on, Uzochi. But I'll remember this when I write your recommendation. Such a good Samaritan."

Uzochi winced at the remark as Sekou pulled him away.

"Hey, man," Uzochi said as the door swung shut behind them. "What's up?"

The hall around them pulsed with students heading to their morning classes. Uzochi swallowed, tension immediately filling his spine. Their thoughts were pressing up against the corners of his mind, waiting for his focus to split so they could tumble over . . .

He wasn't imagining things.

"Dude," Sekou said, jolting him back to the moment. "Your cousin's causing some serious shit, you know that?"

Uzochi bristled. He'd already gotten this from Preceptor Jordan. Did he really need it from Sekou?

"He's pushing Elevation," Sekou continued, his voice harsh. "I saw him dealing near the Rotting Jungle. You know what that shit does to people? My uncle—"

"I don't have anything to do with Lencho," Uzochi said. "We're just . . ."

Blood's just blood.

"We're not close," Uzochi said, trying his best to keep an array of random thoughts from creeping into his head.

"Seriously, man?" Sekou said, looking more frustrated by the second. "You're not going to even try to talk to him? What if he brings that stuff here?"

Uzochi didn't know what to say. And what the hell was he supposed to do, anyway? Lencho didn't listen to him.

Before Uzochi could speak, a buzz went up around them. Voices got louder. People turned. And then, like a wave, they all moved to the right. Chasing something.

Uzochi blinked in confusion, looking back at Sekou.

"I told you," Sekou said. "It's your damn cousin. There's a Spider and a Divine kid about to go at it because of that fight. Your cousin's causing all this beef, man, and someone's gonna get messed up."

"And *I* told *you*," Uzochi said, trying not to get angrier when kids shoved past him as they ran in the direction of the fight. "Lencho and I don't speak."

Sekou frowned, disbelief distorting his features. "I can't believe you, man. I thought you cared about this shit."

And then he took off, leaving Uzochi behind for the crowd.

Uzochi could hear it, the murmur of his peers egging the fighters on, the shouts and dares. Soon, someone would break it up. Just another thing for his teachers to hang over his head.

And Lencho . . . Lencho would get deeper into trouble. Whether the Spider or the Divine kid came out on top, it would come back to Lencho.

Which shouldn't be Uzochi's problem, and yet here it was. Though maybe this time, he could do something, or at least try to say something. Then the school would know that he didn't stand with his cousin. That some Nubians wanted something different.

"Damn it," Uzochi murmured under his breath before taking off in the same direction as his peers.

Finding the fight was easy. It was contained within a hallway around the corner, the burgeoning crowd forming an elongated ring around the pair at the center. Uzochi pushed his way through the throng of students even as they snapped at him.

"What the fuck, idiot?"

Who's the jerk?

"Watch it!"

So rude.

This shit better be good.

Words said, words thought. They blurred together, Uzochi letting language jumble in his mind. He moved into the crowd until he reached the inner circle and saw the two kids. It was one of the Spiders from before, the one with an eye patch. Opposite was a Divine member Uzochi knew as Zaire, a kid who usually got to mind his own business because he was so huge.

This Spider, apparently, was desperate to pick a fight with someone like Zaire. Or pissed. Or drugged out. It was hard to tell as he skipped around the larger boy, twitching and shaking as he spat and shouted.

"Come on, asshole," the Spider snarled. "Big dumb monkey asshole. You even understand me?"

Zaire flexed his fist, eyebrows furrowing. Uzochi looked behind him for Lencho, but he didn't see his cousin in the crowd. Maybe he was being smart for once and staying away. Maybe neither one of the boys would actually make a move. Maybe the Spider would realize this was a fool's errand.

Suddenly, there was a flash of glowing silver in the Spider's hand. An e-dagger.

The crowd grew quiet. Uzochi was suddenly frightened, wondering if it was time for someone to find security. He'd read about electric daggers, how they both sliced and fried, leaving some victims terribly scarred. Completely banned at 104. How did this jerk smuggle it in?

"I'm going to carve you up like a pig," the Spider spat, smirking. "You Nubi loser. Never should've touched our territory."

Uzochi's eyes darted to Zaire. The giant boy didn't move, but Uzochi could've sworn he saw him flinch.

"You know," the Spider continued, pacing before Zaire, "your momma might thank me. Slicing up that ugly face of yours would be a real improvement on your damn looks."

"Shut up!"

Uzochi whirled at the familiar voice. There, on the other side, was Vriana. Her face was furious, her eyes sparkling in the morning light. Uzochi had never seen her look so defiant; her trademark cheeriness was gone.

Zuberi stepped up next to Vriana, appearing beside her like some kind of warrior goddess. Her eyes were narrowed, and Uzochi immediately felt a twinge in his chest. He stared, and after a moment, she turned to him.

This time she looked at Uzochi as if she'd expected him to be there, harboring neither disdain nor elation. Just simple acceptance.

"Stop talking about him like that, you cyclops goon," Vriana said. "I'm warning you!"

The crowd let out an "ooooh" as the Spider hooted with laughter.

"Get out of here, bitch," he said. "See, I'm about to end this fool. And then I'm gonna go find his raggedy family and I'm going to—"

A boom like the sound of lightning in the sky filled the passageway.

Then, a rumble.

At first, it was low, like a growl. Then it was the sound of something tearing, heavy ripping.

The ground tearing in two.

It split below their feet, a single fissure at first that stretched and widened. Around him, Uzochi's peers screamed, both in their minds and aloud. They ran without direction, fighting against each other as soon as they realized the earth was cracking. Some people shouted "Earthquake!" and "Get outta here!" Uzochi fought to stay steady, turning to look around him as bodies struggled against each other. His eyes caught Zuberi's once again; her gaze was wide and focused forward.

No. No. What's happening to me? What am I—

It wasn't her voice that he heard. This was a single voice that smothered the others, low and deep. Uzochi recognized it now.

Zaire.

His head whipped back to the center. The Spider had fallen backward on the concrete and was shrieking as the earth shook beneath him. And in front of him stood a figure that no longer looked like Zaire.

He was still partially the boy Uzochi had just seen, with bright brown eyes and hard muscle, but his skin was no longer smooth. It was . . . hardening. His shape changing, arms and legs sinking into his body, his features erased as he grew more enormous than ever before.

Zaire bellowed, a sound unlike anything Uzochi had heard. It was more than pain, but something guttural, primal. Then his voice was swallowed up as the earth trembled beneath them all.

A screeching alarm began to echo as Uzochi looked around. Most kids had moved out of the way, while a few were still scrambling. All around him, he heard the scattered thoughts of his schoolmates, the instinct to survive at all costs outweighing anything else. Uzochi figured he should be joining them, yet all he could do was look at Zaire.

The boy was gone. In his place was a massive mound of rock shaped like some sort of cracked, distorted starfish melded to the concrete. But Uzochi was sure he could still feel Zaire. The boy was there, somehow fused into rock.

"We have to help him."

Uzochi turned to realize Zuberi was still there, potent as ever. This time, when their gazes met, Uzochi saw how her eyes blazed.

"He can't stay like this," she said, wheeling back to the boy-turned-rock before them. "It's ripping him apart. I can feel it. Can't you?"

Yes. Uzochi nodded vigorously.

"I can see these . . . I don't know what to call them," Zuberi said, gesturing at the air above Zaire. "They're like these phantoms, or spirits. Of him, all around, appearing and disappearing. A couple of them look like what he is there on the ground, but most of them, he's his normal self. Moving around. And, well, I can't explain it, but I think we can help him get back to how he was."

"We have to," Vriana said, appearing beside Zuberi. Her eyes were watery, unsettled. Both girls looked at Uzochi expectantly.

He wanted to tell them that he didn't know what to do. It was the truth, wasn't it? How could he possibly comprehend what was happening in front of them? Why wasn't he allowed to be like the Spider nearby, rocking back and forth as he clung to the still-shaking earth?

Listen to him. Please.

Again, Zuberi's voice in his mind. Was she sending her thoughts to him on purpose? How could she know what he could do?

The earth shook again.

Please.

Zuberi's words were a lifeline in the chaos. They gave him an idea. A weird one, but an idea nonetheless.

A crack in the ground spread to one of the concrete pillars attached to the classroom nearby. There was no time for second-guessing.

Uzochi bent down beside Zaire and closed his eyes, setting his hand on what he thought might be the Divine's arm. In his mind, Uzochi waded through the storm of thoughts around him, looking for Zaire. He operated by instinct, sorting through the hazy world he was suddenly a part of. He reached out for the boy, searching for his voice.

Help.

There it was. A feeble thread, but a thread nonetheless. Uzochi seized it, holding fast, willing everything else to fall away.

Suddenly, Uzochi found himself in a swirl of memories and sensations, experiencing the all-too-familiar images of the shanties on stilts in the Swamp and the constant buzzing of hover cars and the smell of fresh, dewy grass in Central Park and the song of another boy's laughter. Uzochi felt all of this, saw it in Zaire's mind, and forced himself to swim past the memories to enter a murky realm of shadow with a pinprick of light. As he drew closer, the light grew brighter and more vivid, becoming an orb of shimmering, scraggly power. It was solid and looming and massive, yet also soft and airy. Inviting. Something that Uzochi could touch with his mind.

Uzochi reached for the glowing orb, sensing he could hold it, sensing it was the key to connecting with Zaire.

His fingers brushed the glow. He held his breath, stretching his limbs—

Without warning, the energy flared.

The blast threw Uzochi completely out. He ricocheted back through Zaire's mind and into his own, jarred back into the physical world as his side struck concrete.

His eyes flew open. Beside him, a piece of building crumbled. Uzochi fought to breathe, to move, but his legs were lead. All he felt was the pulse of the energy that had thrown him out of Zaire's mind. He looked around, trying to find the other boy in the haze of dust and dirt.

"What are you doing here?"

Uzochi's blood froze. Suddenly, he knew exactly what had severed the tie between him and the Divine. He knew that force of energy.

He looked up, and there was Lencho, his arm thrown around a very human, very groggy Zaire.

"I could ask you the same thing," Uzochi said, his voice low and cold. He wondered if he could read his cousin's thoughts, but he was too exhausted to try. It was taking everything in him to try to stand.

"I'm warning you, man," Lencho said. "You need to get out of here. Now."

Alarms were clanging around the three boys. Uzochi

glanced out of a big, cracked window flanking a stairwell. Preceptors were running around outside, along with a whole bunch of security personnel and a couple of school medics frantically shepherding kids to safety. Uzochi looked around the hallway for Zuberi, but she was gone.

"Go," Lencho told him. "Now."

Uzochi stared at his cousin. He didn't want to run. He wanted answers. He wanted to know why the hell Lencho had stopped him. Still, now wasn't the time.

"We need to talk, Lencho!" he yelled. "Tonight."

His cousin shook his head, glancing over his shoulder at the cracked, crumbling ceiling. Then, after a moment, he turned back to Uzochi.

"Fine," he said. "Now, can you please get the fuck outta here before our asses get squashed?"

This time, Uzochi listened. He forced his leaden legs to stand, then walk.

And then, finally, to flee.

Chapter 16

Zuberi

"Silence isn't going to help you in this case, my dear. So I'm going to ask you again, what was going on in that hallway?"

Zuberi had never been to the principal's office before. She was the girl who kept to herself, who never caused any trouble—at least, until last week. But as far as she could tell, the school administration didn't know she'd been involved in the gang fight at the market. No one mentioned her when they talked about the brawl, and they certainly wouldn't start now. Everyone's attention was focused on the new incident, one that had apparently been interrupted by an earthquake. The event was surrounded by such strange and bizarre circumstances that Zuberi couldn't be sure of the truth.

True, she had spent the past several days—the last week, really—grappling with the strange and bizarre. Ever since the incident with Lencho and the other Divine, she was sure she was losing her mind. When she'd stumbled home that night, she'd been grateful that her dad had been out working a security shift so she could sift through her thoughts in solitude.

She'd turned to her training exercises, as she always did. Not to fighting, necessarily, but to breathing. Centering. Connecting her breath to her body. It was something her father had always stressed, and when she'd been younger, Zuberi hadn't seen much purpose to the exercise. Yet as she'd matured, she realized how essential a centered mind was to staying present in a fight. She'd never realized she'd need the practice to sort out the glowing phantoms haunting her mind.

Then there was the recent development of seeing not just one floating figure but multiple phantoms of the same person. Zuberi could now see an assortment of her classmates' phantoms, running and sashaying and kissing and stumbling and studying and sleeping. She was a witness to random clips of their lives projected just above their heads. She'd gradually learned not to panic over the visions, but to steady her breathing and initiate countdowns in her mind. Sometimes she even got to a place where she blinked and the phantoms were gone. That's when she would take a deep breath and thank Goddess for the break.

But there were also times like today when no amount of blinking would've erased what she saw.

It was different, Zuberi was realizing, with Uzochi and Lencho. They glowed in her presence, each of them giving off something only she could see. Something ineffable that pulsed and called to her, a mysterious light that shone magnificently when Uzochi had bent down beside Zaire. She'd also noticed Zaire's light, dimmer but there, growing brighter as it merged with Uzochi's.

And then Lencho arrived, his red glow like a ravaging

fire, consuming everything in his path. A trio of phantoms floated above his head, the clearest apparitions she'd seen yet. One was angry, his fists clenched, slamming his hand into the ground. Another sobbed uncontrollably over something she couldn't see. And the third Lencho was tearing something apart, his head swinging and eyes bulging as if he was a loon.

That was when Vriana had pulled Zuberi away, only for them to run straight into Preceptor Harold and the principal himself.

"Young lady," Principal Todd said, his voice a high, nasal demand that forced her attention back to him. "Your rudeness isn't going to get you anywhere."

Zuberi wasn't being rude. She'd just been raised by Thato Ragee, someone who told her never to speak before she had a chance to parse through her thoughts. He'd also cautioned her about authority and how some would be eager to twist her words because she was Nubian.

They'd called her father to this meeting, and Zuberi knew he was on his way. Until then, she wouldn't give the principal a thing. She would observe and collect, waiting for backup. Zuberi twisted one of her rings back and forth, melting her anxiety into the metal.

"We know you were on the scene and involved in the altercation," Principal Todd continued. "Our cameras picked up on that."

Zuberi forced herself not to react. She knew that 104 was peppered with cameras. She also knew that not all of them were properly maintained, that students regularly made a point of smudging them with paint or markers to limit visibility. She wouldn't give this man an inkling of reaction until he showed her exactly what he had.

If the principal had seen what had actually happened at the center of the fight with Zaire and the Spider, this meeting wouldn't be happening in the first place. If they'd seen Zaire turn into a rock—the only way Zuberi could describe what had happened—then they wouldn't be wasting their time with her.

"Zuveri," Principal Todd continued, butchering her name per usual, "people were hurt. It's important we get to the bottom of this."

This time, Zuberi couldn't help herself. "Pretty sure more people were hurt by the earthquake," she said, finding it ridiculous that she was being interrogated about gangs after a natural disaster. She kept fiddling with her ring.

Principal Todd's eyebrows knitted together.

"An earthquake that would *not* have been nearly as dangerous if students hadn't been congregating in that hallway," he said, pausing to wipe his dripping nose with his sleeve. "Which is why your information here is key. Now, I know you want to protect your people, but violence at this school won't be tolerated."

Zuberi snorted at the man's use of "your people." To Principal Todd, Zuberi and all Nubians were one and the same. No distinction. One of them being a gang member meant they all were. Never mind that Zuberi quietly earned nearly perfect grades and didn't cause trouble. No, facts didn't matter here.

"Daughter?"

149

The door behind them cracked open and there was Thato. Zuberi let out a sigh of relief at the sight of her father. Now she could breathe.

"Mr. Ragee, thank you for coming in," Principal Todd said, standing to shake Thato's hand. Her father regarded the man in front of him without an ounce of warmth or affection.

"Are you all right?" Thato said, looking down at Zuberi. "I got the call, and after the earthquake . . . I thought you might be hurt."

"She's fine," Principal Todd said, cutting Zuberi off before she could answer. "We're actually here for a disciplinary measure. Please sit down."

Thato blinked, not moving. "A disciplinary measure? *Now?*"

His voice was cold and commanding, the kind of tone that Zuberi went to great lengths not to provoke. This fool had really done it.

"Unfortunately, yes," Principal Todd said, eyes darting down to the empty seat. When Thato didn't take it, he sighed.

"Zuberi may have contributed to an incident that caused more students to be hurt," he continued, clicking a button on his desk so that a holo flared to life behind him. "See here."

As Zuberi had expected, the camera didn't show much. It was smudged over with something and turned slightly to the side. They could see the crowd and, in the very top corner, the circling, frenetic gait of the Spider and the sturdy, steady one of Zaire. Then, from the bottom corner, Zuberi saw what must've been Uzochi darting up to the crowd. He forced his way to the center. That could only mean—

Yes, there they were. Vriana and Zuberi. Vriana's braids were easy to identify, and Zuberi was right next to her. They also moved through the crowd quickly. Zuberi could remember how Vriana had been in a panic, having heard that Zaire was in a fight with a Spider, as if he wasn't a guy who could easily hold his own.

Then, of course, everything had come apart. The Spider's cruel words to Zaire. And . . . the change.

You couldn't see it on the footage. All you could see was the shift in the crowd, how the ground began to crack and shake beneath them. Then, pure chaos. Though the footage was silent, Zuberi could still hear the screams.

A burst of white light appeared, and the camera went black.

"We expect that had something to do with the power being disrupted by the quake," Principal Todd explained as he turned off the holo. "But regardless, you can see what's important. Zuberi, right in the middle of trouble."

Thato still didn't sit. He did, however, place his hand on his daughter's shoulder. His presence was solid, heavy, telling her she would be okay.

"I see my daughter in the footage," Thato said. "But I don't see any indication of her direct involvement in the fight or how she could be responsible for other students being hurt. Frankly, sir, I don't understand why you're wasting precious time with this when there are plenty of students in need of attention."

Principal Todd's mouth set into a hard line. He looked from Thato to Zuberi.

"At the very least, she saw who was in the center of that fight," he said. "And I'm asking, right now, for names. The gang problem in this school needs to end."

Ah, now she understood. He wanted her to snitch on Zaire and the Spider. And probably on Uzochi and Lencho, too. Zuberi just shrugged.

"I don't know any of those kids," she said. "I'm kind of a loner."

"My dear—"

"I'm taking my daughter home now, Mr. Todd," Thato said, his voice like stone. "It's been a traumatic day."

He gave Zuberi a tap on the shoulder, and she knew they were done. She stood up, next to her dad, her gaze rising briefly to Principal Todd. He must have known this was over as well, but he refused to say anything. He glanced back and forth between father and daughter like a nervous rodent.

"I'm trying to protect the student population," Principal Todd said. "As a security man, Mr. Ragee, you must understand."

Thato's eyes narrowed. "It's for that very reason I do *not* understand. Let's go, Zuberi."

They left the office together, and Zuberi took in a deep breath. She looked briefly for Vriana, but her friend wasn't nearby. Maybe she'd been put in a different office. Anyway, Zuberi had a feeling Vriana's meeting would go slightly different than hers, considering Vriana was adored by the staff. Zuberi would text her in a minute.

Zuberi's fingers went to touch her ring again, but she found the finger empty.

"Shit," she said, causing Thato to turn and arch an eyebrow.

"Sorry," she said. "I left my ring. I'm gonna grab it real quick."

He nodded and she raced back to the office. The door was still slightly ajar, and she paused at the sound of Principal Todd's voice before knocking.

"I did my best," he was saying. "She wouldn't talk. I tried to get confirmation, truly, but I don't know. It could be him, but I'm not sure. I'll keep asking."

Confirmation? Zuberi blinked.

"Her? Oh, definitely not. As plain as they come, I'm afraid. No, you'd be wasting your time."

Now Zuberi bristled. There was no doubt who he thought was "plain." She knocked hard then, letting the door swing back from her fist.

Principal Todd's eyes narrowed at the sight of her.

"I dropped something," Zuberi said, edging inside. She saw the glint of metal on the ground and snatched it up.

"You be careful, Ms. Ragee," Principal Todd said as she left the office. Zuberi didn't miss the threat in his tone. It stayed with her, a creepy warning as she caught up with her dad.

"Not here," Thato said just as Zuberi started to open her mouth. "Wait until we're alone."

They got into her father's hover van, dotted with its security features. She knew they were one of the few families from the Swamp to have one, even if her father's was a relic. She sank into the seat and waited as the vehicle drifted down the road, the ride far from smooth. Finally, after several minutes' silence, Thato nodded.

"Now tell me what happened," he said.

Zuberi swallowed. Lying wasn't an option, but there were parts of today that she didn't want to tell him about. It wasn't because she didn't trust her dad; on the contrary, Zuberi trusted Thato more than any other person on earth. But ever since Zuberi had been injured long ago, her father had been intense with his ideas of retribution. She didn't need to cause unnecessary trouble.

"Two gang kids were fighting," she explained. "A Spider and a Divine. Well, they were about to. The Spider kept egging the Divine kid on, saying this horrible stuff about hurting his family."

Thato nodded, but his mouth was a thin line, eyes focused on the road.

"And then . . . I can't really explain it, Dad," Zuberi continued. "Me and V ran forward to try to get them to cut it out, but he kept going. And then the Divine kid, he . . . he changed."

Thato's eyes cut to her. "What?"

"He changed," Zuberi said. "Suddenly, he wasn't a guy anymore. He was this . . ."

Zuberi swallowed, her heart racing as she wondered if she could really reveal what she'd seen without sounding absolutely bonkers. ". . . he was like this gross rock-thing. And when he started to change, that's when the quake erupted. I don't know if they're related, but it sure as hell felt like it." She turned to Thato, his eyes still on the road. "You gotta believe me, Dad. I know it sounds wild, like I'm making up stories, but that's what happened. I swear."

Zuberi wondered if she should reveal more, like how she'd been seeing phantoms for days at school and on the street. But she decided not to. She needed to see if her father believed her when she spoke about Zaire and Uzochi.

"And then this other kid came up, and I don't know what I was thinking, but I told him to help him, to help the Divine kid," she said. "And he sort of dropped down to him, and then . . . and then the kid changed back."

Zuberi realized she was breathing hard at the memory, purposely leaving out Lencho. When she closed her eyes, she could still see the rage and grief and madness coursing through the figures above him.

That memory she simply couldn't bear.

"Who did this, Zuberi?" Thato said, his voice low, quiet. "Who changed the boy back?"

She didn't want to give names. It went beyond snitching. What Uzochi could do . . .

Thato put his hand on hers just as the car came to a quiet stop on the side of the road.

"It's all right, Beri," Thato said, meeting her eyes. "I know."

Zuberi stared at him. She realized that she could see the wisps of a phantom near her father's head, another set of calm, focused eyes trained on her. She straightened up at the sight of them.

"It was Uzochi, wasn't it?" Thato said. "Com'pa's son."

"How'd you know that?" Zuberi asked, her heart threatening to beat out of her chest.

Thato smiled and gently squeezed her hand.

"Time for you both to find out."

Chapter 17

Lencho

Sprawled out next to Lencho on a hard metal bench, Zaire let out a hacking cough. He'd been throwing up what seemed like his entire stomach for the past half hour, straight into dirt and concrete. They were perched on the corner of Second Avenue and Fifteenth Street, ignoring the stares of disgusted passersby and waiting for things to calm down before they headed back to the Jungle. Lencho'd had the good sense to bring Zaire close to Mt. Sinai, the nearest med center to their school, just in case the dude needed a doctor. The kid had to be almost done, which meant it was time to get some answers.

From the scrolling Lencho had been able to do on IMA*, the news was going on and on about "The Great Quake That Nearly Split High School 104," chalking it up to more climate crisis, doomsday bullshit, warning that the world was due for yet another reckoning. There was also talk about how deeply damaged the Swamp seawall was, how it couldn't handle another quake—more reasons for the mayor to take Krazen up on his donation.

"Water," Zaire croaked beside Lencho, head hanging between his knees. "Please."

Lencho passed over the bottle he'd nicked from a food cart on their way out of 104. The seller had abandoned her wares, probably thinking the quake from the school was a threat. Lencho felt a little guilty, knowing he probably wouldn't be the only one to steal from the lady, but that was just the way life went sometimes.

"You ready to talk?" he asked, folding his arms. The burn of the late-morning sun was hot on his neck.

Zaire shook his head. "I don't know what to say."

"How about you start with your transformation?"

Zaire peered up at Lencho. "My what?"

"Your transformation," Lencho repeated in a whisper, not that he thought anyone was listening. "Dude, you turned into some sort of, like . . . stone. What was that?"

Zaire just shook his head again and looked at his hands.

"I . . . I don't know what happened," he said. "One minute, that Spider asshole was talking to me, and the next . . ." Zaire shivered. "Pain. Crazy pain."

Lencho cocked an eyebrow. "Yeah?"

Zaire nodded. "I felt like I was drowning in it, and all I could do was scream. Lencho, man, I thought I was dying. At least, until . . ."

His eyes widened as if the memories were coming back to him.

"Your cousin," he said. "Uzochi. He was in my head."

Lencho bristled. Yes, here was the next part of the puzzle. His cousin.

When Lencho had made his way to the middle of the chaos, he'd found Uzochi standing beside a massive boulder. Uzochi had then fallen forward to the ground, his fingers splayed out. His eyes were shut, and no matter how Lencho had screamed and shouted, nothing moved him. Zuberi was there, too, her eyes wild as she hunkered down with another girl with multicolored braids.

"What the fuck?" Lencho demanded, and Zuberi just shook her head. "Where's Zaire?"

"I . . . I don't know," she said, gesturing. "He was there. He *is* there. I . . . I think that's him."

She pointed at the massive mound of earth strewn out across the hallway.

"Are you kidding me?" Lencho demanded. "What are you talking about?"

She froze then, staring at Lencho, her eyes darting all around him. He whipped around, looking for danger, but there had been nothing and no one save that pathetic Spider whimpering behind them, high on Elevation.

"You're everywhere," she said. "And . . . red. So much red."

Lencho's fists pulsed with energy. How did she know? And what, exactly, did she mean?

"We need to go," Zuberi said, and then she grabbed her friend's arm and pulled her away despite the other girl shouting in protest.

Lencho hadn't had time to worry. All he had known was that energy was continuing to pulse through the space, through *him*, and he needed to act. If the freaked-out chick said the boulder was Zaire, then Lencho knew how to find out for sure.

He'd put his hands on a section of earth and did what he'd done every night before that for the past week: he drained. Only this time, the energy wasn't the sweet flow he'd grown used to. It was potent. Too potent, like a blast of searing-hot water instead of a warm bath.

He'd been lucky not to pass out. It was luckier still that when he opened his eyes, Zaire had reappeared, back to being a boy. Lencho just sat on his haunches and tried to absorb all that was happening, trying to piece together his thoughts even with the ceiling threatening to tumble down.

I'm not alone. Zaire is special . . . like me . . .

And then there was Uzochi.

"What do you mean, my rat cousin was in your mind?" Lencho said, gritting his teeth as he leaned closer to Zaire on the bench.

"I don't know," the other boy said in his usual steady voice. "Only that, with him, I was finding my way out. I'm sure of it. Until . . . something tore us apart."

Something.

Lencho, always the problem.

"And why were you fighting a Spider in the first place?" he demanded, anxious to think about something other than him being a fuckup once again.

Zaire shifted awkwardly. "He . . . he said things about Aren. I mean, he was high as a kite and acting wacky, but still, I couldn't let it go. Too much disrespect."

Lencho stared at Zaire. That was it? Everybody shit-talked the head of a gang. But something on Zaire's face made Lencho swallow the words. Maybe this went deeper than crew loyalty. Either way, Zaire clearly didn't want to talk about it.

"Listen, you can't tell anyone about this," Zaire said, a pleading tone entering his voice. "I mean, that shit was crazy. I . . . can't explain—"

"Let's get back to HQ," Lencho said, rising from the bench. "You can rest there. And don't worry about it, your secret's safe with me. We'll figure this shit out."

Zaire nodded and slowly got up, obviously relieved that Lencho had his back. The two boys made their way downtown, Lencho happy to see that Zaire had regained his strength even though he was clearly spooked, processing everything that had just gone down. And it was all Lencho could do to ignore the bodies of the pedestrians passing by, the call to drain others getting stronger by the day.

With the Jungle just a few minutes away, Lencho found himself trailing behind Zaire, thinking about his cousin yet again, remembering his promise that they would meet later and try to figure stuff out. Something was clearly up with Uzochi as well. Uzochi, who Zaire thought had saved him . . . maybe with a gift of his own? Uzochi, who had a sane parent who'd welcome him home and clean his wounds.

Lencho's hands curled into fists. He'd thought he'd cut ties with this part of his life, carved out a fresh path. And here he was, heading back to family bullshit. There was no way his aunt wouldn't call his parents if he showed up at their place, no matter how estranged they were, not unless Lencho kept it quiet that he'd left home. He could be tugged right back into his old, tired drama.

A ping from his phone made him pause. He pulled it out, expecting a demanding message from Aren or even Lara.

That wasn't what he found at all.

Remember my offer.

The message floated across the screen, its source simply marked as *St. John Enterprises.*

Lencho's eyes lit up with the realization that maybe connecting with his cousin was far less important than what awaited him in the sky. Over the past week, Lencho had returned often to the holo of Krazen St. John loaded into his phone, weighing when was the best time to play this particular card. He hadn't been sure if the crew would be remotely interested in meeting with the Sky King, not when some of them hated what the Up High stood for. But with Zaire obviously coming into his gift, and the chance to learn more about what was going down . . .

He knew exactly what to do. As Zaire and Lencho approached the Jungle, he spotted Aren sitting outside with Lara and Nneka. He walked up to the group, and before the Divine general could say a word, Lencho held up his mobile and pulled up the holo of Krazen St. John for all to see.

"Divine brethren, light be with you, for these are momentous times," he said. "I believe we have an epic opportunity, and I'm here to lead you to it."

Chapter 18

Sandra

"We're coming to you live from Public High School 104, which appears to be the epicenter of today's moderate earthquake, registering as 5.1 on the Richter scale. We've got meteorologists standing by to break down what might be the cause and whether or not we can expect aftershocks. Meanwhile, the quake is having an impact on the surrounding area, from burst pipes to looting. It also cut short one of Krazen St. John's press conferences near the Swamp seawall, another attempt to criticize the city's local government for inaction—"

Sandra hit the pause button on her nightstand screen, the holo-news channel hovering before her. She was curled up on her bed, her hair flowing in loose waves around her as she squinted at the image of the high school.

Her adventures in attending her father's most recent press conference had been enlightening, to say the least. Never could she have imagined that she'd experience an actual earthquake, feeling the tremors even though she was some distance from the epicenter. The timing had been remarkably convenient, though, a clear sign to the people in the lower city that threats to their safety were increasing. Could the seawall withstand another quake, they wanted to know, especially a stronger one? Sandra knew in her heart that their concerns were legitimate.

The boots she regularly wore for most of her lower-city visits of late were slumped in the corner of her bedroom after having been cleaned, a reminder of the unpleasantness of visiting the Nubian Quarter. "It's no wonder they call it the Swamp," Krazen had said over dinner years before. "Despicable the way they choose to live."

It was the sort of thing he would never say on camera, of course. For the holos he was "lifting them out of unimaginable suffering," rather than degrading their homes. He was "praising the vibrancy of their community," rather than disparaging their neighborhood. And, of course, he was never mentioning what, exactly, had landed them down there in the first place.

Sandra was always listening, even when others expected her not to be.

Even at this very moment, no one on her father's team knew she was scrubbing through news and social media footage, hunting for answers. To them, she was wasting another day in her room, a frivolous girl with frivolous distractions.

It was all somehow connected to the kids she'd spotted in the footage. She'd been able to find all four of them with intense detective work—Zuberi, Vriana, Lencho, and Uzochi. All Nubian, all relatively poor, all students at 104.

Lencho, though. Lencho held Sandra's attention the most.

Sandra could tell he was special after reviewing the multiple videos Tilly had recorded of him.

"Zoom," Sandra said, leaning forward on her bed as she reviewed footage from 104 for the umpteenth time. "Right corner."

The screen obeyed, finding and enlarging the two figures on the right side of the frame. Sandra's breath caught at the sight of them, even slightly blurred as they were in the holonews's lower-quality broadcast footage. She spotted Lencho immediately.

Sandra didn't know what was special about the Divine kid, only that she'd overheard an argument between her father and Tilly that revealed their offer had thus far not been taken up. *That* meant that Sandra had an opportunity.

What she was considering was risky, requiring a trip down below—one without the guards associated with press conferences—but the risk was worth it if she could track down the boy and get answers.

Sandra checked the time. She would head to the lower city and find this Lencho, learning more about who he was and what he had to offer and perhaps persuading him to return with her. All it would take would be a positive attitude. She would manifest his "yes" in her mind.

She started to enter standard glam mode, pulling back her hair into her signature ponytail and painting on gold-tinted lip gloss after she'd donned a simple formfitting black bodysuit. She saved the boots for last. It was all she had time for, but it was enough.

She soon left her room, smiling at the few St. John employees she encountered in the hallway, though they all seemed preoccupied with their tablets or holos beaming from their eyes. Sandra caught sight of a large photo on a staff member's screen, glimpsing an image of the boy she'd seen earlier with Lencho via news footage. She also spotted a name. Zaire, his last name hidden by the employee's thumb.

Interesting. Was it possible this boy was also special in some way, like Lencho? But how?

Sandra stopped walking down the hallway. Was she miscalculating, going after Lencho? She could try to get both boys, but if her father was already seeking Zaire . . .

She needed more answers. Sandra resumed her clipped walk down the hall, but this time, she went right, down an emptier part of her father's building, not wanting to waste time walking all the way back to her quarters. She tapped out a pattern on her fingers, the circuitry of her implants coming alive as she deactivated all camera activity in the immediate vicinity. Seconds later, a small holo beamed from her left eye. Her own private computer screen, ready at her command to hack into her father's system.

She had minutes at most before someone noticed the mini video blackout. If the breach was traced back to her, there would be unthinkable consequences.

She typed in the name "Zaire" and clicked "search," then waited as files and data filled her screen. She clicked onto the first folder she saw and then opened the first document, a file titled "104 REPORT." The text was sparse.

Possible N identification. Earthquake confirmed not natural; source possibly N; boy at scene confirmed name Zaire; Divine Suns association; location unknown, possibly investigate Jungle.

Then it was confirmed. He was another of her father's targets. A "possible N." What did that stand for? Sandra clicked out of the system, holding her breath for any kind of alarm.

She couldn't doubt herself now. Whatever this Zaire boy might mean for her father, nothing could compare to the treasure that was Lencho. She had to find him.

Sandra visualized him in her mind as she walked down to the elevators. She saw his eyes and cheekbones and slender fingers that seemed both delicate and strong, images she'd dreamed of for days.

She swiped her hand over the elevator console for her exclusive access, not bothering to hide her moves like last time. Let Krazen know she was unafraid to go down below. So long as she returned with the prize, her actions would be worth it.

I am powerful.

I am achieving my destiny.

I am greatness embodied.

She repeated the mantras, the thoughts turning into a chant. She called together the boy's likeness again and again. She even closed her eyes as the elevator swooshed downward, not minding how her stomach flipped as always.

The elevator floated to the ground with a soft *ding.* Sandra's eyes opened as the door did, and the increasingly familiar sight of Central Park swam into view, broken up by the huge, gleaming elevator towers that connected the two city levels of New York. Sandra looked to the left for the guard who'd been at the bank previously, ready to ignite her charming smile.

Only the guard wasn't around. She blinked at his abandoned post. Then she heard voices, and she swung her gaze forward.

"Don't you see his holo here in my damn phone? How would I get this if I wasn't personally invited? Do you realize how pissed he'll be if you don't let me up?"

Sandra's lips curved into a grin.

Of course he was here already. She'd drawn him here with her intentions, hadn't she? And he wasn't alone. Behind him were several kids. Other members of the Divine, she guessed.

"Mr. Will," Sandra called, her voice high and full of purpose. "I believe you're correct. I'm here to deliver you Up High."

The boy stopped instantly at the sound of her voice. His hand fell from where it had been brandished at the guard. He looked to her, his eyes molten and warm.

Power. That was what he radiated.

"Excuse me?" he said, not sounding the least bit polite.

Sandra smiled wider.

"I said I'm here to deliver you Up High. Won't you join me above?"

Chapter 19

Uzochi

As Uzochi walked uptown, he did his best to sift through the surrounding thoughts. He was still abuzz with energy from being in Zaire's mind, coming to grips with being able to see so much of a stranger's life in a brief moment. There was no denying that was what had happened. Now he listened to the worries and hopes of people on the street, finding individual thoughts and holding them as long as he could while beating back other voices to focus on the one in his possession. It wasn't easy work, and he was already tired, a fatigue that had started to nestle in his bones.

Still, he forced himself to walk home. He passed holo-news screens that showed 104 and the stream of students rushing out after the quake. He kept waiting with dread for videos to appear of either Zaire or himself captured by campus cameras or his classmates' devices, but the only clips he saw from inside the school consisted of shaky hallway footage as debris fell around fleeing students.

The footage made Uzochi wonder if something else had

happened when Zaire changed. At that exact moment, Uzochi had felt a surge of power. Had the surge done something to the cameras, knocking them out? He supposed he should feel lucky that his secret, for now, was hidden.

But what was his secret? What was it that he could do? It seemed like he could delve into people's minds and hear their thoughts. Uzochi looked up at the overcast sky, the truth of this idea settling in.

I . . . I can really read minds. Omigosh . . . Goddess . . .

Uzochi moved, slowly, steadily, toward home, choosing to focus again on the voices of New York.

Wonder if I can get my vendor's license before the summer?

What if we don't make rent? Shit, might need to borrow currency from Ma. . . .

Geez, that dude felt so good this morning . . . will call him tonight. . . .

I can't do this anymore! This relationship is killing me. . . .

I'm going to be great tomorrow at the Barrymore audition. Just wait.

Anxiety and fear and pain, joy and hope and pleasure. Equal parts that Uzochi could find. He let their voices calm him as he trudged wearily to his building and stepped inside.

He'd worried that Com'pa might've come home early, given everything that had happened. He thought she might've seen the news, but their home was empty. Come to think of it, she hadn't sent him a text, so she was probably oblivious to what had happened at school, work consuming her attention.

Uzochi set down his scholar-pack and headed straight to the bathroom after grabbing a set of clean clothes to take with him. He felt disgusting, like he was wearing an actual layer of grime. The small mirror confirmed as much, showing that he was covered in dirt and dust. There were rips in his shirt and a cut that ran from his forehead to his cheekbone. He touched the dried blood absently. He didn't think it would scar, but the cut still gave him pause.

It reminded him of her.

Zuberi.

Again, their paths had crossed, but unlike last time, today they'd been intertwined. He could still hear her voice telling him to help Zaire.

It's ripping him apart. I can feel it. Can't you?

They were alike, somehow. And the power she'd described, like seeing ghosts who weren't dead. Uzochi didn't know how to make sense of it, but he felt a pull to the girl. There was something about her aura and eyes and locs, especially how she often tossed them back from her face in that nonchalant, cool way.

Uzochi touched his cornrows. There were bits of rubble in his hair, clinging to the strands. He shook out as much as he could and grabbed a dry towel to dust the braids off, but still something was wrong. He showered, thinking maybe scrubbing off the blood and the rest of the day would help.

Still, when he stepped out and saw himself in the fogged mirror, his fingers itched for change.

He made the first movement quickly to undo the braid closest to his face. It was too fast, and he winced as the hairs around his fingers tore. He closed his eyes, then reopened them. Rushing wasn't the answer.

So he took it slowly, one braid at a time. He even pulled out the rice water that Com'pa was always insisting he use, spraying the braids before undoing them to help himself get purchase. Eventually, his hair was free around his face, and his eyes seemed to shine brighter when he looked in the mirror.

The sound of voices drew his attention. Uzochi pulled on the clean clothes quickly as he listened. He heard Com'pa's voice, but she wasn't alone.

"I'm so glad you came, Thato," she said. "This will be much easier for the two of them to hear together."

Thato? Uzochi wasn't sure who that was. A deep male voice responded to his mother with words Uzochi couldn't readily decipher, and then he heard another voice that he did recognize.

"Come, let's not linger in the doorway," Adisa all but boomed. "Better to discuss inside."

The elder, here again. Uzochi felt like he was standing over a precipice. Before, his mother had called Adisa after his fainting spell. Now, after the incident at school, he was here again. With others.

So this is where Uzochi lives.

Her. It was her. Her voice in his mind again. She was here, looking for him.

He stepped out of the bathroom into his small living room, now full of people. Four sets of eyes turned to him: Com'pa's, Adisa's, Zuberi's, and a stranger's. The stranger was statuesque and leanly muscled, with eyes that were almost identical to Zuberi's. Her father?

Uzochi swallowed and walked into the center of the room.

"Dear heart," Com'pa said, "you took out your braids."

Uzochi blushed. Of course his mother would say something like that right now. He avoided Zuberi's eyes and chose to cough into the back of his hand instead.

Adisa gave a nod. "Uzochi Will, it's good to see you. Please pardon the intrusion, but I have something I'd like to discuss with you and Zuberi, if you're willing to listen."

Uzochi nodded, slightly embarrassed at how childish he'd acted the last time Adisa was in his home.

"Let's sit," Com'pa said, gesturing to the couch and chair in the living area while she scurried to grab two of the dining chairs. "They'll be here in a moment."

Uzochi perked up. Who else was joining them? He looked at Zuberi for an answer, but she just shook her head.

He couldn't believe she was here. In his home. He purposely sat across from her, leaving the better chairs for his mother and the mysterious guests.

Who, though? Another elder like Adisa? Another Nubian? Had they learned about Zaire? Or was it—

A booming knock on the door.

"You have a visitor," the announcer chirped.

Com'pa dashed over to open the door before a holo was transmitted and was nearly thrown out of the way by the massive figure who entered, his energy rough and coarse.

It had been years since Uzochi had seen his uncle. Kefle was by far the tallest person in the room. He was wider, too, with thickly muscled arms and a mean look radiating from his eyes. Each motion was hard, sharp. His salt-and-pepper hair was buzzed all the way to the scalp, making it easy to see both the tattoo on his neck and the skin that puckered behind his ear from a mysterious wound.

His eyes swept the room as Com'pa locked the door behind her former brother-in-law. His lips curled at the sight of Adisa, but he looked at Uzochi with complete disgust. Kefle glared at the boy with a hatred that seared, threatening to bowl him over.

"Why am I here, Com'pa?" Kefle demanded as he swiveled to Uzochi's mother.

"And a good evening to you as well, Kefle. I see your manners are as impeccable as ever," Com'pa snapped. "You will not befoul my house with your brusqueness. You will treat us all with respect or you will leave."

"Respect?" Kefle repeated, incredulous. "You think it's respect that's brought me over? I'm only here because that old coot sitting over there said he wanted to discuss some nonsense about the rebirth of the kinetic. That as Siran's brother he thought I should be present."

"I'm sorry to hear how you continue to denigrate our traditions," Adisa said, his voice once again quiet yet commanding. "But before you storm out, I suggest you sit down and listen to what I have to say. It is of utmost importance that you get this information to Lencho."

Kefle's mood soured even more. "Boy's been gone for over a week," he said, the bravado leaving his voice. "Complete lack of respect for the rules of my house."

Com'pa looked stunned. "Wait, Kefle, Lencho hasn't been home? Do you know where he is?"

Kefle shook his head, crossing his arms. "My affairs are my own, Com'pa. Now . . . what do you want?"

Uzochi wasn't sure if he should jump into the conversation, letting his uncle know that Lencho was definitely safe and sound and obviously still attending school. In fact, he suspected he was probably squatting at the Divine's nasty ole HQ. But should he tell his uncle that? Would he just make matters worse?

"Kefle, I'm deeply sorry for your familial discord," Adisa said. "But, please, I ask you to be still and listen. An important time is upon us."

Kefle's glare never wavered, but after he glanced at Thato and Zuberi, more of his bravado seemed to fade. Both of them stared at the crazy man with their heads held high. These were two people Kefle couldn't intimidate, and even he seemed aware of that. So he went to an empty chair, pulled it as far away from the group as he could, and sat down with his arms crossed and his gaze averted.

"Right," Adisa said, looking away from Kefle and turning to the rest of the room's occupants. "Now, Zuberi, Uzochi, let's discuss what's been happening to you. And let's not waste time. Your parents have relayed to me what they've seen."

Uzochi glanced at his mother. She was perched on the edge of the couch, watching him as though he was a specimen ready to be dissected. She'd known that night he passed out, whether he'd wanted her to or not, that something major was going on. And after today, he no longer wanted to deny what he was experiencing. Even now, whispers pressed against his mind, the thoughts from occupants of his building threatening to overtake him.

"I can see phantoms," Zuberi said. The words spilled forth, as if she'd been yearning to confess. "I . . . I see multiple versions of a person. I don't know what they are. And . . . I can sense when someone else has . . ."

"It's your gift," Adisa said gently.

Zuberi nodded, then looked at Uzochi. "I knew it the second he ran up to stop the fight with the Spiders."

Uzochi breathed in, not knowing what to say.

"I see," Adisa said. "And these visions, my dear, can you describe them further? Do you see them now?"

Zuberi looked from the elder to the others in the room. Her gaze settled back on Uzochi, though he avoided her eyes.

"Yes," she said. "I see phantoms above Uzochi. One of them is running. Another is . . . I think his hand is on something. And the other—"

"Damn it, Adisa, just tell her," Kefle growled from his corner. "Save the theatrics."

"Kefle," Com'pa hissed. "I'm warning you."

Adisa held up a hand. "No, our brother has a point. Zuberi, I believe you're experiencing the development of a very special gift. A gift that I honestly didn't believe we would see again."

"You too, my son," Com'pa said, and Uzochi met his mother's eyes.

"Yes, child, why don't you tell us what you've been experiencing," Adisa urged.

Uzochi looked down again. It was one thing to have visions, but it was another to read minds. To discern secrets. In fact, what if he revealed what he could do and Zuberi refused to talk to him? What if his gift meant that she couldn't trust him?

"I . . ." He struggled. At the edges of his vision, a blue tinge of light had appeared again. The voices were rising like waves in his skull. He closed his eyes to sift through them again as he had earlier.

He's sad and weak. I knew it.

His uncle's voice, far louder than the others. Uzochi burned with shame.

"He made Zaire change back," Zuberi said, cutting through the haze in his mind. "He knew exactly what to do."

Uzochi's eyes flew open. Zuberi was watching him, leaning forward on the edge of her chair. For a moment, she glowed, and then the light vanished and Uzochi found he could breathe again.

"Explain, dear one," Adisa said, voice gentle but firm.

Zuberi knotted her hands together. "Zaire—that's the Divine kid I was telling you about, Dad—he turned into some sort of rock, almost like he'd fused with the earth. It was during a fight at school. Or, almost a fight. But that's when the quake happened, and I thought Zaire was in pain. I asked Uzochi to change him back, and he did."

The adults all looked to Uzochi now.

"Dear one, is that true?" Com'pa said, her voice bordering on a gasp.

"I don't know," Uzochi said. "I heard him ask me for help.

I saw stuff from . . . from his perspective. I was in his mind, I think. I . . . I don't know." He kept his gaze fixed on the floor.

"You do know, child," Adisa said. "Tell us."

Uzochi forced himself to breathe, feeling terribly exposed. "I can hear people. Their thoughts, sometimes. Not on purpose, but I can. And Zaire, when he had . . . turned, I . . . I tried to help him. But I don't know if I did. Because . . . because something else happened."

He looked to his uncle, who was staring at him again, eyes narrowed.

"This is incredible," Com'pa said, folding her hands together. "An empath."

"A what?" Zuberi asked.

"An empath," Adisa said. "Uzochi can take in the emotions and thoughts and perspectives of everyone around him, including ours right now. And you, my dear, appear to be precognitive."

Thato hugged his daughter and smiled. "A very rare gift, Beri."

"You can see others' potential selves," Adisa explained. "Their possible futures, who they might become or what they might do next. And, it appears, you are particularly in tune with other Nubians and their energies."

Nubians. Energies. The words swam in Uzochi's mind.

"Sorry," he said. "But this . . . this all sounds . . ."

"Insane," Zuberi concluded, and Uzochi couldn't help but smile.

Adisa chuckled. "I apologize. Of course, I realize what this must sound like to the two of you. It's been eons since I've had the honor of guiding two young Nubians through this process of awakening."

His smile faltered only slightly, a hint of sadness taking over his features.

"I've missed the feeling," he said, looking at Uzochi and Zuberi in turn. "Please, allow me to explain. We shall return to the beginning."

He dug into the pocket of his tunic and pulled from it a small, ancient-looking book. Adisa flipped to a page toward the end of the journal, which Uzochi saw was covered with looping script. It had been so long since he'd read anything written by hand, and something inside him itched to hold the book. But he resisted, listening instead as Adisa spoke again.

"My personal journal," he said, still smiling. "When you're as old as I am, it becomes an imperative. To be honest, I've written for many years now off and on, but for the past few days I've been driven to take pen to page all through the night. Perhaps I can share a recent entry."

He read, and as he did, Uzochi could see the pages coming alive in his mind.

From the First Book of Adisa, New York City, 2098

Due to recent events, memories of my birthplace have come to me with an unfamiliar intensity. To say I still miss home would be an understatement; it's an emotion that language cannot contain. But I'll do my best to find the words for those who should know the truth of our ancestral land.

Nubia was wonderful, where happiness suffused the air, where our joy electrified the ether. To the feet of Nubians, the brown-black earth was warm, abundant in vegetation, a fertile soil. We could readily pick guava and naartjies from our municipal gardens or the trees of a neighbor. We would exult in vibrant hues, citizens adorned in tunics and gowns and robes with shimmering wax-print patterns.

From my office window, I looked upon immaculate court-yards, the golden spires of our temples rising above all else. As I walked through the small villages surrounding our city center, I entered simple, refined homes with walls that glimmered. And beyond the villages, when I entered mountain caves, I gazed upon inscriptions carved in stone chronicling the efforts of our catalysts, those grand Nubian heroes who permanently changed the direction of our society. More than one thousand years ago, after violent tremors ravaged our land and homesteads, honored catalyst Komi Assan led our ancestors to create a capital city that endured for centuries. And even further back, more than three thousand years ago, honored catalyst Adwoa Celestine encouraged Nubians to explore the true range of our kinetic gifts, to better understand our potential.

For the citizens of Nubia were graced with abilities that many in the outside world would view as fantasy. We believed these gifts to be our birthright, tied to an uncorrupted communion with a bountiful universe. Some Nubians used their bodies to absorb energy from the sun, walking as nimbuses of gold. Others were able to send their presence across the sky. A young man with elemental gifts could touch the heart of his betrothed as she sailed to the other side of our isle, willing sea-foam to take his form and blow her a kiss. A family member could nurture the spirit of a grieving child who had lost a parent, sending the little one nighttime dreams of her mother singing a lullaby. O precious daughter, listen for my voice on the wind . . .

We were people of the mind, wielders of energy, healers, even shapeshifters on occasion, abilities that manifested depending on the individual. You may believe you're reading the fanciful mutterings of a senile old man, but no, this was reality for Nubians. A glorious existence in a paradise that we kept in peace.

It was during this time of prosperity that one of the Great Storms descended, the likes of which we'd never seen. Nubia had survived all manner of hurricane and monsoon before, natural phenomena that had bowed before the power of our elementals, but this tempest was like a thing possessed, ravaging our city, eradicating villages. Those who controlled the elements were overcome, most sacrificing their lives so the rest of us could flee.

Nubia vanished before our very eyes, our cherished gardens and trees and temples swept away, submerged in cataclysm.

Nubia, my great, glorious Nubia, lost in the storm.

Chapter 20

Zuberi

Zuberi listened to the story of Nubia told in a way she'd never heard before. How many times had she and her father talked of the fighting forms of Nubia, of keeping that tradition alive? But here were traditions deeper than anything she'd studied, waiting for this moment to arise. She simply knew Adisa's words had to be true, feeling it in her gut as relief settled in that she hadn't been losing her mind.

She had the gift of precognition.

Questions bubbled up inside Zuberi with rapid intensity after Adisa concluded reading, but she let the silence sit. It felt wrong to speak, for right now Adisa seemed otherworldly and Godlike, even though she knew he was just a man.

"We'd thought our gifts were gone," Adisa said softly, breaking the silence. "As we fled Nubia and drifted across the sea, adults frantically caring for the countless children first taken to the boats, we could feel our kinetic gifts vanishing. By the time we'd reached the shores of New York, our abilities were lost, like Nubia, and we had no idea why. Many years have passed . . . and still, we don't have our abilities." The grief in his voice was unmistakable.

Zuberi looked at the adults around the room. Uzochi's mother and uncle. Her own father. They had been able to do this, then. Until they were lost.

A strange hope floated up inside her that was almost immediately punctured by grief, warring emotions that both asked for her power to disappear and felt horror that it might go away. She shook them off, not understanding the sensations.

"Why didn't you tell us?" Uzochi said, the hurt impossible to miss in his voice. "Why wait until now?"

"Dear heart, when Nubians came to this city, we had nothing," Com'pa said. "We were sick, hungry, traumatized. We'd lost our homeland and didn't think we would survive the journey over the Atlantic. Some of us *didn't* survive. And for those who arrived, we had to negotiate a new system, a new culture, all while mourning the loss of our homeland and those we cherished. And we mourned the loss of a part of ourselves that was as natural as breathing. Why would we bequeath you that pain when we didn't have to? When we thought you would always be without?"

"The truth of the kinetic wasn't something we felt safe discussing," Thato said, drawing Zuberi's attention. "As soon as we landed here, we were in survival mode. We needed to find homes, jobs, all while being viewed with suspicion by so many. The last thing we needed was our kids saying something at school or on the playground that prompted questions."

"It might've been different if any of you had awoken to your gifts earlier," Com'pa continued. "But that wasn't the case. So we thought, *Ah, this part of our heritage is done.* We needed to move on. Adapt. We decided we would keep our gifts a secret and turn them into the stuff of fantasy and lore."

Zuberi blinked, suddenly remembering once again the story her father had told her about the woman who'd been hounded by ghosts.

Oh my Goddess, that . . . that really happened!

"Our so-called gifts should remain the stuff of fanciful stories as far as I'm concerned," grumbled Kefle, earning himself another cutting glare from Com'pa.

"Wait, what? But why?" Zuberi asked, turning to Adisa. "I don't understand. Why did your powers disappear?"

Adisa considered her. "An excellent question. We simply don't know. We have our theories, but we cannot be sure."

Zuberi wanted to know exactly what these theories were, but her father shook his head ever so slightly, his trademark signal to cease and desist. So instead, she asked another question.

"Why now, then? Why are our gifts awakening?"

Adisa smiled. "Again, an excellent question with an answer that I suspect will frustrate you. We don't know for sure, though we have our theories, but again, theories alone."

The elder looked around the room, even at Kefle, who'd been mostly staring down at the floor since Adisa had finished reading.

"One thing that is certain," Adisa said, "is that we must prepare. The poor child at school who transformed, you two, and young Lencho . . . you are not isolated cases. There will be others." Zuberi noticed that Kefle flinched upon hearing Lencho's name.

"Precisely," said Com'pa, standing up. "Which is exactly why you all need to be trained."

"Trained for what?" Uzochi asked.

Zuberi took him in, his phantoms twirling and twisting above his head as they shone bright blue.

An empath. Someone who could hear thoughts. Was he listening to hers right now, she wondered?

"Trained so that we don't have anyone else turning into boulders and causing earthquakes at school," Com'pa continued. "Mastering your abilities is a key component of control and connecting with who you intrinsically are."

"Now, Com'pa," said Thato, "you can't really think that's the first step. We need to move these kids out of the city, find somewhere safe for them, before we do anything else."

Adisa shook his head. "Brother, that's impossible. This is the safest place for our children."

"Goddess, you can't believe that!" Thato said. "You should've seen the school, the obvious damage to the building just from one Nubian's awakening. What these kids could do—"

"Which is why we're emphasizing training, Thato," Com'pa said. "Training to use their abilities properly. Safely. With our guidance."

At first, Kefle's chuckle sounded like a growl, the low

rumble of a dangerous beast that grew louder in the silence following Com'pa's statement. He laughed for a long time, and then, when his head snapped up, his grin was cruel.

"Properly?" Kefle said, his tone dripping with disdain and mockery. "There's no way to use them 'properly,' you fool."

"Brother Kefle," Adisa said, his voice harboring a warning that Kefle cut through with another bark of laughter.

"Don't 'Brother Kefle' me, Adisa," he said, standing, his bulk seeming to absorb the room's light. "I know how this all works. These things always lead to destruction. To death and carnage."

He turned to Com'pa, whose glare was unrelenting.

"You of all people should know that, Com'pa," he said. "Or perhaps you've forgotten the consequences, willing to offer up your only son to the slaughter?"

Beside him, Uzochi stood, and Zuberi saw a flash of blue roll over his body. He wasn't as tall as Kefle, but in that moment, he looked larger than life.

"Watch it, *Uncle*," Uzochi said.

Kefle shook his head, looking from Uzochi to Com'pa to Adisa. "Incredible. You want to be their lamb, Uzochi? Go ahead. Be like your fool of a father. But my son won't be part of this, wherever he is. And if I find out you've pulled him in, you'll all regret it."

And then he left, slamming the door behind him with such force that the entire apartment shook.

Com'pa tilted her head and reached for Uzochi's hand. "Don't listen to him, dear heart. He's angry, as usual."

Zuberi watched the two of them, mother and son. Their

phantoms appeared above each of them, though Uzochi's seemed to flicker.

"What did he mean?" he asked, his voice quiet. "About Dad?"

It was a private moment, one that Zuberi wanted no part of. She knew what it was like to have only one parent who had to field questions from a child about the other. But Thato's head shook ever so slightly once again and they stayed seated. Adisa stepped forward, putting a hand on Uzochi's shoulder.

"You must understand, Uzochi," Adisa said. "Your father was an incredible human being, a great Nubian. More than that, he was a king to our people. Nubian royalty."

Uzochi's eyes widened, and Zuberi, too, felt the ricochet of the words.

"When the Great Storm hit, it was your father who stepped up to use his powers to save our people," Adisa continued, looking at Com'pa. "At great sacrifice to his family."

A string of tears started to fall down Com'pa's cheeks.

"He was brave, my son," she said, sniffing. "He tried to stop the storm. And while it destroyed our homeland, it did not destroy us. But your uncle still feels guilt. Perhaps he wonders if his brother would still be here if he'd helped stave off the maelstrom. I don't know. But you mustn't listen to him. His grief . . . it's poisoned him, I'm afraid."

"Your mother is right," Adisa said, his hand still on Uzochi's shoulder. "And Brother Kefle, too, has his points. These gifts are both a blessing and a curse, I fear. In Nubia, we would nurture you all together to properly teach you our traditions. But now, our community is splintered, even as we're concentrated in the Swamp. We must unite. And I agree with Sister Com'pa. You must train."

His eyes landed now on Zuberi and Uzochi.

"You are special," Adisa continued. "Both of you. And, Uzochi, I believe you might even be our catalyst."

"Catalyst." The word had been in Adisa's journal.

"It is the Nubian whom every other Nubian is connected to, the one who enhances each of our powers. Who can do great things, just as your father did, Uzochi. The one who can bring Nubians to a more evolved place over generations."

Uzochi's face was unreadable, but the words stirred up a storm of their own within Zuberi.

So much power, just between the two of them. Greater still among the Nubians spread throughout the Swamp and beyond.

"We can use these powers for more," she said, standing up. "We can use them to help those in the Swamp. We can really make a difference. Fix the seawall, stand up to the militia."

"Zuberi—"

Her father was at her side. Again, he was telling her to be quiet, not to push too much. And she'd listened before. But now? She couldn't be silent.

"There's so much suffering," she said, looking to Uzochi. "I know you've heard it, seen it throughout the city. Well, we can do something. This is incredible. *Unbelievable,* but in a good way. Our people need us to use our gifts on their behalf."

"Daughter, your head is in the right place," Adisa said. "But this training is for your safety. We must start small."

"I don't care about starting small," Zuberi said, anger

rising inside her. "And it's my gift, isn't it? I get to decide how to use it."

"This is why we need to leave this place," Thato said. "It won't just be my Zuberi who thinks like this. Others will be reckless as well."

Reckless? Was that what her dad thought of her, after all these years of diligence with the forms? She looked back at Uzochi, watching him. Above him, his phantoms twisted and turned: an Uzochi who was reading, an Uzochi who stared up at the sky, an Uzochi who shouted words she couldn't hear.

The Uzochi in front of her, though, had turned away to face his mother and their elder.

"I'll train," he said. "Whether I'm the catalyst or not, I'll do it. Whatever you need."

Adisa smiled, and Com'pa clapped her hands together.

Zuberi couldn't celebrate.

She took one look at Thato, shook her head, and walked out of Uzochi's home without saying a word, ignoring the calls from the others.

She was no one's pawn and she would use her gifts however she saw fit.

Chapter 21

Lencho

Lencho had seen the sky towers up close a few times over the years. The first was when he was thirteen, on a school field trip to the arts and design museum right across from the park. His preceptor thought it would be a good idea for the class to take a quick detour and check out the towers, where she gave her students a lecture on the history of the columns, including when they were built back in 2067. Others were standing around the columns as well, enraptured by the most prominent symbols of ascendancy in the city. Lencho had felt completely dwarfed by the structures and wanted to leave.

That sense of smallness had returned earlier as he approached the towers yet again with the Divine, spotting a militia squad clad in black with signature berets standing next to a dead tree, with lots of vegetation unable to thrive under the sky city's massive shadow. Typical St. John Soldiers, and Lencho had to remind himself to play it cool. He wasn't doing anything wrong being here. He'd been invited.

It had taken minor convincing to get Aren, Lara, Zaire, and Nneka to come with him. They'd been the only Divine sitting outside the Jungle when he'd presented the holo, but Lencho thought it was enough. At least, this was a decent party to hear Krazen out and learn exactly what he was offering to him and the crew. Still, he'd been extremely embarrassed when the guard had refused them elevator access, unwilling to believe Lencho's claims that he'd met with Krazen before, even with the holo that he produced from his phone. Thank the gods for her.

Sandra St. John.

In all the holo-ads that Lencho had ever seen of the Up High, the people seemed to glow. Their skin was always smooth and clear, not a speck of dirt or a pimple in sight. He'd expected that it was something cooked up in an editing booth somewhere using face-contour tech, and that had to be at least partially true. But Sandra St. John *did* glow, even when she was right in front of him.

Her crimson hair, pulled up in a ponytail, caught and reflected light from every angle. Her cheekbones were dusted with some kind of soft glitter, and there were tiny silver and gold flecks of jewelry adorning her earlobes and fingertips. When she smiled, Lencho swore he'd never beheld such perfect teeth. Her laugh was high, sweet, and when her hand grazed his as she shepherded him and his crew to the elevator, her skin was softer than satin.

"So this is your first Up High elevator ride?" she asked. "I don't want to presume, but I just want to give you a warning. I've heard it can be quite . . . surprising."

191

She batted her eyelashes at him, and Lencho's stomach flipped over entirely. He'd never been this affected by a girl before, and there were plenty of gorgeous girls back at 104. Sandra was unreal.

"Uh, no worries," Lencho said. "I've actually traveled up in one of these before." It was somewhat of a lie, as he'd been totally unconscious when he was first taken to the sky by the St. John Soldiers.

Sandra blinked at him, her glossy lips smiling before she laughed. Lencho laughed, too, hoping his words played like a joke instead of the partial bullshit they had been. Thankfully, the other Divine seemed too nervous and out of sorts to really say much at all.

"Step on in, then," she said, waving him forward so that the group stood in front of a looming elevator door designated as Carrier 22A. The door was closed, but a soft, eerie light emanated from its edges. Sandra tapped the middle of her index finger and the light disappeared. The door swooshed open and she gestured with her hand, saying, "After you."

The elevator was huge and circular with horizontal metal bars lining the sides of the car. The door closed and the car began its swift ascent, a motion that Lencho felt slightly in his stomach.

"I imagine you'd like the outside view?" Sandra said. "It's absolutely *divine.*"

Lencho glanced at her, slightly annoyed at the play on words, but she only smiled her glittering smile. Beside him, Aren chuckled gruffly, while Lara rolled her eyes dramatically. Nneka grinned, looking like an awestruck child as she took in her surroundings, while Zaire stood perfectly still, stoic as ever.

"Uh, yeah," Lencho replied. "Thanks."

Sandra tapped her ring finger and the gray sides of the car vanished, replaced by blue sky and the sight of another sky tower, with the trees of Central Park growing smaller and smaller as the elevator rose.

According to Sandra, special tech had been embedded in the towers that synced with a video camera system in the elevators, thus giving riders the sense of what the towers would be like if they were made from glass instead of steel polymer. Lencho took in the magnificent sights, the reality of his ascension hitting him, the trees and buildings growing tinier and wisps of clouds appearing.

Lencho fought to keep his breathing steady. Now wasn't the time to look like an ass. He needed to appear confident, like he belonged.

Soon, thankfully, the elevator stopped. The door swooshed open again. Lencho stepped forward with Sandra, entering a place he never would have imagined he'd see in his lifetime.

With his fellow Divine, Lencho gaped openly at the glistening edifices of metal and glass that vanished into the clouds, and intersecting paths of silver and concrete where shiny people in metallic clothing and flashy fluorescent hair walked with long and lean droids and short and squat droids and rolling droids. And cars and vans and cycles zipped past in the sky above on invisible lanes, moving much more quickly than the lower city's hover vehicles.

He and the others followed Sandra as they left the elevator

bank to enter an adjoining square. A couple of teens were zooming around the square on hover scooters, their laughter slicing through the air as they weaved through pedestrians. Lencho almost thought they were sparkling—were they gifted, using their powers out in the open?—but then he realized they were wearing T-shirts with some sort of moving star pattern. The members of his crew trailed behind him, the quartet slack-jawed and stunned into silence by Up High opulence.

Several other people walked by, Lencho taking in their tailored clothes and sophisticated accessories and glistening skin and plump, well-fed bodies. A voluptuous woman with a turquoise bouffant had a holo beaming out of her left eye.

He so wanted to touch the people who lived up here. He could feel essence radiating from their skin, calling to his body.

"Hang on," Sandra said next to him. "We're going this way."

Sandra led them through many paths and turns, so many that Lencho struggled to keep them straight. At different points, Sandra needed to flash her hand to gain entry, and occasionally they'd get a look from one of the many St. John Soldiers who guarded the entrances. But no one said a word, and Lencho knew why. Who was going to question the daughter of Krazen St. John?

"Almost there," she said. "Just a little farther."

She led them into what appeared to be the most secure building yet, judging from the number of security protocols they had to clear. The glass-and-steel structure gave Lencho the distinct feeling of a modern office, something he'd only seen on holos, with most lower-city work spaces pretty dank and gray in his estimation. But up here the vibe was, well, odd. Kind of antiseptic. He kept on passing rooms with glass walls and batches of people toiling silently, staring into screens or interacting with holos.

"There he is."

A man was at the end of the room, standing with Tilly; neither of them had yet noticed Lencho and the other Divine.

"Krazen," Sandra called out. "I've brought you someone."

Something inside Lencho heated up at the words, like he was some kind of present to be delivered. But then he caught Sandra's eyes, and the raw pride she felt boiled over onto him. She saw something special in Lencho. Something worthy of presenting to the most powerful man in the city.

Lencho straightened his back and looked straight ahead as Krazen St. John crossed the room to stand in front of him. He addressed a holo beaming from his left eye, the other person on the call speaking in rushed, clipped tones.

"All right, I'll be in touch," he said, and with that the image blinked out. Krazen then turned his attention to Lencho.

"Mr. Will, what a surprise," he said. "Though I am, of course, thrilled we're finally getting back together."

He looked behind Lencho to the other Divine. "And these must be your companions. Wonderful to meet you all."

"Um, yeah, hi," Lencho said. "I, uh. I got your message, and so I decided to finally return. And your daughter . . . uh, she seems pretty cool."

Sandra laughed next to him, which made Lencho smile. Krazen looked from his daughter to Lencho, a neutral expression on his face.

"Of course," Krazen said. "Shall we go to my office?"

Sandra nodded next to Lencho, then gave him a meaningful look. He glanced behind him to the other Divine. Aren still looked slightly queasy from the elevator ride, while Lara's chin was high, as always. Zaire and Nneka were harder to read, but Lencho took their silence as assent.

"Right," Lencho said quickly. "Yeah, that would be great."

"To my office, then," Krazen said. "And, Sandra? I'm sure you have other affairs to attend to."

Lencho had never been in such a plush place. Everything seemed either too heavy or too delicate, and he wasn't sure where to sit until Krazen gestured for him to take one of the large chairs. He sat on the edge, feeling suddenly like he was trapped, until the other Divine took seats near him. It was easier with all of them here.

"We want to hear your pitch," Lencho said, trying to sound tougher than he felt. "Let's talk Elevation and how you'd help us settle up. And then there's the—"

Krazen held up a hand. "Not yet."

He tapped his left wrist, an image appearing almost instantly. There was Zaire on-screen in the center of a ring of people, the Spider standing before him, taunting him.

Then, a flash of light, and the footage went dark.

"Zaire," Krazen said, speaking to the boy in the room. "Your display today was quite impressive. Is that the first time you've shown your gift?"

All heads in the room turned to Zaire, who looked like he wanted to disappear. Even so, he nodded.

Krazen smiled. "Nubian gifts. I'm one of the few in Tri-State East—and possibly elsewhere in the world—to know of them, well, outside the Nubian community, of course. It's my belief that these gifts are resurfacing after lying dormant for some time. They can certainly lead to trouble, like we saw today at Lencho and Zaire's school. I want to help you all navigate this uncertain time."

"Sorry," Aren said, sitting next to Lencho in a padded seat that threatened to engulf his frame. "What'd you say?"

"Nubians were once blessed with extraordinary abilities," Krazen said simply. "They could manipulate light or create storms and earthquakes and fires or send their thoughts to others. And then they came here, and we thought everything was over, that these gifts had vanished. Except they hadn't. Nubians like you, Lencho and Zaire, have power."

The heads of the other Divine whipped back and forth between Lencho and Zaire. The larger boy closed his eyes, placed his hands under his legs, and tucked his head into his chest, hunching over.

"Waitaminnit!" Aren yelled. "Man, what crazy shit are you spouting? What powers?" He turned to stare at Lencho. "Lencho, what is this dude talking about?"

Lencho wanted to follow Zaire and curl into a ball, too, but no, he had to stand his ground. He tried to steady his racing heart as he spoke.

"I . . . was planning to tell y'all, to say something soon.

But, you know, I'd met with Mr. St. John before, and then something happened with Zaire and his power, and—"

"Wait. Zaire's *power*? Bruh, what the fuck are you talking about? Have you lost it? You been watching too much of those sci-fi holos."

"Aren, please," Krazen said, his voice calm yet steely. "Lencho simply speaks of what is. He's come into his gift. As has Zaire, as will the rest of you, as part of a new generation of Nubians. All of you will reveal in time what you can do, I'm sure. But you'll need a place to develop your abilities."

Aren was completely stunned, his jaw scraping the office's immaculate carpet, while Lara stared at Lencho with a fury that was beyond frightening. He imagined that the girl wanted to shank him right then and there. She absolutely *hated* not being in the know. Nneka, on the other hand, let her gaze linger on Zaire, clearly concerned for her fellow Divine, who seemed to have shut down.

"Zaire," she said softly, "what can you do?" The boy didn't respond.

"I'm sure this is hard to comprehend, to absorb, but I'm here," Krazen said, "and we'll be sure to get through these challenging times together." He touched his wrist again. Now there was a new feed, this one of a huge, circular white room with weights and high-tech treadmills scattered throughout.

"I've deeply researched Nubian abilities and paranormal activity in general, and I believe stress can be an effective inducer of your gifts," Krazen said. "We can use the room presented here to put each of you through stressors to help you discover your abilities. Your *power*."

"Wait, you're forcing us to fight?" Lencho said, his mouth suddenly dry.

Krazen chuckled. "Of course not. You're all here willingly, no? Lencho, I have a vision."

He stood, pacing the palatial office. "For too long, the Up High has been an unachievable goal for so many in the lower city. This, I believe, is a squandering of the talent down below. I've always wanted to find a way to provide more paths to ascension for those who deserve it. For those who are clearly special."

He stopped now, eyes settling on Zaire briefly before moving back to Lencho.

"I will train you all to protect our great city," Krazen said. "You and other Nubians like you could potentially be lauded as the next generation of New York warriors, St. John Soldiers 2.0, if you will. I want to offer a secure, clear-cut path to the Up High. I want to offer you a home, Lencho."

Home. Lencho had given up on his home a little over a week ago, exchanging it for the Jungle. Now he was being offered something that most people in his world could barely dream of.

There had to be a catch. Always was, right?

"So we'd be trapped here?" Lencho asked, looking from Krazen to the other Divine.

"Trapped?" Krazen said, laughing again. "Please. Lencho, ascension isn't a prison. You can leave whenever you like. You were invited here, not captured. This is an opportunity, my boy. Not a demand. Please know we would immediately settle your debts for Elevation." He looked pointedly at Aren. "And give you a new home, each of you. All you need to do is agree to train."

"But what if we don't have special abilities?" asked Nneka, a healthy dose of cynicism creeping into her voice.

Krazen smiled. "My dear, all true Nubians have powers. This, I promise."

The Divine looked at each other, a mix of confusion, skepticism, and shock in their eyes. Lencho knew the others needed time to adjust to what was happening, even Zaire, but he already tasted something in the air.

Possibility. Chance.

If only his dad could see him now, sitting across from the Sky King, like they were equals.

"I can't speak for the others," Lencho said. "But I already made up my mind. I'm in."

Next to him, Aren's gaze was heavy. Lencho knew how much pride the Divine leader had in being Nubian. And this . . . this was beyond anything he could've ever hoped for in terms of helping the gang.

"I . . . need some time to think about this," Aren said. "Lencho's down with your deal, fine, but the rest of us need a minute. This is just . . . crazy. I mean, powers?!?"

Krazen St. John nodded, smiling at them all.

"Of course," the Sky King said. "Take as much time as you need. But I'm hopeful you'll make the right choice. The best choice. I'm confident that soon it will be my honor to invite all of the Divine to ascend."

Chapter 22

Uzochi

Uzochi had always loved the cozy nature of his home. He loved that he could see aspects of his family in every corner, from the array of books on the shelves to his mother's meticulous sketches and carvings. He loved that, when he or Com'pa cooked, the entire place smelled delicious, that no corner was left out. He even loved how he could hear the sounds of his neighbors just outside, with an assortment of little kids playing and squealing in the courtyard.

Now, however, Uzochi's apartment had become oppressive in its smallness. The gravity of what his mother, Adisa, Thato, and even his uncle had revealed weighed on him constantly. He replayed their words over and over in his mind, and with those words, he relived their emotions. The sharp disdain of his uncle. The sparkling expectations of Adisa. Even the bitter disappointment of Zuberi when she'd stormed out.

He understood her anger, but what could they possibly do? They were teenagers, not politicians, and they didn't even fully comprehend their gifts, at least not yet. And what was

Uzochi going to do, march up to the St. John Soldiers and tell them a change had come? So Zuberi could see people's future selves. What exactly would that do for the people in the Swamp and the rest of the lower city?

As of now, all Uzochi knew was that he could tune into thoughts and minds, the "control" that his mother had spoken of proving to be elusive. There were moments when he thought he might have a sense of how to handle his power, but then a stray thought or emotion would derail him. That was his life now, grappling with random bouts of hopefulness or buoyancy or lethargy or grief or anxiety from his neighbors . . . all battling for space in his mind and body, all battling to usurp his own thoughts and emotions. Uzochi had begun to understand just why he'd felt so drained at school the more he connected with his gift.

When he began to feel overwhelmed, he made sure to sit down on his couch and breathe, Adisa's words about how to understand his gift playing in his head.

What you're experiencing, the sensations, the emotions . . . see it as a form of energy. The energy of others. Something to control, navigate . . .

Uzochi's eyes remained closed as he followed more of Adisa's instructions and expanded his inner presence, seeing this presence as a barrier, one that could align itself with his body. When emotions threatened to overwhelm, he should concentrate on the barrier and nothing else. He must never underestimate the power of this barrier, for he might one day be able to create formidable fields of force.

And so Uzochi had begun to practice the exercise as often

as possible, a fresh assignment, something to perfect. The exercise helped, allowing him to shut out the noise when he needed a sense of peace. But then he'd realized, as a result of entering Zaire's mind, that his dreams weren't entirely his own. He saw figures from Zaire's memories, places and shapes that he didn't recognize.

Until last night, when he did.

It was the first time he'd experienced something entirely through Zaire's point of view. Not snippets or flickers, but a full memory covered in a hazy gauze.

Zaire was at Primary School 57, the closest school to the Swamp and therefore one of the bleakest in the lower city. Uzochi knew it well, for he'd attended the school, too. He remembered the white floors of the classrooms, how they were gray and sticky with gunk, and how his desk in third grade always wobbled because one of its legs was broken, and how he often had to use standard notebooks because most of the school's cracked tablets had almost no battery life.

Zaire's memory took place in such a classroom. He sat in the back, his eyes fixed on the front of the room where the preceptor was teaching fractions. Zaire looked at his tablet, then at the board, trying to make sense of the lesson. A question read: *If I have two cups of sugar, and I use a quarter cup in a recipe, how many cups do I have left?*

Zaire looked down at his tablet, writing on it with his finger because the device's pen was long gone, figuring out the problem at his own pace.

"Time!" said the preceptor at the front. "Who has— Of course, Uzochi. What did you get?"

Zaire's eyes lifted, and Uzochi saw a small version of himself. A little boy with close-cropped black curls sitting in the front row, his hand extended straight into the air.

"It's one and three-quarters cups, ma'am," said the tiny Uzochi in the memory, his voice squeaking on the last syllables. All around the classroom, the children snickered at the squeak, and Uzochi watched through Zaire's eyes as the younger version of himself sank ever so slightly into his seat.

"Hush now," the preceptor said to the others. "I'll have none of that. I know you're all just jealous that Mr. Will here came up with the right answer. Now, Mr. Will, why don't you show us how you did that?"

She extended a marker for the board, and Uzochi watched himself hesitate just a second before leaping out of his seat to take the marker. He worked through the equation on the board, showing how both the top and bottom of the fraction needed to be multiplied by four before the subtraction could take place. He ended by dividing seven by four, and then he stepped away from his work, looking down at his scuffed shoes.

"Precisely," said the preceptor, clapping her hands together before turning to the rest of the room. "You would all do well to follow Uzochi's example. *He* is going places, and if you want to join him, you should start paying attention."

Zaire looked down at his tablet, still a swirl of numbers. Shame burned through him, Uzochi feeling the sting even in the dream.

Then the bell rang, and Zaire was packing up his things. His eyes were on Uzochi. A boy with black-and-brown curls popped up next to Zaire, and warmth spread through his body.

"Man, that kid always ruins everything," said the boy in a raspy voice. "Must be easy when you're a preceptor's pet."

Zaire didn't say anything, but when he looked at Uzochi, the shame still burned. He only nodded. Together, he and the other boy walked out of the room to the recess area with its metal swings and handball courts tagged with graffiti.

"I'm telling you, someone needs to teach that kid a lesson," the boy said to Zaire. They'd reached the blacktop, where several kids had grabbed balls, many of them slightly deflated, and were smacking them against the courts. Across the way, sitting on a bench, was Uzochi. He had his e-reader out, and Uzochi knew he was watching his younger self doing homework.

"Z, you even listening to me?" said the boy.

Zaire looked at the other boy, his glance a furtive one. Uzochi could feel that looking at this other boy straight-on made Zaire uncomfortable. But he soon met the boy's expectant gaze.

"Yeah, I guess he's annoying," said Zaire. "But what about it, Aren?"

Aren. Uzochi realized with a start that this was the same kid who now ran the Divine. In the memory, he looked stringy and wild, nothing like the cool and collected young man he would become.

"Look at him. What a weirdo," Aren said, shaking his head. "Come on, Z."

Aren marched toward Uzochi, and though Zaire hesitated,

he followed in the end. Aren snatched one of the rubber balls off the ground. Then, when he reached Uzochi, he flung it hard at Uzochi's hands and the tablet he held.

It might've been Zaire's memory, but Uzochi remembered the impact. How the rubber had smacked into his fingers and sent the tablet to the ground. How the delicate screen had cracked, flooding the corner of the device with a streak of black that would make it difficult for Uzochi to do his work.

He watched his young self scramble to grab the tablet and look back up at Aren and Zaire.

"Remember that the next time you wanna show off, preceptor's pet," Aren snapped. "Thinking you're better than the rest of us."

Uzochi watched himself breathe in and out, wanting to say something. Instead, his eyes bubbled up with tears, noticing that others on the playground were watching as well.

Aren turned away. "Come on, Z."

Zaire didn't move at first, his gaze flicking from the crying boy to the tablet. He wanted to say something, too.

In the end, he turned and followed.

That was when Uzochi had woken up, his body soaked in sweat. He'd struggled to breathe, trying to stay as quiet as he could. He knew his mother had been watching him closely, ever since Adisa's revelation days before. She was worried, and the last thing he wanted to do was add to her concerns.

Because he was the catalyst, apparently, thanks to the nature of his abilities. The one who could connect Nubians and push them to a greater future.

Nubians like Zaire and Aren.

He let the prospect of this settle in, that he was expected to help his peers, even after they'd abandoned him or mocked him or made him feel small for being into books. Made him feel small because *they* were small. He knew what he was called by Nubians and non-Nubians alike, and the words had continued to hurt.

Uzochi groggily rose and stretched. It would soon be time to get ready. School had been canceled for the last three days while 104 worked to handle the damage from the quake, but today, Uzochi would be going back. Then, tonight, he would be expected at the first training session to be held in the Carter-Combs Theater, outside of town, away from the prying eyes of St. John Soldiers.

He'd promised to train, and so he would. But as the bitterness of Zaire's memory circled through him, Uzochi wondered if he'd made the wrong choice.

Chapter 23

Zuberi

"I just think it's so cool that you have powers. Add that to all your ass-kicking training, and you're basically a superhero."

Vriana had joined Zuberi in the park early that morning, claiming that her aunt Ekua was on one last night and she needed some fresh air. It happened like that sometimes for both girls. Whether it was Zuberi's dad or Vriana's aunt, adults had a way of obliviously adding to the pressure and stress of life.

Zuberi was working her punching bag, striking it with her fists and shins and feet while Vriana lounged nearby on an old, ratty blanket she'd brought from home. Zuberi had a feeling that Vriana's aunt wouldn't be thrilled that she'd brought a cherished Nubian heirloom out to the park to gather prickers and grass, but she didn't say any of that to her friend.

"Yeah, well, at least it explains my freak-out before," Zuberi said, wiping sweat from her forehead. "If you buy into it all, I guess."

"I think it's awesome," said Vriana, rolling over onto her

elbow. "I mean, it's bananas, with what happened to Zaire and what Uzochi can do. And scary. But like, it's still awesome. Have you figured out exactly what you're seeing? You know, the 'future selves' part?"

Zuberi hit the bag hard with her ankle, wincing at the sting of pain.

"Not exactly," she said. "But I'm trying to study up a bit on temporal realities and timelines. I guess, to keep it simple, there are different paths each person can take, right? Each decision we make produces countless possibilities and potential futures. And . . . well, I guess I can see a very small slice of that."

Vriana nodded. "Have you seen anything cool?"

"Whaddya mean?"

"I dunno. I mean, I have a feeling there's a lot that's about to change, and you're going to see some crazy shit."

Zuberi hesitated to respond. Really, the only phantoms she'd thought twice about were Lencho's. It wasn't so much about what she saw as what she'd felt. The emotions that had boiled over. She shouldn't have been able to experience such a thing, right? That was the power of an empath, at least based on what she understood from Adisa's Nubian Powers 101 lecture. But Zuberi was sure she'd both felt and seen Lencho's energy.

"I guess," Zuberi said. "You know that Lencho guy? His future selves were . . . I guess, they were angry. Really angry."

Vriana adjusted her sunglasses, leaning back so that her body was angled more to the sun. It was just cresting over the hills, Zuberi's sign that they'd need to leave soon.

"He's kinda an angry guy, huh?" Vriana said. "Not like his cousin. That guy is so mellow."

"Mellow." It wasn't the word she'd use to describe Uzochi, not after the other night. Cowardly was more like it.

"Anyway, I know you'll figure everything out," Vriana said. "You're a watcher."

Zuberi sucked her teeth. "I'm a 'watcher'? Because of my gift?"

"I just mean that you see things," Vriana said. "You see people. Not everyone does, you know."

Zuberi smiled. She could tell when Vriana was getting ready to therapize, and this was usually how it started. She returned her focus to the bag, striking in rhythm. One-two, one-two, one-two . . . and so it went for some time until Zuberi's arms ached and she needed to pause for water, looking over at Vriana again.

"Auntie won't talk about it, but do you think all Nubians are going to awaken?" Vriana asked, voice thoughtful as she blinked up at the sky. Today, she'd lined her eyes with light turquoise and added translucent flower clips to her braids.

Zuberi bit her lip. She didn't know the answer to that. From what Adisa had said, it sounded like they would, at least eventually. But here was Vriana, Nubian through and through, and she hadn't shown any signs of having a gift.

"I don't know," Zuberi said, searching her friend's expression for any sadness or jealousy. But, as always, Vriana was nothing but genuine warmth and smiles.

Zuberi checked the time on her mobile. They still had a

good ten minutes. She went back to striking the bag, channeling her emotions into each strike.

"You ever hear from Zaire?" Zuberi asked as she sparred.

Vriana shook her head. "No. I mean, we still don't actually know each other. Yeah, we kinda started talking after that encounter in the Swamp—"

"—because you accosted him after class, if I remember."

"I *greeted* him after class," Vriana said. "And I told him I wanted to get to know him, and yeah, we exchanged numbers. But that was it. I kinda got the sense that he might not be into me that way, you know? Which is cool. I could use a platonic bond."

She touched a nearby dandelion, gliding her fingertips over its fluffy surface.

"Not that Principal Todd believed me, thinking I have all sorts of intel on that boy," she said. "Oooh, that man. Trying to get me to talk shit about Zaire."

Zuberi stopped punching the bag. "What?"

Vriana glanced at her. "Yeah, remember? I told you he kept questioning me about Zaire being in the middle of the fight."

"No," Zuberi said. "I didn't know that. I never told him who was involved."

Vriana tilted her head, thinking it over. "Well, he knew when he talked to me. I don't know how, but he did. And did he have questions."

"Huh. Okay," Zuberi said. Did Principal Todd talk to anyone else? Maybe a few of the kids who'd been on the scene?

Still, if the camera footage hadn't shown Zaire transforming, there shouldn't be an issue . . . unless, maybe, someone else's footage did. And if someone had snitched, then Zaire's gift would've been revealed.

Something bitter turned in Zuberi's stomach. Zaire didn't deserve to be questioned by that creepy goon of a principal. He hadn't done anything wrong besides making unfortunate choices by running with the Divine. Sure, his transformation had sort of . . . wrecked the school. But the administrators didn't know about that.

Or did they?

Zuberi thought about the conversation she'd overheard when she left Todd's office. Who was the principal talking to and why? She thought about bringing it up to Vriana, but she knew her friend would call her suspicions yet another "Zuberi conspiracy theory" that would lead nowhere.

"So you're still not going today, huh?" Vriana asked, standing up to brush herself off.

"To the training? Hell no," Zuberi said. "I'll figure this out on my own."

Vriana rolled up the blanket, not bothering to shake it out. Her silence spoke volumes, and Zuberi glared at her.

"What?" Vriana said, holding up one hand innocently.

"I know what you're thinking," Zuberi said.

"Oh, so you can read minds now, too? Like Uzochi?"

Zuberi rolled her eyes.

Vriana giggled. "Though, to be fair, you don't *need* to be a mind reader to know that that boy has it bad for you. . . ."

"Shut up, V," Zuberi said. "He's so not my type."

"Right, because you have no type," Vriana said, grabbing

her scholar-pack. "Because you're a superhero loner who doesn't need anyone."

"Hey!"

"It's true, isn't it?" Vriana said.

"I'm with you right now, aren't I?"

Vriana scoffed. "Besides me. Sorry, but I'm just saying I think this training thing could be good for you. Even if you don't end up joining their little team or whatever. You go, you learn about what you can do, and then you make the call about what you *wanna* do. But how will you know for sure that you don't want to do this unless you check the gathering out?"

Zuberi opened her mouth to retort but realized she didn't have a proper response. As usual, her friend was annoyingly persuasive.

"Whatever," Zuberi said.

"So you'll go? I mean, I can go with you, if you want. I know I don't have gifts or whatever, but I can be moral support. And it'll be so cool to watch Nubians do their thing. I mean, Beri, this is just beyond!"

Zuberi frowned at her friend and then at the dirt, kicking it for good measure. She knew Vriana was trying to do her bubbly cheerleader thing to encourage her to go.

"I don't know," she said.

Vriana squealed. "Ooooh, that's a yes if I've ever heard one."

"Shut up," Zuberi said again, but she was grinning.

"Come on," Vriana said. "You need a shower, and then I need to study for science."

Zuberi wanted to argue—on all counts, including the

shower—but she found herself suddenly itching with antici-
pation. As much as she hated to admit it, Vriana was right.
The more information she had about who she was and what
she could do, the better.

Zuberi should've expected that, in light of what had happened to 104, someone would be blamed. And, given everything she knew, she should've expected that "someone" would
be Nubians.

She just hadn't anticipated how much worse it could get.

From the second Zuberi and Vriana had walked onto campus, Zuberi had realized that, of course, they'd figured out that
Zaire was in the fight. And even though he hadn't swung a
single punch at that Spider—Zuberi's new suspect for who'd
snitched—it was his fault.

No one could say he caused the earthquake directly,
but suddenly all Zuberi heard in the halls was about how
"Nubians bring bad luck" and how "of course the Divine kid
provoked the situation." She also overheard several preceptors
talking about the continual issues with Nubian gangs, one
teacher even proclaiming "the school is going to hell because
of *those* type of children."

No word about the Spiders, though. They, apparently,
weren't to blame.

It made Zuberi's blood boil. She could barely focus during
her classes, and she was practically a ball of rage by lunchtime.
That's when she spotted a handful of St. John Soldiers on the

premises, telling kids not to congregate in the halls and to "get a move on." She figured they must've been called in for extra security considering all that had just happened, but her intuition told her to pay attention. That perhaps all wasn't as it seemed.

One of the militiamen even let his eyes linger on Zuberi when she walked by. Whether he'd been told by Principal Todd to watch her or was just being a racist, perverted ass, she didn't know. And frankly, she didn't care. All she knew was anger as her fists tightened. She thought she might blow off steam in the gym, but when she got there, the security guard blocked her way.

"Not today," he said. "Just go to lunch."

She resisted the urge to scream. Vriana was taking lunch with her psych preceptor to ask four thousand questions, which left Zuberi alone. She could practically hear her best friend's singsong "Told you so" in her head.

"Damn it," she murmured, looking across campus. She decided to go hide out in the bathroom until her next slate of classes came around, eventually grateful to sit through chemistry and social media ethics with minimal drama save for the phantoms floating above people's heads. By the time the bell rang marking her switchover to final period, Zuberi found that she couldn't wait to get out of 104. She stomped down the steps, ignoring the militiamen with their arrogant strides and haughty glances, and hooked a corner. She started when she heard a familiar voice behind her.

"Um, Zuberi?"

She turned, and there was Uzochi in his standard brown jacket and slacks. He'd braided his hair back again, and she instantly found that she missed the fro. Not that she would tell him that.

"Yeah?" she said, crossing her arms over her chest.

"I, uh, wanted to apologize," he said, his voice low. "For when you were at my place. I should've been more supportive of your ideas about how you want to use your gift. Not cool."

Zuberi arched an eyebrow, remaining silent. Above him, three phantoms appeared, each tinged with light blue. One of them steepled his hands, another kicked the ground, and the last one touched the edges of his braids. All were nervous.

"I know you're pissed about it," he said, kicking the ground. "I wish I didn't know that, but, well . . ."

Of course he knew. The empath. She didn't know why his gift angered her so much.

"Look, I'm just trying to make the best out of a bad situation, okay?"

That made Zuberi laugh. "A bad situation?" She kept her eyes peeled, scanning the hallway for any militiamen who might approach and shoo them away.

He blinked. "Yeah. I don't know about you, but finding out I have powers that my mom never told me about isn't exactly my idea of a good time."

"Uzochi, most kids would *kill* to have powers. You know that, right?"

"Maybe other powers," Uzochi said. "Not this. And with all the schoolwork I've got—"

"Don't tell me you're seriously worrying about homework right now."

One look at Uzochi's face told Zuberi that what she'd said was the worst thing he could've heard at that moment. His features hardened, and he looked away from her. She bit her lip.

"Look, sorry," she said, sighing as she leaned back on one of the school's concrete pillars, suddenly not caring about being late to class. "I'm not . . . I'm not used to this, either. I'm kind of ticked off at my dad and other adults for keeping this big secret, but I kinda understand their perspective as well. You know, I just don't know what to do. And, well, as my friend V likes to say, I'm kind of a loner, so I'm not great at this communication stuff. I mean, I absolutely suck at it."

She gestured between them and made an exasperated face, and to her relief, he laughed. She liked the sound, the way it cracked his typically serious expression.

"I get that," he said. "I guess I'm a loner, too. I've been really focused on making something of myself. Getting a scholarship, making my mom proud. This is just kind of un-expected."

She nodded. When she was younger, she'd thought like him, that she just needed to work hard and claw her way to the top. But then she stopped to watch other Nubians, like her dad or V's aunt, people who worked harder than anyone she knew and still didn't see a path forward to a more pros-perous life. She knew it was because of the system.

But she didn't say that to Uzochi. Maybe it was Vriana in

her head still, telling her to chill out and not blast every new potential friend with her thoughts on the world.

"I decided I'm going to training today," she said instead.

This made Uzochi's eyes widen. "You are? At the theater?"

"Yep," Zuberi said. "I'm bringing V, too."

Uzochi leaned in closer. "What's her gift?"

"Nothing yet," Zuberi said. "Maybe nothing at all. She—"

At once, a flash of purple light burst across Zuberi's eyes. Sharp, vibrant, as if something had exploded right in front of her. She shut her eyes, and still she saw the light. At the same time, a pulse of energy zipped through her, the same feeling she'd experienced when Zaire's transformation had begun. Thankfully, the earth beneath them did not shake.

She opened her eyes to find Uzochi staring at her.

"You felt it, too, didn't you?" he asked, voice breathless. "The energy?"

"Is it another Nubian?" Zuberi asked, looking around. She saw nothing out of the ordinary, just classmates laughing and being silly in the halls.

Uzochi suddenly dropped to his knees, a groan escaping his lips as he pressed a hand to his temple. Zuberi plopped down beside him, putting a cautious hand on his shoulder for comfort and to shield him from passersby.

"Uzochi?" Zuberi whispered. "What's going on?"

"A scream," Uzochi gasped. "They're screaming in my mind . . . pain . . . too much . . ."

The phantoms above and behind him flared with blue light. Zuberi dipped her head back to see them. It was as though the figures were in fast-forward mode, rushing and spinning and gesturing in frenzied movements.

You see people. Not everyone does, you know.

Vriana's earlier comment floated back to her. The phantoms continued their flurried actions, and Zuberi forced herself to watch them all. Just as if she was in a fight, Zuberi knew she needed to sort through the senselessness. She needed to *really* see them, just as Vriana said she could.

Uzochi, on the ground. Uzochi, running. Uzochi, finding someone. Someone . . . someone on the ground.

Focus, girl. Focus on them and see.

Zuberi had only ever observed the phantoms of people immediately in front of her. But now she pushed herself. She gripped Uzochi's shoulder, holding on for her own sanity as she willed herself to see Uzochi and the person he stood beside in her vision.

The figure was shadow. Then, shadow and flesh. Then, flesh and bone. A face appeared. A boy's face, a boy who looked like he'd been running when he fell. He glowed purple when Uzochi's floating phantom touched him, and then—

"Sekou," Uzochi breathed next to her. "It's Sekou. My friend."

He bolted up, and Zuberi might've fallen if she hadn't been holding on to him. She let go when they were both standing, discovering that her breathing was ragged.

"Come on," Uzochi said. "We need to find him. He's . . . I can't explain it. He's not here. But he is."

Zuberi didn't ask for an explanation, simply nodding

before she and Uzochi dashed off. They couldn't run through the school, not with St. John Soldiers stalking the halls. So they moved as quickly as they could, checking hallways and peeking into rooms as a few stragglers made their way to their last class of the day. If Sekou had really collapsed, Zuberi thought there might be others who'd seen what had happened. Or rather what *would* happen. Someone who would've called for security. But the problem was, when in the future would Sekou pass out? And what would happen when he did?

A piercing shriek confirmed Zuberi's fears. She and Uzochi looked at each other and then hurried in its direction just as the bell rang for final period.

They found him by a small crowd of Nubians, passed out exactly as he'd been in Zuberi's vision. Several students were bending over, shaking him and trying to get him to come to. Others were whispering, clearly terrified. To Zuberi's relief, Vriana was there, and she rushed to her friend. Thus far, the area wasn't crawling with adults, but that would change.

"I need you and the others to go distract the militia and security guards," Zuberi insisted. "We can help him, but we can't have anyone see. You understand?"

Vriana didn't need to be told twice. She looked at the others and waved.

"Come on, y'all!" she yelled. "Let's give 'em some space and go cause a ruckus with security, all right?"

Miraculously, most of the kids left with Vriana with no question, save for one boy who Zuberi would've guessed was related to Sekou. They had the same hair, same features, same general height, though the boy had a darker complexion.

He was pushing Uzochi away, the phantoms above his head showing nothing but distrust.

"Hey," Zuberi said, bending down next to him. "I promise, we can help, okay?"

"Fuck off!" said the kid. "That's my brother. He's not breathing. He needs real help, not—"

But Uzochi had already edged in closer to Sekou and placed his hand on his shoulder. Zuberi watched with bated breath as Uzochi's phantoms moved above him. One, she swore, was crying. She refused to believe in that future. The future of failure.

"Sekou," Uzochi breathed. "It's me, Uzochi. I'm here. Come back."

"What's he doing?" Sekou's brother demanded. "What's—"

"He came into his gift," Uzochi said, eyes shut tight. "His . . . he separated from his body. I can't explain it, but he's not in there right now. His soul . . . he's trapped outside his body."

The kid had no idea what Uzochi was sputtering on about, and truthfully, Zuberi didn't get it, either. But she trusted Uzochi. She had to.

"Help him," Zuberi said, placing her hand atop Uzochi's. "Please."

She felt a pulse of energy where her hand touched his. She willed his future to be the good one, the one where he saved his friend.

"Sekou," Uzochi whispered. "Come back."

Then, like when he'd been with Zaire, the Uzochi in front of her became completely absorbed by what he was doing, his body going slack even as he maintained his grip on Sekou's shoulder. His phantoms stilled, becoming more translucent before they vanished.

Zuberi held Sekou's brother back as he began to sob. She fought back her own tears.

What if she was wrong? What if they'd entered a failed future?

She didn't dare to move. Uzochi was hunched over as his chest slowly rose and fell. Sekou's was even more still. Was he even breathing?

"Come back," she whispered. *Come back, Uzochi.*

A pause. A beat. Then, a flicker of blue.

Uzochi breathed, and he wasn't alone.

Beside him, Sekou breathed, too.

Chapter 24

Uzochi

Sekou's mind wasn't like Zaire's. In Zaire's mind, there had been a calm, sturdy quality to every element of his being that Uzochi encountered, even in a state of personal chaos. But Sekou's mind was split into thousands of pieces, each fragment wailing from the pain.

Now, though, Sekou was back in his body. Back in his body and beside Uzochi and Zuberi in the rear seat of a hover van.

Zuberi had messaged her dad the second Sekou had come back to consciousness, declaring it was an emergency and they needed to be picked up. Then, with the help of Vriana and Sekou's brother, Abdul—who still didn't seem to trust Uzochi—they were able to maneuver their way out from 104 to where Thato was waiting to pick them up.

"Adisa wasn't wrong," Thato had said when they climbed into his van. "He said you guys might run into some trouble on your first day back. You okay there, son?"

That had been directed at Sekou, but Uzochi had nodded, too. An embarrassing move that Zuberi definitely saw.

Right now, the hover van trundled above the roads that led to the outskirts of the city. Thato told them they'd be heading straight to training at the Carter-Combs, an older venue that used to be a hotspot for art before anything deemed "worthy" moved Up High, leaving abandoned many theaters, galleries, and other artistic zones still in the lower city. As the Carter-Combs was an iconic theater that hosted a plethora of Nubian artists, some lower city residents had done their best to keep it alive. But soon, public transportation routes stopped going anywhere near the Carter, redirected by Krazen St. John's many new construction projects, and the theater closed for good.

Still, Uzochi had fond memories of the venue. He knew it was named after two twentieth-century performers of stellar talent who'd transcended racism and hood life to become leading business moguls and philanthropists. Honoring the men's legacy, the theater's repertory company had prided themselves on representing people from all walks of life. Com'pa had occasionally taken Uzochi to the Carter-Combs when he was younger, making sure to find family-friendly fare that featured Nubian actors.

"Look," she had said during their first visit to the theater when Uzochi was eight, pointing to an image of Maat Leos, a Nubian heartthrob whose bronze portrait hung among others on the main lobby's brick wall. "He's one of us. That could be you one day, dear heart." Uzochi would soon realize that the Carter-Combs featured old-fashioned portraits of every single performer who'd ever graced its stage, the photos lining the majority of its passageways.

That night Uzochi and Com'pa strolled with other theater-goers into the auditorium, where sculpted stonework was bathed in a fusion of red, blue, and violet lights. The stage was surrounded by a cascading semicircle of cocobolo benches, individual seats marked by numbers and subtle notches in the wood, the layout resembling an ancient amphitheater placed indoors. Uzochi had learned about the venue's history by reading the old-school program booklets he always saved in a box at home after a show, placed in a special corner of his library. Renowned for its massive stage despite being a mid-sized venue, the Carter-Combs was designed to be holistic, offering atriums with benches and floor cushions through-out the building where guests could socialize before and after performances.

Uzochi had watched plays like *The Jaded Glider*, about a cynical Caribbean girl in green garments who could fly, and *My Heart Is Off the Court*, featuring two competitive high school basketballers who fall in love. He'd adored the shows at the Carter-Combs, especially *Glider*, riveted by its story-telling and low-tech tricks.

But the theater closed not long after he'd started attend-ing performances. Now, as Uzochi and his companions exited the hover van and looked upon the old theater, there was no denying that the once-grand place looked beaten down. In fact, Uzochi wasn't sure how it was able to avoid the ever-hungry eye of St. John Enterprises, as it looked ready for de-molition, with its peeling paint and dusty marquee. But then, as they walked closer, he noticed a small placard on the wall that answered his question: PRESERVED HISTORICAL SITE:

"We protect what's important to us," Thato said quietly
so that only Uzochi could hear. He looked at the man, finding
his energy and emotion to be genuine. Uzochi didn't know
what to say, but it didn't matter. Thato was already walking
ahead to greet another one of the adults.

The group was quickly ushered in, making their way
down a narrow, musty lobby before entering the main auditorium, walking through a pair of massive wooden doors
that had been kept open. Uzochi turned to the left, looking for a seat, suddenly surprised when he found that Zuberi,
Vriana, Abdul, and Sekou were following him. Usually, when
he attended assemblies at school, he was alone. Now he traveled with a group. They sat together on one of the benches
that faced the center of the auditorium, where Adisa was
talking to Thato in an emptied orchestra pit. Uzochi knew,
even without reading anyone's thoughts, that Thato was re-
counting what had happened at school. This was confirmed
when Adisa caught Uzochi's eyes and smiled, which made his
stomach twist and turn.

Seeking distraction, Uzochi looked around the space. He
thought he counted roughly twenty other Nubian kids from
school, all with their parents or guardians. Only Uzochi's
group had come alone, and many people looked over at them
as a result. For once, Uzochi wished he had asked his mom
to come with him, but then he caught Zuberi's eyes and took
the wish back. Com'pa already gave him too much grief about

the "clever Nubian precog" and how "charming" she was. This would've sent his mother into a frenzy.

One of the adults walked over to the auditorium's main entrance and released the latch that held the doors in place. A startling boom reverberated through the space as the doors slammed shut.

It was time to begin.

"Magnificent souls, welcome! I am because you are," Adisa bellowed from the pit, raising his arms toward the people who'd gathered before him. All chatter immediately ceased. The elder needed no microphone to be heard. "My name is Adisa Elenkwa. Many of you know me from our community meetings as the old-timer whom your parents often defer to, the one who's provided the tiniest glimpses of our homeland to newer generations. I had not believed that this time would ever come. This moment of rebirth." Adisa clasped his hands and lowered his arms.

"Nubians, beautiful Nubians," he proclaimed in a mighty voice, "the gifts that were once our birthright have been returned to us."

From the audience of Nubians, silence. Stark silence. Uzochi kept his eyes trained on Adisa.

"I speak now directly to our youth. Those of us who birthed you after we came to these harsh shores rarely spoke of the glories of our past, too traumatized by the destruction of our land and the death of our loved ones. Of losses unspeakable. But we possessed an ancient, rich story, complex in its mysteries."

No one else spoke in the theater. To Uzochi, everyone in the auditorium was holding their breath, frozen, their collective emotion a tingling, buzzing thing on his skin.

"I was one of the few scholars to have survived the cataclysm that took our land, one of the few who had devoted himself to our lore and teachings, to better understand how to guide our people. This lore, written by venerated ancestors, has chronicled moments in our history when our community was reborn. Our reality reshaped and retooled through the actions of powerful, heroic catalysts who served as leaders during pivotal moments of our history, moments when we've been laid low only to emerge stronger than before. I believe our next catalyst sits here in this theater."

Uzochi shifted his body, uncomfortable.

No, don't say that now. Please. Don't.

A smile blossomed on Adisa's lips. "Young ones, what we call the kinetic, the glorious talents that belonged to Nubians, is being restored. The power that left the bodies of your parents upon the destruction of our homeland . . . that power has begun to return to the bodies of our youth in a series of awakenings.

"In Nubia, so many of us could use our minds to soar, to literally *fly*. To levitate objects. To bathe ourselves in halos of light or move the winds with the wave of a finger. To send our thoughts to our comrades. And some of us, often the wisest, in fact, could see the future."

Silence. Not a peep from the multitude of viewers watching this thin man. Uzochi tried to observe the faces of those around him. The adults were serious but some seemed on the verge of euphoria, tears welling in their eyes, with trembling chins and fidgeting hands.

But as Uzochi took in the kids . . . he felt their confusion and bewilderment, even their betrayal and anger over not being told sooner. Emotions and thoughts permeated the air in the theater like a soup.

"Now," Adisa continued, "I have heard that at school today, there was an awakening. Young Sekou, would you please stand?"

The room turned to Sekou, who sat beside Uzochi. Immediately, Uzochi felt the boy's fear. The emotion spiked his energy, a warm magenta light. There was a hesitation, and then Sekou stood.

"Child, would you please tell us what happened?" Adisa asked, his voice kind.

Sekou swallowed. He looked around before speaking. When he did, his voice was steadier than Uzochi would've expected.

"A lot was happening for me today," Sekou said, glancing over at his brother sitting next to him. "Some stuff was happening with my family, and it was weighing on me. Also . . . stuff that's changed at school has made it kinda hard, too, you know?"

He then glanced at Uzochi, who remembered their conversation earlier about the Divine and Elevation. When he was in Sekou's mind, it had been too shattered to see much of anything. But he'd felt the fear, a constant thread.

"Sorry," Sekou said. "I'm rambling. My boy Uzochi here knows I do that. But the point is, I was really overwhelmed. Felt kinda messed up. And I kept thinking I wanted to just . . . just get away from it all. Leave and never come back."

His hands began to shake, so he clasped them together.

"I was thinking about it, over and over, at school. At the end of the day, my brother found me and he was trying to get me to calm down, but I couldn't. I just wanted to leave. And then . . . I did."

Murmurs swept the room, but Adisa held up his hand. Instantly, silence fell again.

"Explain, please," Adisa said. "Explain what happened."

"Right," Sekou said. "Well, I'll try. See, when I say I left, I mean I left my body. Suddenly, I was floating above. I was just . . . cruising in the air. And for a moment, it was incredible. I could go anywhere, man."

Uzochi felt the wonder and awe that swept the room. The silence was infinite, stretching with possibility.

Sekou shook his head. "And then I looked down."

He glanced over at Abdul, whose eyes were glassy and fierce.

"It was my body, and my brother was screaming over it," he said. "I knew something was wrong. And that's . . . that's when it felt like everything inside me broke."

More whispering. Adisa held up his hand again, then gestured for the boy to sit down. As soon as Sekou did so, Abdul embraced his brother, tears streaming down both of their faces.

"Brave boy," Adisa said. "Thank you for bearing witness

to your awakening. It is my belief that your gift, Sekou, is the ability to have your soul leave your body briefly to visit the astral plane. This is a rare and powerful ability, not one to be taken lightly. There are many Nubians who have shared your gift and found it difficult to manage. Which is why it's fortunate that someone was there to guide you back."

Now Adisa's gaze swung to Uzochi, and Uzochi's breathing spiked as the whispers around him grew. No, not just whispers. Voices begging to be heard in his mind.

Who?

Who is it?

What happened?

Why . . .

"Uzochi Will," Adisa said, gesturing to him. "Please stand."

For a wild moment, Uzochi wanted to refuse. He was the little boy again explaining fractions, and after he did, they would hate him.

But still, despite his fears, he stood.

"Son, what happened when you came upon Sekou?" Adisa asked.

Uzochi took a breath. "Well, I, um . . . I entered his mind."

The whispers sharpened, turning to hisses. Uzochi began to panic.

"I mean that I found him in the, uh, astral plane," Uzochi said, trying to be brave. He felt a wave of something at his back. Support.

You can do this, buddy.

Zuberi's voice in his head.

"I entered his mind because I'm an empath. And I think a telepath, too. So I called to Sekou, and he came back. It's really not that big of a deal."

The adults in the room exchanged looks while their children whispered. Uzochi wanted desperately to melt into the ground.

"Son, I must disagree with you," said Adisa. "As would any adult in this room, I'd wager. For what you've described is no small feat. It is the mark of someone truly special. Someone, I believe, who is our next catalyst."

"Impossible," said a woman from across the room. "All of this. It's impossible. We all know what happened. We lost our gifts. And my daughter—"

"The awakenings are sporadic as of now, dear sister," said Adisa. "Being so far from home in a wretched land devoid of love, this is to be expected. But I understand your doubt. Today, I mean to quell such anxiety so that we may move forward, powerful, united, fully present for the children of Nubia."

Adisa turned behind him, gesturing for someone to be brought forward. Uzochi watched as Thato guided a girl wearing a SWAMP FOREVER shirt to the center of the pit. Uzochi didn't recognize her, but he felt the anguish in her soul as soon as she stepped to the middle of the auditorium. Her turmoil was clear on her face, from how she clenched her teeth to her closed fists.

"This is young Keera," Adisa told the group. "She has been experiencing unimaginable pain these last two days. Traditional healers have come and gone, unable to help her, for it is not a disease which ails her. It is her kinetic gift, fighting to be free."

Keera cried out at that, falling to the floor. As she did, she began to glow, a deep, molten yellow that burned like gold. The lights in the room began to flicker, and a few people screamed in terror.

"Do not be alarmed," Adisa advised the group. "In Nubia, gifts come in all varieties, and we nurture them all. With the help of our catalyst, Keera will make a peaceful transition."

Now he waved Uzochi forward. He looked at Zuberi, wishing pitifully that she would go with him but knowing he couldn't ask such a thing. So he only nodded at her, and she nodded back at him, sending him another surge of support.

Uzochi walked the short distance from his seat to the pit to stand by Keera, feeling the press of doubt on his back. He looked to Adisa, who nodded, and then to Keera, who was now hugging her body close as she moaned.

He recognized the tiny sun inked on her forearm, the one that meant she was a member of the Divine. He recoiled, looking at Adisa. He couldn't seriously be bringing gang members here.

"Uzochi," the elder said, quietly, so that only he could hear. "This young lady needs your help."

Keera. One of the Divine. Had she been around during the recent fights, egging on the violence? Or perhaps she'd been there a year ago when two Divine had jumped Uzochi for no damn reason and slammed him against the wall, smashing the contents of his scholar-pack?

This was who he was supposed to help?

Keera let out another harsh cry as she rocked back and forth. Guilt rose in Uzochi's chest. When he looked at Adisa, he found the elder's face sharp. Insistent.

"Hey," Uzochi whispered to the girl. "I'm, um, here to help."

Her eyes flashed open at him, solid yellow, glowering. He winced but pressed on.

"I'm going to touch your shoulder, okay?" he said, holding out a tentative hand. "And then—"

"Don't touch me," Keera snarled, standing suddenly and throwing out her arm so that Uzochi lurched back. "Don't touch me!"

"Keera," Adisa advised. "Uzochi's here to help. You must let him."

The girl collapsed back to the floor. Her breathing was ragged, and she twitched there on the ground. The lights flickered again, and the pit began to heat up.

"Now, Uzochi," Adisa said, his voice low and urgent. "You must do it now."

Whatever Keera's gift was, Uzochi had a sense that it was more in line with Zaire's abilities than what he or Zuberi or Sekou could do. And so, fearing for those in the auditorium, he pressed his hand to Keera's shoulder and closed his eyes, tumbling into her mind.

Pain again, coupled with a rage that moved like lava over Uzochi. Keera's memories were as furious as she was, and Uzochi saw them in flashes: cruel words, cutting looks, the hard slap of a hand. Keera's soul rumbled beneath it all, spitting fire that threatened to spill over.

What was her gift?

Uzochi couldn't think of that. He had to call her back.

Keera, he sent. *I'm here. Come back to your body. Accept your gift into your mind. Think of it like a guest, a welcome guest rather than an intruder.*

His words felt like the meditative nonsense his mom was into, but it seemed like the right thing to say. Sekou had inspired the idea when he'd spoken earlier about something inside him breaking. After all, if something broke, it only needed to be pieced back together. That was what Com'pa had told him thousands of times, whether referring to a shattered pot or a cracked screen.

Come back, he sent again. *I'll help you. I promise.*

Little by little, the fire inside Keera dimmed. Her memories receded, and he saw the pulsing yellow core of her energy underneath it all. A brilliant miniature sun that he reached for, holding it in place until Keera could hold it on her own.

And then, with a breath, he left her mind.

The room exploded in applause. Uzochi could barely open his eyes, but when he did, he saw Adisa looking down at him, shaking his head and smiling, reaching down to take Uzochi's hand as he helped him stand.

"My son," he said softly. "This is only the beginning."

Chapter 25

Sandra

Sandra had gradually come to see her primary bedroom, with its softly contoured walls and silken sheets and modern art, as her command center, a place where she could feel safe and scheme. This she knew to be true as she stood by one of her windows, the sun bright and warm on her face, a series of holo-documents floating above her desk just feet away.

A few days had passed since the latest batch of lower-city residents had ascended, a particular cluster of gang members that she was very interested in. Krazen couldn't hide them from her forever.

And indeed, Sandra had managed to find the crew. She'd broken one of her father's biggest taboos and tapped right into the special mics she'd had planted in his office. She listened to every word he uttered, from the mundane to the crass, bypassing the antisurveillance tech she knew he'd installed in the space. The autogenerated transcripts of his talks now floated above her desk, just a few feet from where she stood. She'd studied the documents for hours, letting the truth of what she'd read sink in.

She'd given him the choice, to let her in and reveal what he and Tilly were concocting. But he'd denied her, as per usual. It didn't matter, though. She'd learned what she needed to learn.

Her father was collecting Nubians with some sort of special powers. So, apparently, was someone else—some geezer named Adisa, working out of a rundown lower-city theater. Sandra was fascinated, never having dreamed that she would have access to beings who were paranormals, having heard rumors about people with special powers in other parts of the world. But mostly she wondered what her father had in mind.

He'd told Lencho and his crew that he wanted them all for a specialized militia unit, which was fine. But Sandra had never known Krazen St. John to think small.

There was a larger plan in motion.

Sandra just had to figure out what it was.

Chapter 26

Lencho

Lencho's body burned.

As he jogged around the state-of-the-art track he'd come to love, he realized he was beyond sore. With weeks of intense toil, his muscles no longer felt pain in the traditional way. This wasn't the soreness brought on by running or lifting weights. That had faded after the first few days. Instead, Lencho spent his days feeling like he was a battery, filled to the brim with energy.

It helped that he had a steady supply of opponents to train with and, in turn, drain. He was careful with them all, knowing they were his family. He never let himself lose control. Always, always, he had to keep things locked down.

Most of the Divine had come to Krazen, while the so-called Children had been brought to Adisa by their parents. Lencho and a few of the others heard rumblings about the gatherings at the old theater, the place for Nubians to turn to and learn of their history. Regardless, Lencho had decided to limit news from the lower city. He was starting anew, marking his ascension with a fresh attitude and fresh gear, not thinking about Nubians in the Swamp or his fucked-up family. He'd gotten rid of his decrepit mobile, slowly learning how to use the slimmest, sleekest phone he'd ever handled in his life while constantly observing sky city citizens, checking out how they walked and talked and dressed. Lencho was fascinated by their casual panache and entitlement and nonchalance about their implants. Would he eventually fit in, even with his gift? Could he maybe get implants one day as well?

Those were questions for a later time. For now, the crew had been placed in a former college dorm down the street from the training facility where they would hone their gifts. A domestic staff would take care of all their needs, including around-the-clock cleaning, maintaining a fully equipped kitchen, meal prep, and facility tutorials. Each member of the gang had their own private bedroom and shower scattered across two floors, with some basic wardrobe items already placed in their closets. The building manager, Jack, lived on the top floor and offered the kids a peek into his place, which was an art lover's dream with its assortment of paintings and wall hangings.

On the first night, the Divine had gathered in the big common area, a resplendent open-air lounge that seemed fit for a reality holo. They'd all looked at each other, silence enveloping the room save for the buzzing of two squat janitorial droids buffing the floor. And then Nnneka shot up from the couch and screeched, "We've fuckin' ascended, you mangy beyotches!" right before she disappeared in a puff of purple smoke, reappearing a few feet away. A brief glimpse of what they'd just discovered was her gift. Teleportation.

Aren had knocked Lencho on his shoulder as well, a love tap of thanks, the Divine leader having come a long way since that fateful evening when he sat in Krazen's office. And then pandemonium erupted as the gang started to shriek and shout and play music and party through the night, Lencho's heart swelling with pride.

I did this, he thought as the Divine got drunk and salacious, bouncing off the gleaming gray walls of their new home.

I did this.

Now, as Lencho rose from the bed that morphed itself to conform to his every movement, he blinked, stretching his tight muscles. He still had to take a moment to make sure once again that he wasn't dreaming, that this was now his reality. The roach-ridden baseboards and crumbling walls of his room at the Jungle still lingered in his head even with the blue-silver alloy surfaces that now greeted him everywhere he turned, not a stain or speck of dust in sight.

He was still the first of the Divine to rise in the morning besides Lara, and so, not expecting to run into anyone, he walked into the common lounge area, which was a mess as a result of the crew's recent antics. Lencho padded to the kitchen, wishing he'd remembered to put on socks before getting out of bed, the floor so cold on his feet that it was painful. He waved his hand over the small counter sensor and the kitchen took on a soft yellow glow, light emanating from several panels placed throughout the space.

Lencho opened the fridge door, picking up an oblong bottle of green liquid that he identified as a spinach-berry smoothie with extra protein, remembering Jack identifying the concoction during the property tour. He peered at the mess in the common area, embarrassed, thankful that a custodial manager would come soon with janitorial droids. Once he'd settled back in his room, he did three hundred push-ups and sit-ups. He'd figured out how to enter a state of calm so he could drift off to sleep, but even when he woke up, he could still feel the energy he'd siphoned from others the previous day and night coursing through his body, yearning to be released. He regularly descended to Manhattan on the low at night to find folks to drain. He simply couldn't imagine walking around, leeching folks Up High outside his training sessions.

Lencho walked into his private bathroom and took a shower, trying to remember how to manipulate the array of multicolored sensors embedded in the walls that could control everything from water temperature and pressure to overhead lights. He found the one setting he liked, basking himself in a cool red glow with a misty water pressure option, wishing he could stay in the shower for hours.

The itinerary for the day: continue training. Continue recruiting Divine members and other random kids who didn't want to be up under Adisa to join them all Up High. In other words, the good life of living in the sky.

Lencho had a good ninety minutes before the training would commence, so he opened up the tablet that came with his room, finding that the instructions were intuitive like Jack had said. Everything was presented as a 3-D hologram, even basic articles. Just as he was figuring out how to get on social and close the cascade of holos he'd launched, a starred document popped up from the screen, its title catching his eye.

NUBIAN LORE FOR LENCHO WILL, COURTESY OF KRAZEN ST. JOHN

Whoa.

Lencho immersed himself in the reading, particularly interested when the document got into the specifics of Nubian culture, including how the island's capital city was founded. As he scrolled through the holos, he came across several highlighted paragraphs focusing on the existence of Nubian catalysts, powerful beings who took their society to the next level.

It made him wonder, how did Krazen have access to such information? And why hadn't his parents or other adults in the community ever spoken about this?

He heard a knock at the door.

"Coming," he yelled out, and crossed over to the door, taking a moment to remember that it would swish open if he lightly touched a sensor panel, per Jack's instructions.

"Um, who is it?"

"Sandra, silly."

Of course.

Over time, the girl had become Lencho's confidante, having a way of listening that made him feel, well, heard. And he was happy to tell her everything about the training, how it was going, who was able to do what. She drank up his words while giving him tips about sky city life, like where other kids their age hung out, where to shop and chill.

A true friend who also happened to be one of the most gorgeous human beings he'd ever set eyes on.

"Wanna go for a walk?" she asked the moment he opened the door.

He'd never wanted anything more.

"There're talks of another powerful Nubian," Sandra told Lencho, speaking in a low, breathy voice. The clacking of her silver heels echoed through the glass dome where she and Lencho walked.

The two were surrounded by gardens that stretched from floor to ceiling, every corner of the dome filled with greens, blues, yellows, and reds. They were the flowers and plants that Lencho had read were extinct, wrecked by climate change or deforestation or both. But here, in the Up High, they were kept safe under the glass, a haven for citizens to walk through when they needed space to think.

Or, in Sandra's case, space to speak to Lencho without being overheard.

Lencho hadn't fully deduced the relationship between Sandra and her father. He found it beyond strange that she usually referred to him by his first name, something that would have been unthinkable for most Nubians when it came to their parents. Having lived with Kefle for his entire life, he also knew that some of Krazen's words to his daughter consisted of the sharpest of cuts. He watched how they played out on Sandra's face, any impact wiped clean with her next smile. He'd even figured out that Sandra had discovered on her own that Nubians were coming into their gifts, showing up unannounced at the Divine training facility, much to her dad's dismay.

The only inkling Lencho got of her true feelings was during their walks, when she asked him questions and advised him on how to become, in her words, "essential" to her father.

"Everything is always a test," she'd told him during their first stroll through the gardens. "He wants to see what you can do. No, not your ability. *You,* as a mind, as a thinker. A leader."

A leader. Here, where the Divine lived in a set of dormitories and trained together, Aren retained his leadership role, with Lara still serving as his lieutenant. It wasn't only the Divine who respected them, either. How many times had Lencho seen Aren and Lara pulled into meetings in Krazen's office or invited to lunch? He knew there was credence to what Sandra said.

She was right. It wasn't the ability that mattered. In that way, Lencho outshone them all. But he couldn't just be a powerhouse. He had to be someone Krazen saw as an equal, and that came down to how Krazen saw his mind.

"So who is it?" Lencho asked Sandra, pausing in front of a flower that looked like a bluebird. "Who's the most powerful Nubian?"

Sandra looked around, lowering her voice. "Keera, one of your old gang buddies. She turned Dad down when he offered her a path to ascension, and my sources say she's been training with the Children ever since she awoke to her gift."

Keera. The flighty Divine girl? What could she possibly do?

"Don't look like that," Sandra scolded. "You're being so primitive. Girls can be quite powerful, too, you know."

"Of course. That's not what I was thinking," Lencho said. "I just know Keera. She's a little headstrong, but not particularly intimidating."

"Well, word is she might be able to start fires . . . maybe *explosions*," Sandra said. "And if Krazen could get his hands on a power like that . . ."

She made a move like a bomb going off with her hands.

Lencho's stomach dropped. That kind of power . . . well, it might actually be a problem. He imagined it in the wrong hands . . .

"Of course, I told him I still think he's looking for the wrong Nubians," Sandra said, shaking her head. "He's too focused on the flashy gifts. We need more intellectual abilities."

Lencho laughed. "Sandra, he's building a militia unit. What you want him to do, find someone who's a really good reader?"

She rolled her eyes. "Make fun all you want. If Krazen wants to take this army to the next level, it's going to require him to look a little deeper."

Lencho just shook his head. Here was where he and Sandra differed. Krazen was seeking raw power, which was exactly what he should be looking for. After all, power was the last word in every argument Lencho ever had.

"Say," Sandra said, tapping her chin, "that reminds me. I've also been hearing some whispers about your cousin. Something about him being the 'catalyst.' That mean anything to you?"

Lencho's blood ran cold. It was always a delicate balance for him when his cousin was brought up because it had become impossible *not* to hear about Uzochi.

Uzochi, the empath. Uzochi, the catalyst. Uzochi, who'd "saved" Zaire.

All of it was bullshit.

"It sounds like a fucking marketing tactic for Adisa to get more people to join him," Lencho snapped. "To say he has a savior on his side. Desperation, nothing more."

Sandra arched a perfectly manicured eyebrow. "Relax. It was just a question."

"It's a stupid question," Lencho said, turning on her. "So don't ask it again."

As the words left his lips, Lencho regretted them. He saw the hurt flash through Sandra's light eyes. Sandra, who'd taken him in and told him secrets so that he could impress her father. The person who'd brought him up here in the first place. He opened his mouth to apologize but was cut off by another voice.

"I'm afraid I agree with Lencho," said Krazen, appearing from around the garden's next corner. Lencho knew that, even if he couldn't see them, black-clad militia guards waited in the wings, ready to protect their boss at a moment's notice.

Lencho straightened immediately, dipping his head in a

bow to Krazen. In return, Krazen smiled and stepped forward, clapping Lencho on the shoulder.

"So this is where the pair of you go for your secret chats?" Krazen asked lazily. "Or should I say arguments? Romantic."

Lencho blushed. The last thing he needed was his boss thinking he had the hots for his daughter. Even if, well . . .

"Just hashing things out, Krazen," Sandra said, waving her hand. "And weren't you the one who taught me that opposing views push better ideas?"

He nodded. "Absolutely. And how has Lencho pushed you, Sandra?"

She unleashed a saccharine smile. "I think it's more how I've pushed him."

This was the kind of verbal standoff Lencho hated, the sparring making him uncomfortable. He shifted on his feet, looking away.

"I'm just saying," Sandra continued, "brute force is one thing, and we have that covered. But what about abilities of the mind? What about affairs that need a tad more finesse?"

"Pleased as I am that you have thoughts on this, I am *not* interested in altering my plan," Krazen said, his voice an icy fist.

Lencho could see Sandra's point. He could. But he also knew that Krazen wasn't going to budge, at least not until they had someone supremely powerful join his militia.

Someone like . . .

"We should ambush them," Lencho said suddenly, his mind whirring. "Grab Keera and maybe anyone else who'd be an asset. The most gifted."

Krazen blinked, his brows knitting together. Next to him, Sandra's face was unreadable.

"We know they're meeting at that run-down theater, right?" Lencho continued when neither of them answered. "Training or whatever. So we wait, maybe stage some kind of diversion, and then we grab 'em."

"I can't look like I'm kidnapping children, Lencho," Krazen said. "Remember, you came of your own accord. That's important."

Sandra's eyes flashed at her father, but she said nothing.

Lencho pressed on. "We'll do it without you or any of your guys. Divine kids only. They'll think it's gang stuff, and no one will know it comes back to you. And the kids that we bring . . . we'll just show them that it's better. Once they're here, they'll want to stay. How could they not?" He paused, glancing over at Sandra, knowing he was about to reveal something that he suspected she didn't know. "Think about how I was first brought to the Up High. I . . . I didn't have a choice, but look what ultimately happened."

"I'm sorry, Lencho, but your idea . . . sounds ludicrous," Sandra said. She looked away, seemingly uncomfortable as an awkward, long silence descended upon the group.

"Actually, it's not a bad plan," Krazen finally said, seemingly paying no mind to his daughter's comment. "And you can convince Aren to do this?"

"I'll do it," Lencho said. "Aren can . . . support this time. Because I really think I can pull this off. You know, with my connections and everything."

Uzochi.

That was the connection he wasn't naming but that they all knew he was talking about. He was offering to use his cousin to get them the information they needed. To betray his own family.

No. Not betray. After all, this was his home now, and this was his family. Blood was nothing to Lencho. Was it ever?

"Sandra," Krazen said, his voice soft. "Leave us."

Lencho glanced at the girl, looking for that familiar, telltale hurt, but her face was as undecipherable as ever as she nodded and turned on her heels. Only when she reached the end of the path did she look back, a scowl on her lips, and then she was gone.

Krazen sighed after she disappeared. "She's been spying, I'm afraid."

Lencho peered down. "Well, yeah, I mean . . ."

Krazen waved his hand dismissively. "It's fine. An annoyance that I'll one day have to . . . correct. But honestly, she would have found out about the Divine and gifted Nubians eventually, so perhaps I could have been more transparent with my intentions. My daughter, though quite intelligent, is sometimes too ambitious for her own good. I can't have her interfering with my affairs."

"I guess you're not so crazy about us hanging out, huh?" Lencho replied.

"Lencho, please, don't worry about it at all," Krazen said. "As I said, my daughter is smart. I figured if you formed a connection that you would confide in her. She's a valuable resource, especially for someone who's recently ascended. But that isn't why I wanted to speak to you."

This was all so . . . odd. Not only was Krazen admitting that he'd been wrong to keep a secret from his daughter—something Lencho could never imagine Kefle doing—but he was also telling Lencho that he trusted him.

Lencho felt dizzy.

"I need you to know that I have faith in you," Krazen continued. "You've been right about everything from the start. Your plan to sell Elevation at the school . . . impressive. Strategic, rational, unsentimental. The revenue would have been quite small, of course, but such operations can lead to bigger things."

"I have to admit I was shocked you knew about that."

"It is my business to know everything about my products," Krazen said. "And yes, they are my products. My way of giving a piece of the Up High to those down below."

Something in Lencho ran cold at those words as he struggled to comprehend what the Sky King was telling him. Elevation . . .

Elevation came from Krazen?

"Power is a complicated beast," Krazen said, turning to look at the greenery around them. "To hold it, you must have multiple pieces on the board. People will always look for ways to chase new highs, especially if they feel lost dealing with our altered world and are unable to actually live Up High to find peace of mind. I thought, why not give them something to help them chase *this* particular high, to indulge in this fantasy of sky life? The demand was there, and I could provide the supply."

Lencho suddenly felt off. He couldn't erase what he'd seen of those he'd sold to, the way the drug changed them. He'd always known Elevation came from somewhere. But . . . from the man who ran St. John Enterprises?

"I'm telling you these things," Krazen continued, starting to stroll, "because I know I can trust you. You have a mind for all of this, and it's time to put it to use. Like this plan. It has its merits, but you need to be the one to convince the crew to embrace the plan as well, the same way you sold them on the notion of moving to the sky. Let's not waste time. All of you need to think about securing your future."

Lencho nodded. "Yeah, I get it. I know my crew might be rough around the edges, sir, but we're not looking for hand-outs. We're hard workers. They'll understand the plan."

"And they'll be okay confronting your own people at the theater?"

Lencho shrugged. "I don't know if those kids and elders are my *people*, like you said. The Divine's my family now, but yeah, I'm fine with it."

Krazen stopped walking and looked at Lencho. It was a deep stare, one of complete concentration.

"You're extraordinary, Lencho, and not just because of your gifts," Krazen said, pausing briefly to let the words settle. "It's because of who you are, your mettle and vision. If I'd been blessed to have a son"—Krazen looked to the sky, letting out a deep breath—"I certainly hope he would've been someone like you."

Lencho had never heard such words before.

"I think it's a damn shame how your own people have treated you," Krazen continued, his voice deep, resonant. "I don't know why you joined the Divine, but I do know that people who feel safe and loved don't end up squatting in a tenement. You were abandoned by older generations of Nubians and left to suffer. Atrocious. You owe those people nothing. You understand me? Nothing."

Lencho couldn't hold it anymore. Tears streamed down his cheeks, and he glanced around, hoping that whatever soldiers were nearby couldn't see him crying like a pathetic kid. His own father treated him like dirt tracked in from outside, but Krazen St. John saw his potential.

"I believe in you," Krazen said, placing his hand on Lencho's shoulder. "And I don't believe in just anyone."

The words stirred something powerful inside Lencho, robbing him of his voice.

"I'll leave you to plan," Krazen said, dropping his hand. "Good luck, my boy."

The words burned through Lencho, lighting him on fire as if he'd just drained someone. He felt everything coming together, a future that he would lead.

A future where he was special, anointed by the Sky King himself.

Chapter 27

Sandra

"You can't really believe his plan will work."

Sandra was done playing nice. After Lencho had left the garden, she'd marched straight to her father's office and waited until he arrived. Now that he was here, she was through. If he was going to let Lencho ruin absolutely everything he'd been working toward, then there needed to be a confrontation.

Krazen settled down at his desk, tapping the back of his neck so that the door to his office closed and blended into the wall. Sandra was happy for the privacy. The last thing she needed was that leech Tilly wandering in.

"So you're not hiding any longer?" Krazen asked. "You're admitting to me that you've been actively looking into my business with the Nubians? I knew you'd discovered they were gifted, but what else do you know?"

Sandra took in a breath. "Yes, I know about the Nubians and your militia," she said, not caring about her father's anger for the moment. "But this is a terrible way to operate. You must know that."

"Is it?" Krazen asked. "I think everything's going supremely well considering we didn't know there were any Nubians with gifts left in the world."

"Which is exactly why you shouldn't be acting rashly! This is uncharted territory. This is . . . this will be life-changing. You can't really be considering Lencho's awful plan."

"I see you're emotional," Krazen said. "Are you sure you want to discuss this now?"

"I am *not* emotional," Sandra snapped. "I'm passionate because you and I both know that this is going to end in chaos."

"Do we?" Krazen said lazily, steepling his hands.

"Yes!" Sandra shouted. "Lencho has big dreams but didn't even have the wherewithal to call you or that numbskull Tilly before deciding to ascend. He just *showed up* at the elevator towers. What would've happened if I hadn't arrived to escort him to the sky? I mean, he's just so green. And you're relying on him for tactical advice? People are going to get hurt, Father. You're throwing kids into the fire who've been training for, what, two or three weeks? Not even a month. They're not ready!"

"Of course they aren't," Krazen said, a smile twitching on his face.

"So then you agree!" Sandra said, slamming her hands down on his desk. "You know they'll hurt each other. Hell, they'll probably blow up the damn theater and a good chunk of Manhattan!"

Sandra breathed hard. She'd never shouted at her father before. Never smacked a desk or a table. She saw that strands of her ponytail had come loose and now floated in her line of vision.

Krazen didn't speak right away. He leaned back in his chair, watching her, the silence so suffocating that she feared she would drown.

When he did speak, his voice was level. Calm.

"My dear daughter," he said, "you really think I don't know this?"

Sandra glared at him. "Of course you don't. You're so fixated on building a new militia now for whatever reason, and you're not thinking of the future. What you should be focusing on is convincing Uzochi—"

Krazen laughed. "And upset Lencho? Sandra, Sandra, when you have a person like Lencho in your grasp, you keep them there. As long as we have Lencho, we don't need his cousin."

"But Nubian elders say Uzochi's the catalyst."

"So say the elders," Krazen said. "The same elders who have no explanation for why these powers have suddenly reappeared among a new generation. All of this is a happy accident, Sandra, and we're playing this game as it develops. But so far, I've been right about all of it—and you would do well to trust me."

Krazen glared at her now, his eyes harboring the look that said he was about to deliver his worst blows. Sandra steeled herself, unafraid and defiant.

"Actually," he said, "now that I think of it, there is one thing I've been wrong about quite recently."

He leaned back in his chair.

"I told those Divine urchins that all Nubians have gifts," he said. "But it would appear I was wrong."

"What are you talking about?" Sandra spat.

"You, my daughter," he said. "Your own mother was Nubian. And yet here you are, not a gift in sight."

All around Sandra, the room seemed to spin. The words her father had just spewed . . . didn't make sense. Because Sandra's mother had died when she was young, so young that she didn't have memories of the woman. So young that . . .

"No," Sandra whispered. "You hate Nubians."

"'Hate' is a strong word," Krazen said. "And a false one. Nubians are useful. Take the Nubians here, training. For a long time, they served me in a minute way by dealing Elevation, though of course they didn't know that I made the very drug they were scrambling to sell. Now they serve me by preparing to join my militia. I couldn't hate people who help me so. Every piece in the puzzle has a purpose, Sandra."

Words. Endless words, but she only heard the dull roar in her ears.

"But yes," he said, "your mother was Nubian. Beautiful, headstrong, powerful. Yet it appears she hadn't passed down *all* of her traits. Of course, it's funny that you're so focused on Uzochi. I've heard the boy is helping others to awaken. Maybe he could help you . . . but no. I would've known if you had special abilities. I've seen enough to know that no Nubian gift resides in you, unless that gift is stubbornness."

The words felt like a slap across the face, and Sandra willed herself not to cry. She shut her mouth and tilted her chin down. A traitorous tear slipped down her cheek, but she turned her back to her father so that he couldn't see. Behind her, he spoke.

"You think I'm being harsh, but this is what you need to hear," Krazen said. "You think you've outwitted me, but you haven't. You're playing a game. I'm running an empire."

Now Sandra turned. "I'm playing the same game you are, Father. And I know you're wrong."

He chuckled. "Do you? As I told you before, I know Lencho's plan will fail—at least, in the way he intends it. There will be destruction. In fact, I'll make sure of it."

Sandra blanched. "But why?"

"Why?" Krazen shook his head, pressing his wrist implant so that a holo appeared between them showing video footage of people running and screaming outside a building. It was the footage Sandra knew too well, shown every year.

The UN Massacre.

"Every few years, Sandra, they get restless," he said. "I have to remind them what I am to them. Who I am. People are simple, so their reminders must be clear. You must show rather than tell."

Sandra blinked, not understanding what her father was saying. She looked from him to the holo, which cast a glow across his face.

"They will be a means to a greater end," Krazen said, "a way for this city to see just how much they need me and how dangerous these Nubian brats potentially are to their safety. Only by fighting fire with fire will we be safe, and thus I will be as indispensable to them now as I was all those years ago."

It dawned on Sandra, then, what her father intended to do. How he intended to use Lencho and the others.

Just as he'd used a terrorist attack all those years ago.

"Make yourself indispensable, Sandra," Krazen said simply, clicking off the holo. "That is how you win."

Chapter 28

Uzochi

"Catalyst." The term spun constantly in Uzochi's head, something he'd heard almost every day since the gathering with Sekou and the others. "Catalyst." The word that tumbled from so many adult tongues and rose to the surface of people's minds as he walked by. Uzochi had barely gotten used to hearing the word "empath." Now his own mother no longer called him "dear heart" but "my noble catalyst," her eyes twinkling.

Uzochi Will was the youngest catalyst in recorded Nubian history, the one who would surely lead his people to the next stage of their evolution, though no one seemed clear about what exactly that might be.

He thought the concept was ridiculous, that he had absolutely no idea how to take Nubians to the next level. Adisa declared it wasn't something that could be forced, that his role in shaping Nubian destiny would become clear over time.

The elder had so many things for Uzochi to do or learn

or practice, and that was on top of the constant awakenings he had to deal with. Never mind how each one left him weak with unfamiliar, haunting memories gleaned from someone's mind. No, Adisa didn't care about those things.

Not that Uzochi asked. He didn't need to. That was his curse, after all. In every moment he spent with Adisa, he heard the urgency of the man's thoughts. How he wanted more from Uzochi, even though he barely had anything else to give.

It had gotten so bad that Uzochi had started to hide out on his own. Thankfully, the theater had several classrooms once used for workshops, with the third floor offering a small commissary and living quarters for performers who needed housing while they starred in a production.

Uzochi was sitting in such a room now. He stared down at his mobile, reading the administrators' text sent from 104 for the twelfth time. The student affairs office wanted to know if he wished to have his credits validated to receive his diploma. He understood the unspoken assumption: that after being absent for so long, perhaps he'd decided to leave school permanently, that he wasn't coming back.

It had been all Uzochi could do to keep from crying when he'd received the message. For the past few weeks he'd had almost no time for schoolwork, not even able to switch to homeschooling protocols, not considering the assortment of Nubian kids who'd awoken to their powers after Sekou and Keera, not when he seemed to be the only one who could immediately guide them to the inner expressions of their gifts, easing them through their trauma and confusion and revulsion. Not when he had to sit in meeting after meeting with the elders and learn as much as he could about Nubian history and lore and subtextual prophecy and how the kinetic *used* to operate and how the kinetic *might* operate now, with no one understanding why teens were awakening to their gifts after the kinetic had abandoned a previous generation.

Everybody needed Uzochi. No one seemed to worry that it would cost him his dreams.

He stared at the text again, his chest tight. According to his guidance counselors, Up High universities generally wanted to see a full four years of high school on a student's transcript before making scholarship offers to lower-city residents. Would they make an exception for him?

He could validate his credits and graduate now and still be competitive elsewhere, getting a scholarship for a college in the lower city. Or maybe he could figure out other options to get to an Up High university if they wouldn't compromise about their four-years rule. *Others have it worse,* he tried to tell himself. Maybe he could talk to his counselors, see if he could come back in the fall after things had settled down with the awakenings.

A sobering thought hit him: the awakenings might never end and he would be stuck like this forever.

"Damn it," Uzochi said, slamming his fist into a nearby wall. Immediately, he regretted it. Nothing happened to the plaster, but his fist stung.

"What'd that wall do to you, buddy?"

Uzochi whipped around to the open doorway where

Zuberi leaned. One of her eyebrows was raised, a grin playing on her face. Uzochi looked away. He didn't want her to see him like this. Pitiful.

"Hey," she said, striding into the room. "Sorry. I was just trying to be funny."

He nodded. "Yeah, no, I get it. And I'm the one who's sorry. Just not really in a laughing mood."

"I've noticed. You're working a little too hard, you know."

He nodded again, unable to find anything that didn't sound terrible to say back. So he pulled up the message from 104 and turned it so she could read it herself.

Waves of care radiated from Zuberi. "Uzochi," she said. "You don't have to be here all the time. You can go to school. The rest of us still go."

He shook his head. "You don't get it, okay? I have to be here. I have to train every day, and be there for the others. And no one cares what it does to me."

"Excuse me?" she said, eyes narrowing. "Pretty sure I'm standing right here, caring."

He laughed. He hated how cold his laugh sounded. Like his cousin, or even his uncle.

Had his dad laughed like that? And how had he handled being a catalyst? Probably better than Uzochi. His dad had faced down an unimaginable storm for his people, but he was crying over goddamn schoolwork.

"You don't have to be a martyr," Zuberi said, stepping closer to him again. "And look, I get it. It's hard being alone. But you have people here who want to help you."

"Do I?" Uzochi said, the ghost of the laugh still on his lips. "Because I'm pretty sure I can hear what everyone thinks of me. And guess what? None of it's changed. They see me the same way they always did."

A loser. A Goody Two-shoes. Someone who got lucky. Someone who would fail. A show-off. A weirdo who listened to your private thoughts.

As if he had a choice in any of this.

"Then maybe you're listening to the wrong people," Zuberi said, her voice softer now. She touched Uzochi's chin lightly with her fingertips, turning his face so that she was looking right into his eyes. "I don't think of you that way. And neither does Vriana or Sekou or Keera. Hell, you've even grown on Abdul."

And Uzochi knew she was telling the truth, for he could feel it. Zuberi believed in Uzochi completely. She had ever since that first moment when she'd asked him to help Zaire.

But Zuberi didn't know that Uzochi hated the burden of being catalyst. She didn't know how often he wanted to run away. She believed in Uzochi, the hero, but she would loathe who he really was.

A coward who wanted to leave.

"Look, I know this is hard," Zuberi said with a sigh. "We never expected this, right? But we're doing the best we can. And, hey, we know each other because of all this now, don't we?"

Her face was so close that he could see just how silver her scar was up close. Her eyes shone brighter than ever, and

Uzochi could've fallen into them. She made him want to stay. She made him think that, maybe, he could endure it all. As long as she was there to anchor him, maybe he could handle the pressure.

Zuberi's energy was warmer, and she glowed softly in his mind. He had learned, through his training, to raise the shield and tune out certain voices. As much as he didn't want to, he tuned her out as well. He did so out of respect, and, to be honest, out of fear of what he might discover.

What did she want from him now? It would be so easy to find out. He could just peek. She wouldn't even know.

His mind brushed against hers as they moved closer.

Zuberi's eyes fluttered shut.

Maybe he wouldn't need to look in her mind after all.

"There you are!"

Uzochi and Zuberi snapped apart. It was Sekou, and his face paled at the sight of the two of them in the empty classroom.

"Shit," Sekou said quickly. "Um, sorry, I can—"

"No, it's cool," Zuberi said. "Was just giving a pep talk. I, uh, have to meet V anyway."

She looked back at Uzochi. "You cool?"

He nodded. He was cool. Feeling a tad murderous toward Sekou, but otherwise, cool.

"Right," she said. "I, um, I guess I'll see you."

And that was it. She bolted, leaving Sekou grimacing in her wake.

"Man, I am so, so sorry," Sekou said. "Adisa just told me to come get you and—"

Adisa. Of course. Because Uzochi could never have a moment to himself.

"What does he need now?" he asked, not bothering to keep the harshness out of his tone.

Sekou grinned. "It's my brother. I think he's awakening."

Another Nubian for Uzochi to help. Another person who needed him. At least it was Sekou's brother, which made it easier for Uzochi to nod and smile even though annoyance prickled at his mind.

As soon as Sekou turned, though, Uzochi let the smile fall. He was tired of giving so much of himself for so many.

What would happen when he had nothing left to give?

As Uzochi expected, the awakening left him drained. His head pounded, crowded with the memories of yet another person, though he was happy to see that Abdul was revealed to be an elemental who controlled air, earth, fire, and water. He'd barely sat down on a bench in one of the theater's labyrinthine hallways when Adisa ran out of a meeting room to be at his side, the elder pacing and full of energy.

"You're getting better, Uzochi," Adisa said. "Swifter. It's just as we discussed before. You're navigating the energy rather than letting it overwhelm you."

Normally, Uzochi would have glowed at such praise from a teacher. But he was too tired, and Adisa's words rang hollow to him. He could barely nod.

"Uzochi? Are you all right?" Adisa said, pausing his pacing to look down at Uzochi.

No. Of course he wasn't. He was running on fumes. Wasn't that obvious?

"Just tired," he lied.

"Is it your field?" Adisa asked. "Are you maintaining it? Practicing? Visualizing emotion as energy?"

Uzochi resisted the urge to scream. "Yeah, Baba. Always."

"It should feel natural. Remember, never allow yourself to be consumed by the chaos of those who surround you," Adisa continued. "Maintain your field so that the energy of others becomes inconsequential. Eventually, you could even expand to a—"

"Baba, I get it," Uzochi snapped. "It's not the field, okay? It's just been a tough day."

Uzochi knew he sounded rude. More than rude. To talk to an elder this way was unacceptable, and he'd eventually hear it from his mom for his behavior. But at the moment, he couldn't care. He was nearly shaking with rage, with anxiety. With everything. He looked away from Adisa, unable to bear the elder's judgment.

"Uzochi," Adisa said, voice softening as he settled down next to him. "I'm sorry. I should've realized the strain all of this would put on you. If there were more time, I'd give it to you. But we must act swiftly in rebuilding our community."

Uzochi said nothing.

"I know how challenging this must be for you, child," Adisa said, "but you've been exemplary in mastering your abilities and helping the others. Your finesse with the kinetic is un-precedented. You would have been a prodigy at our temples back in Nubia."

"Yeah, well, you know what?" Uzochi folded his arms. "We're not in Nubia."

There, he'd said it.

"What?" Adisa lurched backward on the bench.

"We're not in Nubia, Baba!" Uzochi uncrossed his arms and fidgeted as his voice rose. "We're . . . not . . . in Nubia. You and the elders keep on talking about the rebirth of Nubia, the future of Nubia, what the return of the kinetic means for reestablishing Nubia . . . Nubia this, Nubia that. But we're not in Nubia. We're in New York." Uzochi took a deep breath. "Baba, can't you see, Nubia's gone."

Adisa reclined his head. "Uzochi . . ."

"I . . . I'm sorry, but I've been trying my best to go along with everything that's happening and follow instructions and learn," Uzochi said, his voice becoming quieter again. "But everybody keeps on talking about Nubia's rebirth and the importance of us kids carrying on the ancestral traditions that were destroyed in the storm. We have no idea what that means."

"That's why I'm here, child," Adisa said. "That's why I have you meet with the elders, why your mother has been telling you about our history."

"It's barely been three weeks since I awoke to my gift. You can't just snap your fingers and expect me to be perfect and want to immerse myself in the traditions." Uzochi tried to build up his courage again, balling his fists in the pockets of his jeans. "And to be honest, almost no one in this theater gave a damn about me until I became somebody they could use."

"Uzochi, that simply isn't true. I've seen the respect you command over your peers. Tasha was telling me how you helped her with schoolwork even before she came into her abilities, and Zuberi clearly adores you."

Uzochi kept his gaze planted on the wooden floor, but his insides burned.

"Baba, uh, maybe we can speak another time? I . . . I'm sorry, but I don't want to have this conversation right now."

"Uzochi—"

He spun away from Adisa and charged forward, bypassing the elevator at the end of the hallway and opening the door to the stairwell that would lead him one floor down into the wings of the stage. He briefly looked over his shoulder to watch the elder reentering the meeting room, his body hunched over. It was the first time Uzochi had been so confrontational with Adisa, committing a monumental breach of one of the most important Nubian rules he'd been taught as a child: Never, *ever* disrespect your elders. His tone seconds ago—unforgivably blasphemous.

But he didn't care. Right now, he just needed to get away. He went down the stairs and entered stage left, swiftly skirting the proscenium and pivoting to face the rest of the auditorium. The Carter-Combs's immense stage had been cleared for some time now, with the cyclorama that served as a performers' crossover removed, creating even more space. During the afternoon, the kids who had so-called physical reality/energy gifts were allowed to practice there. Two guys walked around with glowing bodies, shifting to the same color every few seconds, their chests puffed out and grand smiles on their faces as they called out to each other "Lime green" and "Red-brown" and "Gold," cueing their color shifts.

If only Uzochi's power had been so simple, maybe he could've enjoyed it like the others.

He kept going, deeper and deeper into the Carter-Combs, down different hallways, just to keep his legs moving. He kept going, and it wasn't until something shadowy lurched across his mind that he stopped.

Sadness. Deep, powerful sadness. Then, the soft sound of someone crying.

"I can't give you any more than that, okay? I've done enough. These people . . . they've tried to help me."

Uzochi paused. He was near a tiny cluster of classrooms on the opposite side from where he'd been with Zuberi earlier. The voice was familiar, feminine, but the crying made it hard to distinguish.

He shouldn't be eavesdropping. Already, some of the other Nubians were suspicious of him because of his empathic abilities. This was an even more egregious violation.

"Lencho? No. I won't."

Uzochi froze. What did his cousin have to do with this?

"I'm begging you. Please."

Uzochi edged back. He needed to leave. He couldn't hear this. He moved as quietly as he could.

Unfortunately, his right sneaker squeaked across the old linoleum.

Keera appeared in an instant, her cheeks slick with tears

as she clutched her mobile. She looked at him with wild, desperate eyes. She was going to scream at him, just as she'd done when she'd awoken.

Except, suddenly, Keera rushed over and grabbed Uzochi by his shirt, shaking him.

"You have to help," she said. "Please. I'm begging you."

Uzochi pulled away from her. He'd been right before. She was Divine, through and through, and clearly, she was planning something. Something to hurt the Children.

"What're you talking about?" he asked.

"I need help," Keera said, sobbing now. "The Divine. They want me to get back with them. They say . . . your cousin says that they have a setup now that we wouldn't believe."

Uzochi shook his head, perplexed. "Wait, you just spoke to my cousin? Where is he? And where are the Divine?" Dread began to fill his heart. After all that had gone down, he hadn't had time to think about his cousin or question the whereabouts of the Divine. But for the past few weeks Lencho had been nowhere to be found. And Zaire had vanished as well.

Keera let out a cry and fell to the floor. She was shaking all over, on the verge of convulsing.

Uzochi bent down to help the girl, reluctant to get too close. She'd made it clear that she absolutely hated having Uzochi in her mind, even after her awakening. "I don't know where your dumb cousin is, but don't you get it?" she snapped, a bit of the old Keera in her voice. "I'm not going back to being in a fuckin' gang. I'm trying to fix my life, get on a higher path. Awakening to my gift is a sign."

Uzochi nodded, trying to convey a sense of sympathy, though he wasn't remotely in the mood for the girl's antics. "Well, Keera, maybe you should've thought about the consequences of running with the Divine way before now. I mean, they're a gang. This sort of thing happens."

Fury. That was what Uzochi felt, waves and waves of it coming from this girl, who slowly rose from the ground.

"You . . . you dumb jerk!" she yelled. "You've always judged me for being with the Divine. You don't know my life, Uzochi, what I had to do to survive. Some of the Divine are pretty cool and helped me out. But something's up . . ."

Uzochi's field was gone, Keera's barbed thoughts and emotions tearing into his body.

He'd simply had enough.

"You know what? I'm done! DONE! I'm so sick of trying to be there for folks and being told off for not saying the right thing or being the right way. *You're* the one who got involved in a skanky drug-dealing gang. *You're* the one who dated a crazy brute and got messed up by doing body work. Not me, sis! Not me!"

"Uzochi!"

He spun around, and there was Adisa. Even though he was in the same red tunic as before, his white fro as wiry as ever, he looked fiercer somehow. Angrier.

Disappointment licked off him like flames.

Uzochi knew why. There was Keera, clearly shaken, with Uzochi shouting at her, yelling to the world the secrets of her life, which he'd only learned when sifting through her memories.

The ultimate betrayal.

Uzochi didn't need this. He didn't need this judgment or the stress.

Fuck these people.

"I'm gone," he said, shaking his head. "Do this without me."

He ran for one of the exits and left without looking back.

Chapter 29

Zuberi

Zuberi strolled down an unkempt sidewalk eating a veggie-beetle wrap, taking her time on her way to meet Vriana. Seeing as the Carter-Combs was on the outer fringes of the city, it was roughly a twenty-minute walk before she reached any kind of civilization. Zuberi and Vriana had found a coffee shop that had clearly seen a boom in business ever since Nubians started using the theater. They usually spent their time gossiping about the latest awakenings or catching up on classwork, but today, Zuberi had a particular topic in mind.

Uzochi.

With every awakening, she grew more impressed by him. He was rising to the challenge of being the catalyst. More than that, he was easy to talk to—or, in some cases, not talk to. How many hours had they spent now just sitting near each other in silence? Zuberi would watch the figures above him spin lazily back and forth. She'd wondered, in the beginning, if he'd been reading her mind, but she knew he wasn't. So often, she'd had boys who thought they were entitled to every piece of her. But Uzochi, even with all he could do, respected her.

She appreciated the boundary.

The thought made her touch the scar on her face absently. She quickened her pace, anxious to get to the shop and Vriana. Oh, V would be insufferable. That was a given. But she would also be helpful. Like, should Zuberi go for it, even with everything else going on?

Zuberi was so lost in thought that she nearly ran right into another person on the street. It was only at the last second that she heard the crunch of boots on gravel, and looked up just in time to step to the side. There, standing in her path, was a St. John Soldier. With her black clothing and gear and helmet pulled low, it was hard to make out any features other than her light eyes and smooth skin. Still, the look of suspicion was easy enough to read.

"Sorry," Zuberi said, even though she wasn't. She had every right to walk here, after all.

The woman nodded and smiled, suspicion erased. "My apologies. I believe I was in your way."

Zuberi cocked an eyebrow. A militia member apologizing? Might be a first.

Zuberi stepped away from the woman, her eyes sweeping the area. The street was mostly empty—the coffee shop was just across the way—but down one of the alleys, Zuberi saw the unfortunately familiar sight of a small squad. She didn't know what they were doing out here, seeing as the area was mostly vacated. Still, a closer look down the alley showed at least one of their obsidian squad vans perched on the curb.

Maybe it was nothing, but considering what was going down with Nubians, the timing seemed off.

Something continued to pluck at Zuberi's consciousness. A tinge. A tug. The sort of sensation that had become increasingly familiar since she'd awoken. As if something wasn't right, or there was a puzzle to decipher. As if she needed to just pay attention.

Zuberi tried to shake it off as she walked up to the coffee shop. Vriana was seated outside, easy to spot thanks to the puffy pink sweater she wore and matching ribbons she'd used to tie back her braids. When she spotted Zuberi, she waved and grinned.

"There you are!" Vriana said. "I was beginning to worry that something happened."

It was like Vriana was talking underwater, from what Zuberi heard. Because even as she sat, all she could do was stare down the street at the St. John Soldiers. Above their heads, phantoms marched back and forth or reclined against invisible walls.

Vriana followed Zuberi's gaze. "Oh yeah. Kind of a buzz-kill, right?"

"Why are they here?" Zuberi asked, not taking her eyes off the militia.

Vriana shrugged, taking a bite of a pastry. "I dunno. They've been here ever since I got here, though. Just hanging out."

No. St. John sociopaths were never just "hanging out." Only Vriana would describe a group so sinister in such a way.

"It's bad enough in the Swamp," Zuberi said. "This was supposed to be our safe place. I'm going to need to tell my dad."

Vriana nodded, taking another bite. "That's a good idea."

Zuberi hated how placating her friend sounded. It was the same tone that Adisa and the elders used when she tried to bring up her concerns about Krazen.

"There are so many Nubians awakening to their gifts," she'd told Adisa just a couple of days ago. "I mean, there's one guy who can literally move things with his mind. Why don't we start making demands? Show the people what we can do, maybe start confronting the problems in the Swamp . . . like the seawall, for example. We could fix that. Between the telekinetic dude and Abdul's elemental powers, easy-breezy. And then we could challenge the militia—"

"Child," Adisa had said, sighing as he pressed a finger to his temple. "I appreciate your passion. But we're not ready for anything yet. We must focus on our fellow Nubians first. Uzochi is still coming into his own."

"But he's not the only one here who can do something," Zuberi had said, feeling her anger rise. "The rest of us have gifts, too. It can't be all centered around Uzochi because he's catalyst."

Adisa had looked at her then, old eyes swirling with emotion that she couldn't decipher.

"We cannot rush these things, young Zuberi," he'd said. "We must be patient and wait. Moreover, most of the world has no idea about who Nubians are and what we can do. Once our gifts become public knowledge, our lives will become tremendously complicated. We're simply not ready."

He'd dismissed her then. Always, she was dismissed.

Enraged at the memory, she tossed the remaining bits of

her wrap in the nearby trash. Some of it bounced off onto the ground. She knew she should pick it up; instead, she folded her arms.

"Beri," Vriana said, reaching out to touch her hand. "What's going on?"

Zuberi felt the sting of tears. She hated weakness. In all her training, both with the fighting forms and now her gift, she was always pushing harder, never wanting to be a victim again. How many times had she toiled to the point of exhaustion to make sure she remained strong?

And here she was, crying. The most obvious sign of weakness there was.

"It's just everything," Zuberi said. "No one listens to me. I mean, no one except you."

Vriana nodded, squeezing her hand. "That must be so hard."

It was hard. Zuberi could literally see the future—blurry and in figures, sure, but still!

"I just . . . what's the point of having power if no one cares what you can do?"

Vriana gave her a soft smile. "I know what you mean."

"No," Zuberi said quietly, pulling her hand back. "Actually, you don't. You're not gifted. You *can't* understand."

Zuberi watched the hurt flash across her friend's eyes. Vriana's smile faltered, her hand still hovering in the air. Above Vriana, soft, pink figures looked down on her with wide, glassy eyes.

"Need . . . help . . ."

A rasping voice nearly made Zuberi jump, and she whipped around. An unhoused man was crawling toward them on his hands and knees. His clothes were tattered, his long beard unruly and singed. His eyes were wide and marred with cataracts, and he grabbed at the air as he moved toward them.

"Help . . . ," he begged. "Water . . . please . . ."

Zuberi stared at the man. The phantoms above him were nearly still, shaking or rocking back and forth. Behind her, Vriana's chair screeched across the concrete as she jumped up and rushed forward.

"Here," Vriana said, handing the man her own bottle of water. "Drink this."

The man grabbed for the bottle and downed it, sitting back on the concrete. Vriana helped him straighten his back and adjusted his legs as he drank.

"What do you need?" Vriana said, her voice steady. "Tell me."

"Food," he coughed out. "Food, please."

Zuberi looked at the remainder of her wrap in the trash, consumed by shame. She'd grown up knowing what it was like to not have enough, and here she'd thrown away food because of a tantrum.

But Vriana was already grabbing what was left of her pastry and handing it to the man.

"Eat," she said. "Slowly."

Zuberi watched as the man took slow bites of the food. His shaking gradually decreased. He leaned back slightly, supported by Vriana's hand as he stared up at the sky.

"Drink some more water," Vriana said, her voice gentle but firm.

And then Zuberi noticed it, an aura so subtle that she

almost had to squint to fully make it out. There, so close to her best friend's skin and clothes as to be almost invisible, was a soft, pale pink glow.

Vriana *was* gifted.

With each gentle command she gave, the glow intensified at her lips before fluttering through the air toward the man. Vriana's phantoms watched, glowing brighter with each uttered word.

"You're telling him what to do," Zuberi said in awe. "And he's listening?"

Vriana's eyes cut back to her friend. "Zu—"

"He's going to hurt me again," the man said, the tremors starting again. "He's going to hurt me, and you have to stop him. *Please.*"

"Who's going to hurt you?" Vriana asked, attention back on the man as she pressed the water bottle toward his lips. "Drink, and tell us."

He did as he was told, and the shaking lessened for a moment.

"The boy," he said, closing his eyes. "He will come, and he will take everything I have left if you don't stop him."

His eyes flew open again, and Zuberi looked into the white clouds that rested there.

"You must stop him," he begged. "You must!"

His voice rose. Down the street, Zuberi saw one of the militia members turn curiously toward them.

"V, you've gotta keep him quiet," Zuberi whispered, dropping down so as to block the man from view.

"He's distraught," Vriana snapped back. "Can't you see that?"

"Yeah, well, he's going to be even more distraught if a bunch of St. John Soldiers cart him off to who knows where."

Vriana's face softened. "Right. Okay. Hey, friend, please, try to be calm. We'd really appreciate it, and we're here."

As Vriana spoke, she touched his hand. Like her, he softly glowed pink, and his face went slack as he smiled.

"Of course," he said. "Anything for you, wondrous queen."

Vriana bit her lip, glancing at Zuberi. "Sorry. Might've overdone it a bit."

So many questions zipped through Zuberi's mind. How long had Vriana been able to do this, and what exactly could she do? But then the man groaned quietly, jolting Zuberi back to reality.

"Don't let him hurt me," he said again in a raspy voice. "Please."

Zuberi felt the tears coming on again. She wanted to tell Vriana to ask him to repeat what he meant, but she knew they probably wouldn't get a better answer than before. She glanced up, finding hazy gray phantoms above the man.

No.

Not just gray.

Zuberi refocused her mind and saw them clearly. Mostly gray phantoms—the man, asleep or passed out or in pain. But there, in one future, she saw that he was joined by a different figure. One tinged with red.

Lencho.

Lencho bent over the man and grabbed him by the shoulder, remaining there as the man sobbed and wailed, energy from the gray phantom flowing to the red phantom. The red figure burned brighter then, a frightening flame of power that grew and grew.

Zuberi's mind flew back to the first fight, how Kal had been reduced to nothing after Lencho put his hands on him. Had it been more than brute strength? Did Lencho have the ability to drain others?

"Goddess," she said. "But then—"

An explosion of yellow light erupted in Zuberi's mind. She winced at the pain, feeling it rocket over her, dread coursing through her veins.

Something had happened. Whether it was an awakening or something more, she didn't know.

"He's going to hurt me," the man whispered feebly. "He's going to hurt me."

Zuberi looked from the man toward the Carter-Combs, her heart in her stomach. She looked back at Vriana.

"We need to go," she said. "I think something happened. Or will happen."

Vriana's eyes were glassy now, just like her phantoms. She shook her head.

"I'm not leaving him, Beri," she said. "He needs my help. I think he's . . . Omigosh, I think he's transitioning. I can't let him be alone."

At the words, the man shook again, convulsing. Tears slipped down both Vriana's and Zuberi's cheeks. Zuberi saw only one phantom drifting above the man now. Asleep, peaceful.

"I'll help her."

Zuberi looked up suddenly. It was the militiawoman she'd spoken to before, her features uncharacteristically soft and youthful. Gently, she removed her helmet and bent down next to them. Her crimson hair was knotted back in a bun, and her eyes shone with her own tears.

"We'll call one of our medical teams," the woman said. "Whatever we can do for this poor fellow, we'll do it."

Zuberi had never trusted the militia members. When she'd been hurt, crying for help, they hadn't come to her aid. And how many Nubians had they hurt themselves, or incarcerated? She wouldn't be fooled by anyone.

Still, Zuberi didn't have many options. Her eyes darted up to the phantoms above the woman's head. They were no longer marching. Instead, a couple were bending over, comforting the distraught man. And a third phantom was laughing with another figure—a soft pink one that must be Vriana. She was hugging the girl.

Safe, Zuberi thought. *This person is safe.*

"Thank you," Zuberi said. And then she turned to Vriana and said, "I'll message you later, okay? And you message me, too. Don't keep me in the dark."

Vriana nodded. Then, suddenly, she wrapped Zuberi in a hug. Zuberi felt the warmth again and realized that this power had always been there. Vriana had always had the ability to comfort. An inherent gift that she'd known how to use all along.

Let it be that way for me now, Zuberi thought. *Let me trust that I'm making the right call.*

With a final nod to the group, Zuberi turned and bolted. She took out her staff and extended it to its full length. She channeled energy into each vertebra as she ran, knowing— without knowing—that, whatever had happened at the theater, she needed to be prepared for a fight.

Chapter 30

Lencho

It was strange being back in the lower city after spending so many weeks Up High. Lencho felt the difference in energy down here, the kind of energy that had sustained him before. Now Lencho took the essence of others during his training sessions and while sparring with the Divine. He'd become adept at taking just what he needed in the moments when his fist or ankle touched his sparring partner. They were all so powerful that a little went a long way, charging him through the rest of the fight.

Still, as Lencho moved through the streets of the lower city, he found himself drawn to familiar targets. He recognized several of the people he'd drained in the past. One of them—the blind stranger Lencho had first drained—must have felt Lencho's presence when he crossed by him in an alley, for the man immediately began to mumble and pray.

"Don't hurt me," he'd begged. "Don't hurt me."

The plea made Lencho's gut twist.

"All right there, Lencho?"

It was Tilly, speaking to him via his earpiece from her sky office. Part of him still jerked at the sensation of hearing a voice this way. He didn't know how any of the Up High people handled having a constant stream of voices in their implants. This earpiece—which had been fused to his auricle so as to be temporarily immovable—was already annoying as hell.

"Yeah, I'm fine," he said. "Just taking the scenic route to make sure the area's clear."

"Let us know when you're ready for the others to be sent in," Tilly reminded him. "Time is of the essence."

Lencho didn't like Tilly's tone. In fact, he didn't like Tilly at all. He could tell when she was briefed on this mission that she wasn't feeling it. She'd glanced at Krazen, speaking without speaking, but Lencho could guess what she was thinking, that the Divine were too dumb and inexperienced to handle this type of venture, that it was too complicated. That *he* wasn't capable.

Lady, please, he wanted to say. *No one's better at hustling and figuring out logistics than gang kids.* But he held his tongue, wanting to be a pro, needing to make Krazen proud.

He'd nearly reached the Carter-Combs Theater. Shit, the place had gone to the dogs. When he'd heard through the grapevine that Adisa was using the venue to help awoken Nubians with their gifts, he'd thought it was semi-fitting to use such a relic. After all, Adisa must've been primeval at this point. Lencho had heard his dad rant about the elder almost all his life, calling him a "misguided fool who was blinded by old Nubia."

Lencho paused down an alley at the sound of voices. There, in the shadows, was a kid holding his hands out, playing with a light that pulsed.

A gifted Nubian.

He was younger than Lencho by maybe a year or so. Lencho wondered why he was out here, but, of course, it was obvious. He was practicing with his powers without the press of eyes, just as Lencho had done in the beginning. Lencho could easily discern how raw and new this kid's gift was. He licked his lips, feeling need suddenly course through him.

He needed to drain. He didn't dare walk into this situation without the right amount of energy. It was imperative that he be operating at his best, right? And here . . . here was a chance to drain a gifted Nubian. Not in bits and pieces during a brawl, but in one big gulp. A rarity for him.

Lencho strode quietly toward the boy. He held out his hand, keeping his breathing steady, nearly silent. He was nearly there.

His fingertips brushed the boy's hoodie.

"What the—"

The boy whipped around, brown eyes going wide at the sight of Lencho, the light in his hand popping out into darkness. He tried to run, but Lencho was too fast, snatching the kid by the shoulder. With his free hand, he pushed up the boy's sleeve and closed his hand over the boy's wrist. The boy didn't get out another word before Lencho began to drain.

He leeched mercilessly, the boy's eyes rolling in his head as his hands loosened from Lencho's neck and he keeled over. Lencho swirled from the fast infusion of energy, coruscating colors taking over his vision, the smells of wood, mint-honey, and metal reaching his nose, a tinny ringing in his ears . . .

He felt . . . titanic. Like a god.

"Lencho?"

He jolted, dropping the boy's arm. It was Tilly in his head again, and he was breathing hard.

On the ground, the boy was slumped over, passed out completely. Lencho stepped away. He felt Nubian energy tingling in his veins and distorting his vision and he wanted more so very badly, more than almost anything else he could imagine.

He forced himself to breathe.

"I'm here," Lencho said. "Right around the corner."

He was pure energy now, and it sizzled on and under his skin. Nothing could stop him. And anyone who dared would suffer.

"I'm sending in the rest," Tilly said after a pause. "Good luck, Lencho."

Luck. He didn't need it. Luck was what cowards wished for, cowards who wanted what Lencho already had.

Power.

Chapter 31

Uzochi

The moment Uzochi got home, he slammed the door shut behind him. It was something he'd never done before, knowing that even the smallest action in his apartment could reverberate down the entire floor. He didn't care. *Let them feel this,* he thought. *Let them share a small piece of it.*

"Uzochi!"

His gaze snapped to the kitchen table, where his mom sat. He hadn't expected her to be home, but one look at the clock told him it was late afternoon. She'd finished her shift by now. He didn't care. In fact, the sight of his mother only added to his anger.

"Yeah, sorry," he grumbled. "I'm going to shower."

"Young man, you will give me a real apology for treating our home that way," Com'pa said, standing up and coming around the table. "What's gotten into you?"

In his mind, memories that belonged to him swam with memories that did not. His own anger at Keera, at Adisa, at all of the elders, at his mother—pitched like an angry sea. He looked from Com'pa to the rest of the apartment, furious again at how small it all was. He didn't even have his own room to retreat to, not even a corner of a place where he could catch his breath. His eyes lit on his discarded scholar-pack in the corner, his frustration rolling through him, slamming into his mind because the sanctuary he'd had at school had been ripped away from him, too.

"Did something happen during training?" Com'pa asked as she stepped toward him. "Did you—"

"Ma, don't you get it?" he shouted, stepping back from her. "I'm done with being their catalyst. *Your* catalyst. I'm done."

He'd never raised his voice at his mother. Never, not once in his life. But everything around him was so loud and unceasing, the noise in his mind overwhelming. He would explode if he didn't shout.

"Well, well," said a cold voice. "Look who's finally got something to say."

Uzochi turned and saw his uncle coming out of the bathroom. He still hadn't gotten used to how big the man seemed now. Weren't adults supposed to get smaller the older you got? And here was Kefle, more intimidating even with the bits of gray now flecked in his beard and hair.

"I don't want to talk to you," Uzochi said, hating that his uncle had heard the exchange with his mom. All their lives, it was Lencho who threw the tantrums, Lencho who was the brat.

"Yeah, well, I didn't come here to talk to you, either,

arrogant pup," Kefle said with a smirk. "But while you're here, why don't you tell me where the old guy's hiding my son."

"Kefle . . . ," Com'pa warned.

"He's not there," Uzochi said, touching a hand to his temple, trying to stave off the poisonous waves of emotion from his uncle.

"Bullshit," Kefle said. "I've looked everywhere for my boy. Called him, texted . . . his blasted line is dead. Even went to the damn Jungle after figuring out he'd been running with the Divine. Disgraceful. He's not there, so that only leaves working with you all."

Uzochi shook his head. "He's not at the theater. Maybe try looking on the street, since both of you act like dogs."

Kefle's eyes narrowed dangerously. Before he could move, Com'pa stepped in front of him.

"Kefle, you know he doesn't mean it," she said, dismay in her voice. "It's the pressure of being catalyst."

At that, Kefle barked out a laugh, his eyes flashing mean and bright in Uzochi's direction. Hatred coursed through him, a steady energy that smothered the room and blocked out everything else that Uzochi had felt. Kefle's presence was so heavy, like a callused finger snuffing out a flame.

"Of course he means it," Kefle growled. "He's finally saying things that he wouldn't have said before when he was nothing but a helpless nerd. He means every word. Don't you, boy?"

Uzochi's fingers flexed. Kefle was too close to Com'pa. His emotions were murkier now, threads of something else swimming near the bottom.

"You don't have to tell me," Kefle continued. "I know.

How many times did Siran get a pass for being an ass? All because he was dealing with 'the pressure of being catalyst.' Well, I've got a secret for you, Uzochi. Your dad said some pretty terrible things, too. And he meant every word as well."

Com'pa glanced from Kefle back to her son. "Don't listen, dear heart. Your father was a man, and all men say things they don't mean. But he was good, through and through. Don't let your uncle's jealousy—"

"Jealous?" Kefle roared. "Jealous of Siran?"

Com'pa stepped back, closer to Uzochi, her eyes blazing.

"Yes, Kefle," she said. "I'm saying what you don't want to hear. But it's time for you to grow up. You have a family, you have Leeyah, you have Lencho—"

"Don't talk about family to me, Com'pa," he snapped. "Not when you're willingly throwing your son into this mess."

Com'pa scoffed, flaring with her own emotions, ever protective and loyal.

"You don't even know where your son is!" Com'pa said. "I know you, Kefle. I know how unnecessarily cruel you've been with that boy of yours over the years. How you've never let Lencho's light shine because of your own bitterness toward the world. Tell me, how is that being a good father? And now you say you want to protect your son? I say he's finally escaped you, thank Goddess!"

Uzochi had never heard his mother speak so brazenly, but her words now rang out like a siren in the apartment. For a moment, Kefle only seethed, glaring at her. Then he straightened, looking back at Uzochi.

"I won't let him be ground up and spat out," Kefle said,

eyes never leaving his nephew. "I will protect him, whether you like it or not."

Com'pa made something between a sigh and a groan of frustration.

"You aren't protecting him by hiding the truth," she said. "You know that, deep down."

Uzochi took each of them in, their twirling energies in the room. He looked at each adult, and then he looked back at the sketch of his father. His father, who'd stood steady when others wouldn't. He was a hero. Nobility. He wasn't someone who ran and hid.

Uzochi realized with a sinking stomach that he was behaving like his uncle, not his father. Hadn't he always accused Lencho of being unwilling to work hard, of making excuses? How ashamed his father would be of him now.

"I'm proud to be part of this, to be catalyst," he said, looking back at Kefle. "It asks a lot, yeah. But I can do it. I'm not afraid."

But Kefle's lips curled with cruel laughter. He shook his head as he stared at Uzochi.

"My brother said the same thing," he said, and now Uzochi could pick out the thread he'd felt before. It was deeper than sadness, deeper than regret.

It was grief.

"They want you to think like that," Kefle continued. "Put yourself before the rest. Be a hero. But it's going to break you."

Uzochi shook his head. "No. I'm . . . I'm strong enough to help our people. And if I'm not yet, I'll get there."

He glanced at the portrait of Siran again, and Kefle followed his eyes. The grief was sharper now, overtaking every other emotion in his uncle's body, nearly shaking Uzochi with its intensity. Then, slowly, as Kefle took in the sight of his brother, anger pulsed through his limbs.

"No," he said slowly. "You won't. Because that's the thing Adisa isn't telling you, isn't it? That the burden of catalyst isn't simply difficult. It's the nature of what you can do. It's power that's impossible to control."

Uzochi felt a sharp twist in his gut. He willed himself to believe that Kefle was lying, though he sensed nothing but truth.

"Kefle—" Com'pa said, but his uncle wouldn't be silenced now.

"Your mom ever tell you what your dad could do?" Kefle asked.

Uzochi looked at his mother. No, he hadn't asked. He hadn't wanted to dredge up her sadness, the very thing emanating from her skin now.

"He was an elemental," Com'pa said, her eyes watering. "The most powerful elemental Nubia ever saw."

An elemental, Uzochi repeated to himself. *Like Abdul.*

"And what type of elemental was he?" Kefle asked, his voice a deadly quiet.

Com'pa wiped away tears. "He . . . he communed with the forces of nature. He controlled the weather."

Then she reached out and grabbed Uzochi's hands, her eyes pleading with him.

"Oh, dear heart, if you could have seen what your father could do, the passion with which he wielded his gift, befitting a Nubian prince serving as sire of our land," she said, voice breaking. "You must understand. He stayed behind on the island with most of the other elementals during the cataclysm, trying to use their abilities to stave off the waters of the storm. They sacrificed their lives, buying time for the rest of us to flee. I begged your father to come with me to the boats, but he said it was his sovereign duty to protect our land and people. He was a hero, Uzochi. He was."

"Don't lie to the boy," Kefle said. "You and I both know, Com'pa, that that storm wouldn't have gotten where it did if Siran had left well enough alone. If he hadn't pushed and pushed because he was the damned catalyst!"

Com'pa dropped Uzochi's hands. She turned away from him, eyes continuing to well as she pointed at Kefle.

"My husband was trying to save Nubia," she said. "He did more for Nubians than you ever did, and he gave his life to save us. You despicable, horrible—"

"My brother let his ego get in the way," Kefle said, now looking at Uzochi. "He thought he could control his gift, but he couldn't. He died saving us from a storm *he* created with his supposed gift. That's the real burden of the catalyst, isn't it? Pushing to take us to the next level, no matter the cost."

With one move, Kefle crossed the room. He grabbed Uzochi's wrist, even as Com'pa cried out. His eyes, creased at the corners, bored into Uzochi.

"See," he demanded. *"See."*

And so Uzochi saw.

Rain fell on Uzochi's skin like tiny needles as water whipped all around him. A storm thrashed the ground, leaving it slick and muddy as Uzochi struggled to find purchase with his feet. Distantly, he heard screams. But he moved forward. *Kefle* moved forward, for this was his memory.

"Brother, you have to stop," a younger Kefle demanded. "The boats must leave."

And through the haze and rain, Uzochi saw his father.

Sturdy muscles rippled through his back and arms. His tunic was torn, his braids whipping behind him in the furious wind. He held out his hands as if he was gripping some invisible force, and his chest rose and fell as if he held a weight in each hand.

"Then you need to get to the boats," Siran said, his voice steady. "And hurry, Kefle. I can't hold this much longer."

Kefle's fists shook at his sides. "Siran, stop! Give this up, please. Nubia's going to fall. You have to let go."

Siran's lips quirked in a small smile. "Not until my baby brother is safely on those boats."

"Siran," Kefle repeated, voice breaking. "Come. Your son will be born soon. Give this up. Now."

Uzochi's father looked over his shoulder as slivers of water whipped around his face. "And your son as well. Which is why I need you to go and watch over them both."

Kefle's shoulders shook. In the relentless rain, it was impossible to see the tears that fell, but Uzochi felt them. He felt them all.

"Go, Kefle," Siran said, his voice a steady command. "Go!"

A bolt of energy threw Uzochi out of the memory, leaving him gasping for breath as he stared at his uncle. Kefle's hard expression was enough, words not necessary. He knew what Uzochi had seen, that his father had chosen Nubia over his family.

But then something else rippled through the air. Something potent that built up into a cacophony.

Fear.

Uzochi's pocket buzzed, and he pulled it out.

A terse message from Zuberi.

Carter-Combs under attack. Divine with powers. Help.

Uzochi looked up at his uncle and mom. Her face was smeared with tears and makeup. His uncle's expression was unyielding. He knew what Kefle expected, that the memory would show Uzochi that he needed to walk away.

But it wasn't Siran who'd failed in Uzochi's eyes. It was Kefle, a man who'd never honored his brother's request to watch over their family.

"I need to get to the Carter-Combs," he said. "And fast. They're under attack."

He looked pointedly at his uncle, then turned Zuberi's message to him. "Maybe we've found Lencho."

Com'pa straightened. "I know the way. I'll call Thato as well. Come on, son."

Uzochi nodded as his mother grabbed her keys. He turned to look at his uncle, but Kefle was already halfway to the door, leaving without a word.

Uzochi met Com'pa's eyes. "Dear heart—"

He shook his head. "Later. Right now, we need to go."

She bit her lip and nodded, and they left the apartment together. Uzochi forced himself to breathe as he followed his mother, pausing only when they got to the hover car so that he could type out a message to Zuberi.

Hold on. I'm coming.

Chapter 32

Zuberi

Zuberi arrived at the Carter-Combs just in time. She'd barely crossed over the threshold of the main auditorium, shouting for Adisa as the massive wooden doors slammed behind her, when Sekou also appeared, reporting that members of the Divine were heading their way.

"I was floating up in the astral plane," he said. "And I spotted them down below. Definitely Divine with those sun signs that are like super easy to see. Some militia folks are close by, too, but they weren't together."

"I saw them as well," Zuberi said, gathering her breath after her sprint. "But Baba, it's more than that. There was . . . something. A vision. A warning. I think the Divine are coming to attack."

Adisa looked at the two of them, his eyes grayer in the dim light of the theater. Behind him was a table of other elders, each of them looking curiously at Zuberi and Sekou.

"I appreciate this concern," Adisa said. "But the Divine

are children. If they're coming, we should be ready to accept them with open arms."

"No!" Zuberi said. "Baba, you need to listen to me. They're not coming for help. They're coming—"

"She's right. They're coming for me."

All of them had whipped around to see Keera struggling forward out of the shadows of the stage. Zuberi had never seen the girl look so distressed, except right before her awakening. She was slick with sweat or tears or both, which was frightening. Keera's gift was just too volatile. Ever since she'd awoken, she had only trained privately with Adisa.

"My child," the elder said, approaching her. "What's going on?"

"They want me to go with them," she said with a sniff. "I told them no, but they're coming. Baba, you need to leave. All of you. The others . . . they're gifted, too."

She looked at Zuberi then, and Zuberi saw above her phantoms that danced. Keera, screaming, then running, then shaking, then . . .

Was it possible?

On fire?

Adisa turned toward the other elders, all of whom started speaking in hushed tones. Then he looked back at Sekou and Zuberi, his features hardened.

"Thank you for alerting us to this," he said. "We should use the tunnels. Sekou, gather up the elders and the Nubians who haven't awoken. Get them out. Zuberi, assemble the others. We'll need to guard Keera."

Questions swam through Zuberi—tunnels?—but she nodded anyway. She sent off a message to Uzochi as quickly as she could, and then she moved to gather the others.

The building rattled beneath her feet.

She remembered that sensation.

Zaire.

"They're going to break in," she said, whipping back to where Adisa still stood. His eyes were set on the entrance. Behind him, Sekou was trying to move the elders, but they'd paused, hands covering their mouths, seemingly undone. Zuberi watched as a couple of others hastily tried to barricade the doors with whatever pieces of furniture they could find in the auditorium.

Adisa turned back to them. "Did you not hear me? I said get to the tunnels!"

Now the other elders hurried, rushing to a nondescript door found to the left of the stage. Zuberi looked back, ready to be chastened for not gathering the other Nubians, but there was no need. They were filing into the emptied orchestra pit from all corners. A ragtag group, Zuberi realized. She counted five, plus Keera, Sekou, and herself.

Uzochi wasn't among them.

Adisa turned to the young Nubians as the building shook again.

"These are not our enemies," he said. "These children are confused. Their minds have possibly been poisoned against you, but they will see the truth in the light. Protect each other, but do not harm them."

Zuberi stared at the elder. Had he ever been in a fight? If the Divine had come here today, they'd come to brawl. And she would protect herself and her friends above everything else.

"Keera," he said, waving to her. "With me."

The girl looked back at Zuberi, and Zuberi saw her phantoms twisting above, engulfed in fire.

No . . .

The theater shook again, just as Adisa and Keera fled the room, leaving Zuberi standing before the other Nubians.

Fear was in their eyes.

"I don't care what Adisa said," Zuberi said, her voice rising. "Your job right now is to protect each other, you understand? Don't underestimate them. If they come for you, you show them exactly how strong we are."

Before her, she watched as each of the Nubians began to glow, readily discerning the energy of their gifts at play. Some flickered while others grew brighter. They spread out, each of them facing the entrance. Each of them ready.

"In a fight, you want to focus!" she yelled. "Don't let them distract you."

Several of them nodded at her. She recognized them as her neighbors and classmates. Standing together, following her.

A boom echoed through the building, and it wasn't just the front doors that came down.

It was the entire wall.

As debris rained down, a figure stepped forward, glowing bright red.

Lencho.

"Nice hiding place," he said, looking around at the mess. "Though, I've gotta say, it could use a bit of a face-lift."

Behind Lencho, several other figures appeared. A girl with purple hair. Another girl who smirked at the sight of them. Then Aren. Zuberi had expected his cocky ass. But then . . .

Zaire.

He walked up slowly behind them all, something between boy and rock, moving with heavy, weighted limbs that sent an eerie, cracking sound throughout the auditorium.

It was horrible . . . and wondrous.

"Lencho, I don't know why you're here, but you need to cut it out and leave," Zuberi said, gathering her courage. "This isn't some petty turf shit."

The boy laughed, and the other Divine grinned and joined in, all except for Zaire.

"You think we still care about *turf*?" Lencho chided. "We're beyond that. Don't you know? All of the Divine have ascended."

Ascended? Up High? Impossible. Lencho was talking out of his ass. But then Zuberi caught how Aren's gaze cut to Lencho, the indication that maybe he'd said too much.

"Anyways," Lencho said, ignoring the look, "we're missing somebody, and we thought we'd come grab her, maybe bring some of you others along for the ride."

"You're not getting anyone," said one of the Nubians behind Zuberi. She looked back and recognized Ibrahim, a guy who'd only recently awoken to his gift of telekinesis. She appreciated his gumption, even if he spoke with a shaking voice.

Lencho smirked. "Oh yeah? Well, since I'm feeling generous, I'll give you the option to let our Divine friend leave with us."

"Come out, Keera!" shouted the smirking girl. "Stop hiding."

"She's not going anywhere," said Sekou, glaring at the Divine girl.

Zuberi held her breath. She hoped Keera had managed to get far away with Baba, that they were moving fast.

"It's all right, Lara," Lencho said. "We figured they'd be stubborn. After all, y'all know my cousin . . . which, by the way, where is the Goody Two-shoes?"

Zuberi forced all emotion from her face. She wouldn't reveal that Uzochi wasn't here, not while she worried about where, exactly, he was.

One of Aren's phantoms began to emit a dazzling light.

"I'm giving you one last warning," Zuberi said. "Leave now, Lencho, before someone gets hurt. I get that you want to buck the system, but this ain't right. You can't just take people and force them to do what you want."

She hoped he understood that she was also referring to the man he'd drained. Zuberi hadn't heard from Vriana, and she was worried.

Lencho's red glow flared.

"Don't tell me what to do," he snarled. "I'll do whatever it takes to survive. I don't need to buck the fuckin' system. I *am* the system." He turned to Aren, shouting, "Now!"

A blinding, luminescent glow overtook the Divine leader, beaming through every corner of the theater. Zuberi hit the ground just in time, avoiding the burning light as others fell beside her, shielding their eyes.

"Someone get him!" she shouted, just as she turned and saw Ibrahim raise his hands and send one of the tables straight for Aren. It struck him in his stomach, throwing him backward into a pile of debris. The light faded immediately, and the Divine kids scattered. One girl—Lara—moved purposefully to the left, and Zuberi had a sinking feeling she was going for Keera and Adisa.

"Stop them!" Zuberi called, rising and pulling out her staff. She leapt up just as Sekou sprinted past her.

"On it!" he called. "I'll get her while you handle this."

Right. This. Two Divine kids were still up and about, Zaire and Lencho. Behind Zuberi were Ibrahim and Tasha, the shy girl Zuberi barely knew from classes. The others had disappeared.

"Tasha, go get help," she told the girl. "Fast, okay?"

The girl looked back and forth, but eventually, she bolted. Then Zuberi turned her attention on the most dangerous person in the room: Lencho. Her target. They locked eyes, and then he turned and looked at Ibrahim.

"I think I'll drain him first," he said, grinning wildly.

No. Not after what she'd seen with that poor man. She wouldn't let him do that to Ibrahim. She ran for Lencho, but his swiftness was unfathomable. He ran as if he was on hyperspeed, laughing maniacally as he charged.

"Watch it!" shouted Ibrahim, and not a moment too soon.

Tipping her head up, Zuberi saw the cables above the pit snap. She dropped and rolled to the side just as a chunk of rigging plummeted down. Lencho also dodged the rigging, his eyes narrowing in fury at Ibrahim, who'd snapped the cables.

"You think you can handle me?" Lencho roared. "Let's see!"

Ibrahim scurried backward, and Zuberi raced forward, thrusting her staff out so that she caught Lencho in the face. He tumbled back, and Zuberi assumed her favorite defensive position from the forms, staff raised in front of her. The telekinetic quickly stood and came to her side.

Lencho grinned at her, blood dripping down his nose.

"You're good," he said. "I remember that. But two against one isn't exactly fair."

"I don't need anyone to take you on," Zuberi said.

Lencho shrugged, oddly nonchalant. "Maybe. But we'll see. Nneka, you got her yet?"

Suddenly, there was a puff of purple smoke and a Divine girl appeared onstage. In her grip was Keera, struggling and screaming.

"Get the hell offa me, bitch!" Keera screeched. "Let me go! How can you do this?"

"Chill out, Keera," came a slippery voice, just as Lara appeared around the corner, dragging someone behind her. "You wouldn't want to get too *heated*, would you?"

Zuberi's stomach dropped when she saw who Lara had grabbed. It was Adisa, the old man's hands tied behind his back. Above him, his phantoms were calm, hands steepled. Each figure looked at Zuberi as she struggled to breathe.

Goddess . . . damn.

"Lara, let him go," Keera said. "You have me. Just let him go."

Lara smiled. "Oh, Keera. You should've just come with us. This was a huge mistake."

A desperate look overcame the former Divine, almost as if she was cornered. Caged.

"Stay out!" Keera screamed. "Stay out of my—"

Zuberi heard a rumbling, the theater's ancient pipes exploding right where she stood, no doubt from the pressure of the building crumbling around them. Still, Zuberi focused on Keera, held by the grinning Divine girl called Nneka. Above them both, yellow light burned through Nneka's purple phantoms.

"Children, this is a mistake," Adisa warned. "Your abilities are not meant to be used this way. It is an affront to nature to wield your gifts against one another—"

"Shut it, Grandpa," Lencho said. Behind him, Aren was stirring, groaning under the weight of the collapsed wall. With one hand, Zaire lifted the rubble off him so that the Divine leader could stand.

Lencho looked at Zuberi and the other Nubians.

"I'm offering y'all a choice here," he said. "Come with us. Ascend and be great. These people . . . they just want to use you."

"Wrong," said a voice behind them.

Zuberi's heart lurched.

Uzochi.

He'd finally arrived.

Chapter 33

Uzochi

Uzochi stepped into the swirling dust that was the center of the theater. He stood beside Zuberi, feeling how her energy shifted at his presence. He stared at his cousin, hatred coursing through his veins.

In the tunnels that led from the scrapyards in the Swamp to the theater, Uzochi had thought about his cousin and his uncle. How pain and abuse had shaped Lencho into who he was. But none of it made what Uzochi found in the theater forgivable. As he looked from Keera, who was shrieking, to Adisa, whose gaze was steady on Uzochi, he felt nothing but fury.

"Give it up, cuz," he said. "I know you're scared. This isn't right."

Lencho only laughed, gesturing at Keera and Adisa. "Looks like I'm the one getting to make demands, *cuz.*"

It was true. Behind Uzochi, he knew the other Nubians were tired and afraid—all save for Zuberi, whose passion filled the room. They couldn't seize Keera from a teleporter, and Uzochi didn't know what Lara's power was. Whatever her gift was, it was submerged by a warped emotion that he could barely identify.

"I'm asking you to do the right thing," Uzochi said, looking from Lencho to Zaire and Aren. Uzochi felt hatred course through his veins at the sight of them both, but he forced himself to stay cool.

Lencho only grinned. "Oh yeah? Because you say so? Sorry, I don't take orders. Not even from the catalyst."

Beside Uzochi, Zuberi's mind shifted. He sensed the change, as if she was demanding that he listen. He met her eyes and, almost imperceptibly, they widened.

Get Adisa.

Her voice, clear as a bell, giving Uzochi the moment he needed.

"Now!" he shouted.

From the rafters, Sekou dropped like a bullet, holding on to the cables as his legs smashed into Lencho and sent him flying. Zuberi sprang forward, her staff whirling as she cornered Aren and spun in front of him, keeping him from using his gift. Ibrahim surged forward, too, throwing sheets of rubble back at Zaire to keep him in place.

Uzochi grabbed Adisa's hand and yanked him from Lara as she tumbled, thrown back by more rubble sent forth by Ibrahim.

"Nneka!" Lara shrieked.

"Get the girl!" Adisa shouted. "Uzochi, save her!"

Uzochi whipped back to where Keera was held by Nneka, the two girls grappling. Uzochi couldn't understand why

Nneka hadn't teleported away yet, but he couldn't stop to think about it. He charged forward, determined to hop onstage and tackle them both to the ground if he needed to.

But then Nneka cried out.

She was flung back, away from Keera, her screams echoing in the auditorium as she stared at her hands. Uzochi saw them, red and blistered . . . burned.

He looked at Keera and found that she didn't just glow yellow. She burned. Already, her hands were consumed by fire, the flames shifting from yellow to orange to jade.

A wave of searing heat followed by fire snaked from her hand to her head, her hair floating around her head. She tipped her head back as flames covered her completely, save for her eyes, which burned yellow.

She looked at Uzochi, and through the fire, he saw her smile.

"No!" Adisa cried, just as Keera sent flames in every direction.

Uzochi dove out of the way, rolling into a dusty nook at the edge of the pit. He peered up, smelling that his hair was singed, and realized that several rows of seats had been set aflame.

"Save the girl!" Adisa said. "Save her!"

Uzochi thought Baba must be out of his mind. What was he supposed to do? Keera was on fire. No one could touch her. Even Lencho, thrown to the side, was staring at her, wide-eyed.

Above them all, the Carter-Combs was crumbling. Cracks were appearing in the ceiling, sending down waves of debris.

A large chunk of brick clipped Ibrahim's shoulder, sending him to the floor. Uzochi watched as Zaire extended his arms and caught more rigging, dust raining down on everyone on-stage before he tossed it aside. Soon, it wouldn't matter what Zaire caught. They would all be buried.

A puff of purple smoke told Uzochi that Nneka had tele-ported. Another told him that she was grabbing the Divine members one by one. When he looked toward the collapsed wall, he saw that Aren and Zaire were gone. They were aban-doning the Carter-Combs—which was exactly what Uzochi and the Children needed to do.

"Zuberi, get them out of here!" he yelled. "To the tunnels in the back! Sekou, help!"

Sekou grabbed Zuberi, and together, they hauled Ibrahim up and out of the room. Zuberi looked back at Uzochi, and he hoped she knew he wasn't running just yet. He was going to fix this. He was going to—

Keera howled, and more fire shot forth from her body, nar-rowly missing Uzochi. A crash reverberated, and he watched as a piece of the ceiling smashed down directly next to Adisa. Uzochi rushed to his mentor's side, dodging debris and barely avoiding being burned by flames.

"Didn't get me," Adisa said, waving Uzochi off as he struggled to stand. "The girl, Uzochi. I keep telling you—"

"Baba, we've got to get you out of here," Uzochi insisted. "Come on."

Uzochi's eyes swept the room. There was Keera, in the center. All of the Divine were gone, save Lara and Lencho.

His cousin was struggling to stand under rubble, and Lara was watching Keera with wide eyes and a horrified grin.

"Lencho!" Uzochi called. "Come on. You've got to—"

One of Keera's streaks of fire shot straight for Lencho, striking him in the chest so that he tumbled back. Uzochi hollered at the sight, rushing forward.

It didn't matter what Lencho said about blood. Uzochi wasn't going to watch him die. He wasn't.

He dropped next to his cousin, grabbing his hand. Lencho was breathing, struggling.

"Lencho, you've got to get up," Uzochi told him. "The building's coming down. Where's your damn teleporter?"

A small smile crept over Lencho's face, most of it covered in dust from the building. Then it was as though Lencho realized who Uzochi was, and he yanked back his hand.

"Get away from me," he snapped.

"Lencho, don't be stupid," Uzochi said. "We've gotta go."

Uzochi. The girl. Save her.

He whirled at Adisa's voice, seeing then that Adisa was walking toward Keera, his arms outstretched, talking to her. Trying to get her to calm down.

No. He was too close to the fire. He was . . .

Adisa turned and met Uzochi's eyes.

Save her.

"But how?"

Uzochi looked from Keera to Lencho. He didn't know what Adisa was asking him to do. Unless . . .

Her mind. Of course.

"I've got to get into her mind," Uzochi said aloud. "Okay, Baba, I'll try!"

But wading into Keera's mind now wasn't possible. He couldn't touch her. He could try to send forth his thoughts from a distance, but as he did, he found that her soul was an angry, raging thing, full of shattered memories that cut and bit as he tried to sort through them to find her. Wherever he went, he found obstacles.

Uzochi breathed, returning to his body, sobbing. He wouldn't be able to get to her. She was lost.

Suddenly, beside him, Lencho stood. He ran straight for Keera, threw out his hands, and seized her arms. Uzochi screamed for his cousin—Lencho's pain was blinding and swept through the room.

"Lencho!"

Keera's fire raged, thrown out in every direction. Uzochi's heart broke as the fire bloomed and the building shook. He was watching his cousin die. He was Kefle watching Siran in the tempest, only this storm was unbearable heat and flame.

But then . . .

Slowly, slowly, the flames faded. Slowly, Uzochi could see to the center where the stage was burned black. Where Keera slumped against Lencho, breathing slowly.

In the corner of the room, a purple puff of smoke. All of the Divine were gone, except for Lencho.

Uzochi, quickly, send to me . . . there's no time . . .

Adisa's voice again. Where was he?

Uzochi's heart sank when he saw the elder, crushed

beneath a beam from the ceiling that had pinned him across the chest.

"Baba!" Uzochi yelled, rushing to him.

Adisa coughed. "You . . . you must leave, child."

"I've got you," Uzochi said, trying desperately to move the beam. "Come on."

But when Uzochi finally pushed it away, he saw that Adisa's old body was terribly battered, the elder's crippling pain practically unbearable.

"You brave boy," Adisa said. "I wanted to prepare you . . . give you more time . . . what's coming . . . it terrifies me."

"Baba, you need to—"

"We don't have time," Adisa said, voice straining. "I hoped to keep you safe from what is coming. But now . . . you must try to understand—"

The elder's words were drowned out as he coughed again, this time with blood spilling over his lips. Tears filled Uzochi's eyes as he held up Adisa's head.

Adisa grasped Uzochi's hand and peered into the boy's eyes. Uzochi knew that Adisa could speak no more. But when he heard the elder's thoughts in his mind, the words were clear, ungarbled.

Uzochi, you must place your consciousness into mine. . . . Enter my mind. . . . I will show you.

Uzochi closed his eyes immediately. He dropped all remaining threads to this world and focused solely on Adisa. With a rush of blinding blue, his thoughts unraveling, the elder's voice echoed in his head.

Ah, now I can let go . . . be strong . . . for what's coming . . .

Uzochi's head spun and spun some more and then the blue faded. He had the briefest moment when he thought he saw his cousin's face, bobbing in space. He reached for Lencho, but then there was nothing but shadow. Movement, a scream somewhere. The ground felt rough and cold and Adisa's blood was on his hands and then . . .

. . . and then . . .

. . . .

Chapter 34

Lencho

Lencho dreamed of screaming. It followed him even after he blacked out, covered by the wreckage of the Carter-Combs.

There were different screams in his mind. Keera's, the girl who'd burned. He'd thought she would burn through him when he drained her, but when he looked at his hands after, they were devoid of any marks or blemishes. Another side effect of his gift. Accelerated healing. The thought left him hollow.

There were Adisa's screams, echoing alongside Keera's. He'd carried them both to the tunnels, Keera and Adisa. The elder had been heavy, a body that no longer held a soul. Lencho had known this the second he lifted the man. That's when Lencho had screamed, too.

There was Uzochi, also yelling in his mind. He'd carried his cousin out, too. With his enhanced strength, he'd carried the three of them to the tunnel entrances, dropping them off with the horrified man who'd demanded to know who Lencho was and what he'd done. But Lencho couldn't have answered. He didn't know what he was doing. He was acting without thought, pure energy, nothing more.

Then Lencho had run back to the center of the theater. He'd waited for Nneka, but she hadn't returned. The building had fallen down around Lencho, snuffing out the remaining fires with debris.

Now Lencho felt cool air. He looked up. He was no longer in what was left of the theater but could see the wreckage. He was looking down at the ruins from a hill. He scanned the ground near him and found scratchy grass and dirt.

"What the hell were you thinking?"

Fear seized Lencho instantly. He looked up and saw his father crouched against a wall off to the side, covered in dirt and ash.

"You could've died, Lencho," Kefle snarled. "Do you understand that? Does death mean anything to you?"

Death. Lencho had certainly seen death today. He'd carried it.

Yes, death meant something to him.

"I don't know what you're playing at, boy, but it ends now," said Kefle.

Lencho stared at his father, the man who'd made their home a place of fear and pain. And now he was acting like he was worried about his son?

"Fuck off," Lencho said, shaking his pounding head. He'd never felt so weak. So dizzy. The world was fuzzy.

"You think this is a joke, don't you?" Kefle demanded. "Everything is to you. When are you going to wake up?"

Suddenly, Lencho's ear buzzed. He tapped at it, realized that the earpiece was still fused to his auricle. Sounds were coming forth—distorted and staticky.

"Hello?" Lencho asked. "Hello?"

"Lencho," Kefle said, stalking over to point a finger in his son's face. "I'm trying to talk some sense into you right now. I didn't pull your ass out of that goddamn theater for you to ignore me."

Lencho froze. His dad had done what? No, wasn't possible. But then, when he took in Kefle's clothes . . .

"Lencho?" Tilly's voice was in his head. "You're there? Double-tap and send us your location. We need you back here immediately."

He tapped the earpiece, then looked at his father. How had he never seen how weak his dad was? How he chose to live in misery? Then again . . . Lencho might have his own problems to face. He'd failed today. Failed so horribly that he wondered if Krazen St. John would revoke his ascension outright.

"These gifts aren't true gifts," Kefle said. "They're going to eat you alive. Don't you understand?"

A tired smile found its way to Lencho's features. Oh, if only his dad knew what he could do. Not true gifts? He'd been the one to save Keera. Uzochi had failed, but Lencho had succeeded.

A problem, though, given Lencho's objective. But he made it out alive. Maybe Krazen would understand. And maybe Krazen would have something for his pounding head, because Lencho felt like his skull was about to burst.

In a puff of purple smoke, Nneka appeared. She glanced at Kefle once, then back at Lencho. Her raised eyebrow was the question, and he nodded his assent.

"No," Kefle said, moving to block Nneka. "No, not my son. Not my—"

Lencho reached out, and Nneka took his hand. In a moment, they were gone, the girl making multiple jumps through the lower city before reaching Central Park. The whole enterprise left Lencho queasy, and he quickly blacked out again.

When Lencho opened his eyes, it was to see Krazen St. John at his office desk. Tilly was beside him.

"Lencho," Krazen said, his eyes widening. "I was worried we lost you."

Lencho struggled to stand. He was so weak. So, so weak. Sandra was right. The plan had been terrible. And where was she? He felt if he could see her . . . maybe he could get his thoughts to align . . .

"He's dazed," Tilly said. "That much exertion—"

"Quiet," Krazen said. "Let him have a moment."

Behind them, silent news footage played. Lencho blinked, for a moment not understanding. Then he realized it was the Carter-Combs. It was Keera, on fire onstage as others screamed and ran. Then it was the Nubians fighting . . . Zuberi and Aren and the others. A caption scrolled across the bottom.

Dangerous Nubians destroy historical site, but Krazen St. John promises a return to safety with his private gifted militia. . . . Special meeting with the UN coming soon. . . .

There was Lencho, seizing Keera's wrist. Lencho, carrying

them out of the room. Lencho, buried in the rubble as a drone camera popped out and zoomed around the scene.

"You've done beautifully, dear boy," Krazen said. "Better than I could've ever imagined."

But Lencho didn't understand. He didn't secure Keera. He destroyed the theater. And Adisa . . .

"He might have a concussion," Tilly said, gaze flicking from Lencho to Krazen.

"You're right," Krazen said, standing up. "We'll get him fixed up. Quickly. An examination and rest are in order. But Lencho, I want you to know that I'm so proud. And we got everything, thanks to the cameras Nneka planted. So don't worry. You were incredible."

Incredible. The word filed through Lencho's mind on repeat, even as he struggled to understand the images on the screen.

"I'm afraid I have to ask for more of you," Krazen continued. "I'm about to leave, and Tilly will escort you to where you need to go. You'll know what to do when you're there, I'm sure. Because you're incredible, son."

More? Lencho didn't know if he had more. But he could dig deeper for Krazen. Because he was incredible.

Incredible, incredible, incredible.

Lencho barely felt the needle Tilly injected into his neck. And when he succumbed to darkness, he felt safer than he'd ever been.

Chapter 35

Zuberi

Zuberi barely made it through the tunnels to the scrap-yards before she collapsed. She hit the concrete ground hard, her body crying out from the exertion. Everything she'd left behind spun in her mind, and she craved peace. She'd run straight past Thato, even though she'd wanted nothing more but to cling to her father and hold on tight. He needed to stay in the tunnel, and she needed to get out. To get to where it was quiet and screams didn't tinge the air.

But as Zuberi fought for breath, she realized that the sounds of the scrapyard weren't quiet. They were alive.

Alive with fear.

Many of the Children who'd run through the tunnels now were slumped against discarded metal, but others were stand-ing and pointing to the sky. Zuberi realized with a start that something was there, above them. A massive holo, with Kra-zen St. John firmly at the center. His hands were spread wide as he addressed a group of people tucked into the shadows of the projection.

A booming voice filled the air, echoing from every speaker in the street. It was duller in the scrapyard, but still horrifyingly clear.

"This is Helios News, and we're going live as Krazen St. John addresses the United Nations. We've been asked to project this important and essential meeting so that every person in Tri-State East is aware of what's at stake today. This comes as word of an explosion erupting in the area is still being investigated. Let's go live now—"

Zuberi drifted toward Krazen's image in the sky like a girl possessed. What would this horrible man say about what had happened today?

"My friends," Krazen's augmented holo said to his audience of UN representatives. "I come to you today as a man who fears for my home. Today is another example of the atrocities that global governments are unwilling to face. First, the discovery of a horde of paranormals right under our nose. Then, the destruction of one of our esteemed historical sites. But the issues run so much deeper. Our city and country have been plagued by crime, by drugs. I have done what I could, but the mayor refuses to accept my help, and even those higher up in government do not work with me. It's clear that I do not have the power necessary to—"

A hysterical cackle drew Zuberi's attention. She held up her fists by instinct, and she kept them up when she saw who was laughing. There, on the ground, was a battered Aren, his face turned up as he laughed and cried at the same time.

"Aren?" she said, stepping toward the Divine cautiously. She knew now what his gift was, how dangerous he could be.

"Did you know?" he said, nearly choking on the blood in his mouth as he looked up at Krazen. "Did you know he's the one who supplies us? The Elevation. All this time. I found out it was him."

Zuberi stopped in her tracks as the words hit her. Krazen was behind Elevation? But . . .

"I had rules," Aren said, swiping at the blood on his mouth. "But then . . . I found out. It was him all along. My rules didn't matter. He's been pumping this entire city with the shit."

"To keep us in the same cycle," Zuberi said, realization dawning on her. "Where we need to be."

She'd known she hated Krazen. Hated him for the ways he always made ascension seem like just a matter of hard work, hated his racist militia and how they turned her home into a constant war zone. But this . . . this went beyond.

"I had Nneka take me here," Aren said. "I couldn't go back. I couldn't. I—"

Suddenly, Sekou was racing across the scrapyard, drawing Zuberi's attention. She saw a couple of his phantoms ahead of him, morphing so quickly he became a blur.

"Zuberi!" he called out. "Zuberi, hurry . . . I just spotted something while zipping around in my spirit form. We've gotta get to the seawall. Now."

"Why?" she demanded. "What's happening?"

Sekou's face was grim, shaded by the light of Krazen's holo above them.

"It's better if you just come see."

So she raced with him, defying fatigue, dodging metal and Nubians who sank, crying, against the adults who were scattered about. Zuberi wished she could tell them it was all over, but in her soul, she knew it wasn't.

When they reached the seawall, it took Zuberi a moment to realize what, exactly, Sekou was showing her. The area was empty, eerily quiet. It was her first sign that something was wrong, actually—there wasn't a St. John Soldier in sight. The only thing she heard was the voice of Krazen echoing all around her.

"These problems are multiplying," he was saying. "What will we lose tomorrow if we don't have proper leadership? For too long, we in Tri-State East have struggled to have our voices heard. But we've waited too long. With your help, we can rectify this. I can do what is necessary to save our fine country."

On those words, Zuberi noticed what Sekou had led her to see.

There, nestled in the corners of the seawall, were tiny black circles, webbed to the wall with some kind of metal guard. Zuberi thought, for a moment, that they were high-tech, meant to fix the wall. It was what any Nubian would've assumed, given the constant repairs.

"Can you see?" Sekou asked, his voice tight. "When I was up there, astral surfing, trying to see if I could find any Divine in the Swamp, I realized what those things were." He ground his teeth. "Fuck."

She looked closer, noticing the blinking red dots on each of the circles.

Bombs.

"What will happen if we do nothing?" Krazen continued, his voice a mighty boom across the Swamp. "What will we lose next if we choose to wait?"

It was then that the first bomb exploded, tearing a hole straight through the center of the seawall.

Chapter 36

Uzochi

Uzochi didn't know where he was. His mind was consumed by shadow as he struggled for consciousness. A hollow place in his heart told him he'd just endured unimaginable pain. But when he awoke, it was because of a loud, resounding *boom*.

Adisa's voice echoed inside him, telling him he needed to be brave for what was to come. He wanted to stay with the voice, to sink into it.

But when he opened his eyes, he was greeted by chaos.

Someone had carried Uzochi back through the tunnels to the scrapyard. Someone had left him there, but they were gone. Now, when he stood, he saw a holo in the sky—but it wasn't just any holo.

It was a live feed of the seawall being ripped apart.

Uzochi didn't think. He forced his muscles to run, to bolt for the Swamp. His instincts proclaimed this was insanity—he should be running away from danger, not to it—but he also knew that something had to be done.

As he reached the seawall a couple of minutes later, debris

fell around him, torrents of water gushing from the breach and filling the streets. Several shacks on stilts had already collapsed. Flying bricks hit another home, which plummeted to the ground. He saw Sekou bravely leading a cluster of elders away.

Uzochi heard more yells and cries. Some people were frozen, in shock, while others had begun to flee. He peered up at the breach, and something in his mind flashed. He remembered the shields he often relied upon to block out the thoughts and emotions of others. Something inside told him to bring the barrier forth now.

No, not something.

Adisa.

He'd told Uzochi before, hadn't he, that Uzochi could make the field physical one day if he tried, if he practiced relentlessly.

Uzochi didn't know how, but there wasn't time to think. He called upon his mind to create a shield of force, something he'd never done before.

And then the water stopped, cupped against his barrier, curling upward almost as if being swept up by an invisible hand. He pushed the water back, and back some more, and immediately felt a pounding in his head.

The pressure . . . would sever him in two. But he held it there for as long as he could as people darted around, trying to reach safety.

"Everybody, you've got to run!" Zuberi shouted from nearby, nearly breaking his concentration. He saw her there, gesturing and waving to the people. He wanted to run to her, so furiously happy that she was all right . . . but no. He needed to stay where he was, maintain the force field.

A stampede began, people seeming to fully comprehend what was about to happen. Wails of terror filled the watery streets. Zuberi cupped her hands to her mouth, shouting as loudly as she could to the shacks on stilts.

"GET OUT AND RUN! PLEASE! RUN! A FLOOD IS COMING!"

He wanted to close his eyes, Zuberi's shouts piercing his skull. The pressure in his head . . .

. . . was unbearable.

He couldn't hold back the waters much longer, but thankfully, the people were listening, bolting. An old man stumbled, screaming and screaming, the throngs of people running and jostling becoming a stampede.

Suddenly, there was a puff of purple, and Uzochi saw several Nubians flash from the scene.

That Divine teleporter is whisking folks away, Uzochi realized with a jolt, wondering why she was helping. Even so, no one could teleport all these people to safety.

From the corner of his eye he saw a blurry figure whiz by, grab two more people, and whisk them away from the wall.

More water began to pour forth from the breach. Water began to rise around Uzochi, his feet completely submerged.

He panted and centered, letting go of his physical pain and embracing the lessons learned when he was fully in his mind.

Go within, hold on . . .

. . . find your core . . .

. . . find the strength through your breath . . .

Adisa's voice, carrying him on. Guiding him.

Uzochi let go of the pain in his head and arms and shoulders and the rest of his body, just trying to make sure he was breathing.

He opened his eyes once again, only to see more streams of water gushing from the fissure, flowing through cracks in his shield. The water had risen to his knees. He heard the continual cries of people behind him, waves of fear smashing into his back.

They were going to die. He was supposed to be a protector of Nubians, like his father once was, and he was going to fail them, just like his father.

They were all going to be swept away.

His knees began to wobble, his control over his body gone. He hoped other Nubians knew that he'd tried. That he wanted to be there for his people. Was Zuberi still behind him? Had she gotten far enough away?

Oh, Goddess, please, please, please let her be safe. Goddess, please take care of my mother. . . .

A blurry figure slashed through puddles of water and zipped past Uzochi, circling around him and stopping several feet to his left. It was the same figure he'd noticed just moments ago getting folks to safety.

Lencho.

His cousin looked a mess. There was no other way to say it. His eyes were wide—too wide—and he kept whipping his head back and forth, maybe seeing whom he could help?

Something was off, but Uzochi didn't have time to figure out what.

An idea hit him.

They'd been able to save Keera together, hadn't they? Perhaps . . . perhaps they could figure out a way to save the seawall, too.

"Lencho!" he called out over the roar and the panic. "Lencho!"

Lencho turned to Uzochi, clearly bracing himself for his cousin's usual disdain. But for once, it wasn't there.

"You!" said a furious voice from behind. Uzochi looked back only to see Zuberi rushing toward Lencho, her staff at her side. She'd nearly collided with the boy when Uzochi saw his cousin's eyes narrow and his hands rise.

I won't be stopped. I won't let anyone get in my way.

It was his cousin's voice, furious, maniacal, louder than Uzochi had heard any voice before. But there, under the noise, was something else. The contours of Lencho's gift, pulsing brighter than anything he'd witnessed at the theater.

"No!" Uzochi called, stepping between them, his gaze firmly on Zuberi. "We need him, Beri. We need him to save the Swamp!"

"Do you know what I'm seeing right now?" Zuberi shrieked into the wind. "Every other phantom floating around is dead. And it's all because of that asshole."

Her mind was a mass of rage, slamming into Uzochi. He looked at his cousin, who was breathing hard. Uzochi expected to feel rage from him as well, but most of all he discerned . . . shame?

Yes, shame laced with determination.

"There's no time," Uzochi said. "We have to work together. Lencho, we need to merge our gifts to save the seawall."

His cousin still looked dazed, but as he turned to the collapsing wall, he nodded.

"He told me I could do it," Lencho said, voice heavy. "So, yeah. Whatever you need. I'll help."

Uzochi didn't understand, but Lencho had given his consent, which took precedent over all else. And so, without further discussion, Uzochi flew into his cousin's mind, barely able to send forth his consciousness as he held back the waters, going past Kefle's venomous words and Kefle's slaps and Kefle's fists and the roaches in the Jungle and the siphoning of people on the street and shame over the gift that had become an addiction and the magnificently poised young woman known as Sandra St. John and the perennially gray and silver and glass walls of the Up High, getting to the energy at his cousin's core, the energy that represented Lencho's gift. A magnificent scarlet energy that bristled and pulsed and writhed, terrible in its power, ready to consume, the most frightening expression of the kinetic that Uzochi had ever witnessed.

Yet something there was inviting, something that drew Uzochi closer, promising invigoration and renewal.

As was his way, Uzochi immediately understood what Lencho could do.

"The lights are trying to merge," Zuberi said from somewhere far away. "You need to come together. . . . Lencho, let Uzochi in! Give him your power!"

It was what Uzochi had felt, too, and now, with Zuberi's words, Lencho acted with no hesitation. He gave fully to Uzochi, allowing them to combine their gifts into one.

Uzochi opened his eyes and gasped as Lencho sent waves and waves of energy into his body, the rush so dramatic that he almost thought he would swoon. What his cousin felt like when he absorbed essence from others.

Uzochi turned toward the breach, and a glistening blue field of force erupted to cover the hole in the seawall, mighty, resplendent, the pressures of the waters no longer vexing Uzochi's mind.

He adjusted himself, turning to fully face the seawall, and Lencho placed his hands on his cousin's shoulders, continuing to channel energy.

The infusion of power bolstered Uzochi's consciousness so much that he once again saw the bristling core of energy that he knew to be an expression of the kinetic, this particular expression a rich, shimmering turquoise sun. Uzochi's own personal manifestation of his power.

And that energy reached forth and touched all the gifted Children and all the gifted Divine in the Swamp. His ability was to wield the kinetic in all of its varied forms, to ask those who were gifted to share what they wielded.

Through Lencho's boost, Uzochi understood who he really was as well.

Uzochi's mind floated about the Swamp, above the screaming and dismay and confusion, trying to allay the fears of his people, thinking of when he was in the Carter-Combs, reaching out to so many different minds. But he had far more power now. This kind of gift . . . he could make it so no one ever hurt him or his loved ones again.

Uzochi's consciousness floated higher above the Swamp, taking in the totality of the city, people starting to look like ants. He could stay up there forever, could exult in the kinetic forever, could remain safe and free and mighty, could eliminate anyone who dared to not fully see him, to not worship him for everything he could be.

And he heard a voice from within . . .

Do not lose yourself. . . .

Baba.

From the lofty heights of his mind, Uzochi saw that the danger to his people had ended, the flood had been held at bay. Baba was right.

He dissolved the strings he held to the Children and Divine. What they had was not for him to take.

As Uzochi's consciousness returned to his body, Lencho's hands still on his shoulders, he entered a zone of numb awareness, feeling like he would hold his shield up for eternity if it meant making sure that the people of the Swamp were okay. Time lost all meaning, though he understood on some level that time was still a thing, as people continued to run to and fro, a plethora of shouts in his ears.

Barely aware of anything any longer, he focused on his shield, keeping still, not turning away from the wall, relieved when he soon saw Ibrahim and Abdul using their gifts to repair the breach. Abdul created compact, thick mounds of earth that Ibrahim diligently floated up to the wall to serve as a makeshift patch, the boys repeating the process again and again and again until the water leaking from the wall had become a mere trickle.

And that was when Uzochi knew he could finally release his shield.

He stumbled to the ground, barely able to acknowledge his cousin, who was still by his side. Uzochi closed his eyes, the water at his knees no longer frightening but cool. Refreshing.

A place to rest.

Chapter 37

Sandra

"Well, it looks like your plan worked."

Sandra smiled up at her father. They were walking through one of her favorite places, which wasn't as bright and colorful as the gardens. In fact, the space's concrete walls and steel doors were downright dreary. But Sandra had learned long ago that she could work with anything as long as she had a vision.

"You sound surprised," Krazen said, his bare feet padding beside her heels. She clicked loudly throughout the halls, the sound echoing all around them. Most of the space was empty, leaving so much room for sound.

"No, you were right," Sandra said. "I realized it after I left, of course. And it was masterful, you know. Using the theater as a distraction so you could rig the seawall. Making sure your 'special' militia would be there to help fix the problem."

"I had to accelerate things," Krazen said, "once I realized the Children were on hand and might eventually interfere. They hadn't been part of the original plan, since I'd thought they'd be thoroughly occupied with the fallout from Keera. But those tunnels . . . I couldn't have known. They did well, regardless. Played right into our hands."

Sandra nodded, choosing to ignore her thoughts about the scores of Nubians who would've been killed if the Children hadn't come through. "They were a . . . as you like to say, 'happy accident'?"

Krazen chuckled. "Yes, especially Uzochi."

Sandra knew how spectacular a moment this was. Mayor Culliver had stepped down, the failure of the seawall the final death knell for his administration. An emergency election was already in the works while Krazen continued to pull strings and orchestrate the world to his liking.

But Sandra wasn't finished.

"You did give me an idea," she said. "You know, about being indispensable."

Sandra walked past the St. John militia guards, turning left down the first hall. On her right, she took in the floor-to-ceiling windows that showed the small rooms dotting the hallway. Well, perhaps "rooms" was a generous name. They were pens. Pens in a prison, honestly. The windows were see-through glass, titanium-strength, that looked out through the room to the sky. It was the view that made it hard for Sandra to really call this place a prison. Prisons never came with such majestic views.

"You've piqued my interest," said Krazen. "But you know I loathe waiting."

Sandra nodded. "Just a little longer."

It had taken some convincing for Sandra to secure what

she needed from the guards. Not many of them were her size, after all. But eventually, she'd found a militia member who was willing to let Sandra borrow her uniform for a hefty sum. And she'd found another who let her sneak onto their patrol on the day of Lencho's attempted kidnapping of Keera.

From there, it had been timing. Timing and manifesting. Of course, she couldn't have dreamed that one of Lencho's former targets would stumble onto the girls. She'd only hoped that Zuberi would rush off and leave Vriana behind. The old man had been a bonus.

Timing. Manifesting.

"There," Sandra said, waving her arm with a flourish at the glass. "There she is."

Krazen squinted, taking in the prisoner inside. Sandra had made sure that Vriana was given a proper bed, a sink, and a screen for privacy to change. She'd even given the girl her best dresses to wear, though Vriana refused to even glance at them. Truly, she cried most of the time, but Sandra knew that eventually, she would see things the right way. After all, if she wanted her friends and precious aunt kept alive, she'd have to listen.

"Who is this creature?" Krazen asked.

"Well, don't be mad," she said. "I know you said powers of the mind weren't a priority. But after I saw Vriana . . . well, I knew you'd have to have her."

Krazen glanced at Sandra.

"She can persuade people to do absolutely anything she asks," Sandra said, not able to keep the hunger out of her voice. "And the best part is that she can give them a sense of euphoria while she exercises her gift. So they're *happy* to listen to her. Just imagine. Any Nubian who doesn't want to join you . . . well, they just have a little chat with 'V' here and, boom! Right on your team."

Krazen's lips curled into a smile. Not a mocking or cruel smile, but a proud one. Sandra's heart beat faster as she continued to talk.

"I used every one of your tricks to get her here," she continued. "I told her we had a distress call about her friends. That she needed to come right away. She was so trusting. I mean, look at her. She really cares, this girl."

Through the glass, Vriana could be seen sitting on a chair, staring straight ahead back at Krazen and Sandra. Tears slipped down her cheeks. She spoke, but her words were muted, unheard through the glass.

"She can't see us, of course," Sandra said. "And we can't hear her."

"But how did you get her in there without her using her gift?"

"You've always said that meeting in person is more effective, right? Our chat was very convincing," Sandra replied. "I told her that if she used her gift on me, we had a squad of St. John Soldiers waiting to attack her friends and family. And, of course, Lara's been helping, coming up with ways we can use her abilities to keep V in line."

This made Krazen's head turn. He stared at his daughter.

"What?" she asked innocently. "Lara told me long ago about her gift. How she can not just read minds but short-circuit them, too. She told me about your whole plan to, you know, use her to make sure Keera went fire-crazy and destroyed the theater. Excellent touch, along with the bombs at the seawall. How she was actually the first Nubian you found, even before Lencho. People like to talk to me, Father. You don't know how lonely it can be up here, especially for us Nubians."

Krazen blinked, looking back at Vriana.

He cleared his throat.

"I . . . underestimated you, Sandra."

"Oh, I know," she said, tossing back her fiery hair. "But it gave me ideas. Made me better."

She turned and took a few steps back the way they'd come before pausing and looking over her shoulder.

"Though I will say, Father, you might not want to underestimate me in the future."

She let the words hang before smiling her glittering smile, turning on her heels, and clicking right back down the hall.

Chapter 38

Uzochi

When Uzochi woke up, he still expected to be in the scrapyard or by the seawall. The memories were so vivid, burned into him. He dreamed of the scrapyard again and again, finding himself amid broken-down hover cars and metal piled high. It was all Swamp garbage, a place where no one would expect secret tunnels to be hidden. The passages had been Adisa's idea, Com'pa told Uzochi, all the way back when the Carter-Combs Theater had first been used. A way for Nubians to always find their way home safely.

Now, because of Uzochi, the tunnels had been discovered, the Carter-Combs was destroyed, and Adisa was gone.

Grief hit him like constant blows to the chest. With each waking breath, he relived the ugly comments he'd made to Adisa. He heard the old man's voice again and again as he died. Uzochi would sob with every memory, drawing Com'pa over for comfort.

"It wasn't your fault," she told Uzochi as he clung to her. "It wasn't your fault."

But he knew it was. He had entered Keera's mind too late, let her cause too much destruction. And even before that, she had asked for his help. If he had listened, they could have avoided all of this destruction. If it hadn't been for him, Adisa would be alive.

Uzochi wondered about Lencho, too, the moment he awoke. Was he really living Up High now? He was confused about his cousin, who had apparently disappeared with the rest of the Divine after Uzochi passed out at the sea-wall. Com'pa told him it was Lencho who'd dropped Uzochi, Keera, and Adisa's body at the edge of the tunnels. He'd left them with Thato and then run back to the theater only to mysteriously reappear later, as Uzochi had seen.

"But why come back?" Uzochi had wanted to know. "And why help us in the first place? And how did he make it out of the rubble if he didn't take the tunnels?"

That last part, Com'pa hesitated to tell him. Eventually, she admitted that it was Kefle who'd saved Lencho before he'd been taken back by the Divine. Or at least, that's what Uzochi's uncle claimed when she spoke to him after the fire.

"You must understand, dear heart, that I wept and wept for your father as we fled, as we witnessed Nubia vanishing in the tempest, the few elementals on our fleet of wooden sailboats barely able to protect us from the weather," she said, wiping her eyes. "I sat next to your uncle Kefle on one of these vessels, along with your aunt Leeyah, who was quite pregnant with Lencho by this time. We had just witnessed your father's death and your uncle shed no tears, offered me no succor or words of support. He simply sat there, rigid, silent, clasping a bundle of possessions in his lap while Leeyah tried to control her breathing, frightened she might go into labor. I tell you this: if I'd had the strength, I would have thrown that contemptible louse off our boat to join his brother in the depths."

She grabbed his hand and held on, her tears falling down her cheeks.

"That man is so . . . lost, Uzochi," she said. "And it doesn't make a piece of what he's done right. But your uncle may finally be trying to heal, to make amends. I don't know."

Lencho hadn't stayed with Kefle, though. He had gone back to the Divine, back, Uzochi now knew, to Krazen himself. Even after everything . . .

He needed to talk it all out with someone who understood. His mind searched for Zuberi but couldn't find her. She wasn't near, and the thought hurt deeper than any of his actual wounds. He'd expected her to be waiting for him when he woke, after what they'd been through, but instead, all he could do was watch the holos and try not to think of Adisa while his mom held whispered conversations on the phone.

"Several residents of the Nubian Quarter and other parts of the lower city continue to rally against the newly identified 'paranormals' that we've been made aware of recently. While Krazen St. John promises his gifted militia unit will serve the city, residents have questions. He points to their efforts at the seawall as evidence that they can be trusted, but others aren't sure. Still, there's no denying the calamity that would've happened without them. We go live to Krazen St. John's most recent press conference—"

The Helios News anchor was replaced by a shot of Krazen St. John presiding over a swarm of reporters.

"We want each of you to feel safe," he said. "It's come to our attention that certain Nubians have particular gifts, some of which are dangerous, as seen with the incident at the historic Carter-Combs Theater. In fact, we have our own force to thank for saving lives that day. Just witness here how one of our own rushed in to save a Nubian who'd lost control of her powers."

The holo flashed to footage of the Carter-Combs, of Lencho grabbing Keera and drawing her out of her state. There were also brief shots of his cousin at the seawall rushing bystanders to safety, though Uzochi noticed that he himself had been edited out of the footage.

"We will need them in this strange, distressing time. The seawall was on its last legs, woefully damaged because of the recent quake. I tried to save the wall and thereby the Swamp through discussions with our recently departed mayor, but it's clear that we are beyond discussions. We need action. Now. Thankfully, I now have the backing of the United Nations and other governmental authorities to make real change here. We will use our gifted militia to keep us safe, and if any of these new bands of paranormals pose a threat, my forces will deal with them accordingly."

Uzochi's mind spun with Krazen's incredible lies. His orchestrations. Zuberi had been right all along. He was the threat to their way of life, and he'd now marked every Nubian not aligned with him as a target.

He turned off the holo and sought solace in sleep, but it was no use. His mind was a mess of memories, particularly Adisa's. He woke with a start after each one, unwilling and unable to relive the elder's life. Not yet.

"You all right, buddy?"

He turned at her voice, finding her kneeling close to where he lay on the couch. He sat up and, without thinking, opened his arms. She crashed against him, hugging him tight, and he drank in the feeling of holding her. Her mind sparked with feelings—relief, joy, grief, worry . . .

"Your mom let me in," she said, pulling back to look at him. "She stepped out to give us some time. Said she'll take in a matinee at the holo-theater."

Uzochi smiled. *Subtle, Mom, always subtle.*

Zuberi nodded at the table and Adisa's journal, which Uzochi had just been reading.

"You doing okay?" she asked. "With everything?"

"I feel like it's all I have left," he said. "And . . . I have a responsibility. He was right about something bad happening. Somehow, he knew the seawall was going to collapse. So I owe it to him to learn everything I can."

Uzochi felt broken, especially when Zuberi's lip began to quiver. Did she blame him for what had happened?

"I tried," he said quietly. "To save him."

She nodded, looking down. "I know you did. Because that's what you do. Help people."

He stayed quiet. She didn't know how close he'd come to running away.

Then she looked up at him, and her gaze was fierce.

"That's why I need your help now, Uzochi," she said. "Because they've taken her. They've taken Vriana."

Uzochi felt cold seize him. "*What?* No . . . Who?"

"The Divine," she said, standing and pacing. "Or Krazen. They're one and the same now, I guess."

"But—"

"She's gifted," Zuberi said, pausing her pacing. "She can persuade anyone to do as she asks. She did it with this unhoused man we met right before the Carter-Combs was attacked. I think . . . I think this militiawoman was following us and saw what she could do. And now those St. John pigs have her. And, Uzochi, I can't do it. I can't live without her. She's my best friend."

Zuberi dropped to her knees, shaking with sobs. Uzochi sat up and put his hand on her back, wishing he had Lencho's ability to take away her pain.

Except, no. That wasn't true. Lencho's so-called gift involved taking what wasn't his.

"I hate feeling this way. So powerless," Zuberi said. She let out a deep breath and pulled her knees to her body as she wiped away the tears. "When I was younger, Uzochi, I was attacked. I was on a school field trip slightly north of the Swamp, walking at the back of the line with my classmates before being grabbed by a bunch of hooligans. There was a group of Elevated crazies known for doing this at the time, targeting Nubian kids for no fuckin' reason. They just snatched me and ran down several blocks, laughing and hooting, and pulled me into an alley.

"I was held down and cut across my face with something sharp. I think it was a broken bottle, but I'm honestly not sure. What I do remember was the burning pain and the fear, and then they tried to . . ."

Uzochi's chest flared with rage, remembering her fight with the Spiders near 104. He looked at her with tenderness, and she tapped her scar.

"I'm so sorry, Beri," he said, her awkwardness over sharing the story intertwined with his own. "I . . . I didn't realize. I wish . . . I'd like to be of support."

Zuberi nodded. "I appreciate that, buddy." She kept her gaze on the floor. "I was able to get away and was immediately taken to a med-center, but I felt so . . . defeated," she said. "And my dad . . . he was beyond furious at those creeps. He went a little insane, to be honest, feeling like he'd failed me and the memory of my mother. But I was furious because I'd been caught unaware, because I could've been taken out by some stupid punks. So I've spent my whole life training so no one would be able to hurt me or my friends again."

Her eyes welled up with more tears and she rubbed them away.

"Only now, it doesn't matter how much I've trained," she said. "Because the goons who have V are up in the sky and I can't do a damn thing about it."

She slammed her fist into the couch.

Uzochi took her hand and held it, looking into her eyes.

"We'll get her back," he said, wanting to be there for Zuberi the way she'd always been there for him. "I promise."

"How?" Zuberi asked. "My dad wants to leave. He's done

with all of this shit. With what they're doing to the Swamp, everything. He doesn't want to risk another seawall collapse and he believes some people will start to hunt Nubians once they discover who we really are. I had to beg to get him to stay for even a day."

Uzochi took in a breath. He didn't know, exactly, what they could do. They were still newly trained Nubians with a long way to go before they could fully comprehend their gifts.

He tapped the journal in his hand.

"We can do it," he said. "We can fight back. You were right before. We need to fix things, especially as more of us awaken."

Zuberi let loose a sort of sad smile. "I don't just want to fix problems anymore, Uzochi. I want to stop *him*. We need . . . we need a revolution to take that man down."

Uzochi agreed. He thought of his father in the memory, holding back the storm. This was a storm, too, wasn't it? A different kind.

"We train harder than before," he said, turning his attention back to Zuberi. "We take the fight to them. And we show the world who the real Krazen St. John is—a kidnapper, a manipulator."

Zuberi's lips quirked in a smile. "Sounds like you're talking revolution there, Catalyst."

That made Uzochi pause. Because the name needled at something inside him. Something about what had happened with Keera.

"I don't know about that," he said. "I'm . . . I'm starting to think I'm not the catalyst."

Zuberi stared at him. "What?"

He ran a finger over Adisa's journal.

"Maybe Lencho is."

He didn't know what she would do when he said it, but he knew that ever since Lencho had been able to force him out of Zaire's mind, he had been wondering who was more powerful: him, or his cousin. And after the events at the theater and the seawall, especially when he and Lencho combined their talents, Uzochi thought he had his answer.

Zuberi set her hand on his. The touch sparked energy between them, and they met each other's gaze.

"It doesn't actually matter," she said. "You know that, right? Whether it's him or you, what matters is how you wield that power. And I've seen you, Uzochi. You're a leader. You're the only one who can handle all this."

It was that burden of power again, pressing down on him. He felt it in every crevice of his mind, every held memory.

But this time, instead of resisting, he leaned into it. Every Nubian he'd helped awaken had shared a piece of themselves, pushing him, guiding him, even now.

He wouldn't let them down.

"Then let's do it," he said, holding tight to Zuberi's hand. "Starting with Vriana."

Zuberi smiled. "First Vriana, then revolution."

Uzochi nodded, grinning in spite of the pain and suffering that rolled inside him. For he was not alone.

"Then, revolution."

From the First Book of
Adisa, New York City, 2098

I've sat with all that I've written so far in this journal. I've sat with Uzochi's words and his unwillingness to blindly accept the label of "catalyst," an act that must have presented its own personal challenges for him.

And thus, I've decided that I will privately convene with the other elders and declare that we must meet with the awoken Children in a special tribunal, perhaps with their guardians by their side, perhaps not. Or perhaps they should speak among themselves with gentle Uzochi or mighty Zuberi as their representatives, who could later meet with the elders and present statements establishing how the Children would like to use their gifts going forward. Our young people should have the right to express what *they* want, to grapple with *their* future. What are the questions that have now seeped into their consciousness? How have they changed as a result of awakening? How do their experiences compare to what we once knew in Nubia?

The answers to these questions may not be what I would have envisioned for our people, but I must allow the bravery of the Children to inspire me, to force me to be brave and open to a future that's fluid and uncertain.

Something is coming. Something that we must be ready for, even if we do not feel ready. The destiny of all Nubians depends on this, and for that, we must put our faith in the Children, in what they can do, and how they must rise to the challenge of the future.

Faith is what I return to. Faith in ourselves. Faith in our heritage.

Faith that we have done enough to prepare for what comes next.

ACKNOWLEDGMENTS

First off, I'd like to thank my copilot, the wonderfully talented Clarence A. Haynes, for taking this journey with me to bring *Nubia: The Awakening* to life. Though it was challenging at times, I think we're both better for it artistically and personally. I've earned another friend in you, and that's much appreciated on my behalf.

Secondly, to our incredibly capable and well-respected editorial team at Delacorte Press: Krista Marino, Beverly Horowitz, and Lydia Gregovic, thank you for lending your absolute expertise, and for ultimately believing in the vision of *Nubia: The Awakening*. It couldn't have happened with you. As well, thank you to Josh Redlich and the entire marketing team at Delacorte. All your hard work is much appreciated.

Thirdly, thank you to Todd Shuster and Erica Bauman at Aevitas Creative. Your counsel, guidance, and patience have been invaluable from the beginning of this endeavor. Thank you for your contributions.

Lastly, I'd be remiss if I didn't also thank Adeyemi

Adegbesan and Casey Moses for creating such an amazing piece of cover art, one that will influence readers for years to come.

To my family and friends, thank you for the consistency of your support through the years. I love you all.

ABOUT THE AUTHORS

Actor and producer **OMAR EPPS** was first introduced to audiences as Q in Ernest Dickerson's cult classic *Juice*, opposite Tupac Shakur. He has gone on to star as Quincy in the beloved romance *Love & Basketball*, as Dr. Eric Foreman in the massively popular TV show *House*, as Jeff Cole in *In Too Deep*, as Isaac Johnson in *Shooter*, as Darnell in *This Is Us*, and in many, many more television shows and major motion pictures. His self-published memoir is *From Fatherless to Fatherhood*. *Nubia* is his first novel.

CLARENCE A. HAYNES has worked as an editor for a variety of publishers, including Penguin Random House, Amazon Publishing, and Legacy Lit, an imprint of Hachette Book Group. He has edited top-selling fiction titles such as *The Hundredth Queen, Scarlet Odyssey, Legacy of Lies*, and *These Toxic Things*, as well as the *Washington Post* and Amazon Charts bestseller *The Vine Witch* and its two sequels. He is also the author of the nonfiction work *The Legacy of Jim Crow*, published as part of Penguin Workshop's True History series.